GOLDEN
TALES FROM
FLAUBERT

GUSTAVE FLAUBERT was born at Rouen in 1821, and was educated in his native city, which he did not leave until 1840 when he went to Paris to study law. His famous novel, *Madame Bovary*, was published in 1857, and his Carthaginian romance, *Salammbô*, appeared five years later. *La Tentation de Saint Antoine*, of which fragments had been printed as early as 1857, was issued in complete form in 1874. In 1877 he published in one volume *Trois Contes* consisting of *Un Cœur Simple*, *La Légende de Saint Julien L'Hospitalier* and *Hérodias*, translations of which appear in the present volume, together with *La Tentation de Saint Antoine*. Flaubert, who was one of the greatest stylists that France has ever produced, died in 1880 at Croisset, near Rouen.

GOLDEN TALES FROM FLAUBERT

WITH A PREFACE BY
GEORGE SAINTSBURY

Short Story Index Reprint Series

 BOOKS FOR LIBRARIES PRESS
FREEPORT, NEW YORK

First Published 1928
Reprinted 1972

118497

THE TRANSLATIONS

A Simple Heart, *The Legend of St. Julian the Hospitaller* and *Herodias* are translated by John Gilmer.

The Temptation of St. Anthony is translated by A. K. Chignell.

INTERNATIONAL STANDARD BOOK NUMBER:
0-8369-4133-0

LIBRARY OF CONGRESS CATALOG CARD NUMBER:
73-38720

PRINTED IN THE UNITED STATES OF AMERICA
BY
NEW WORLD BOOK MANUFACTURING CO., INC.
HALLANDALE, FLORIDA 33009

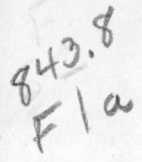

PREFACE

WHEN, some dozen years ago, Flaubert's representatives at last made up their minds to publish the mass of his early (and by himself suppressed, or rather never uttered) novice-work, there were those who thought they did well to be angry: and perhaps they were not wrong. It is always rather doubtful business to publish what an author has not published: but in Flaubert's case there seemed to be worse than doubt. It was perfectly well known, from his own confessions as well as from the testimony of those who knew him, that though he was not, in the German phrase, one " who could never be ready," he was probably *the* one of all men of letters who took most trouble in getting himself ready, and was most ruthless in sacrificing what he thought was *not* ready. The extraordinarily silly as well as vulgar taunt of Edmond de Goncourt that Flaubert just got the best epithets *de tout le monde*, while he, Edmond, and his brother, Jules, only used such as were their own private invention, is in reality an almost grovelling admission of his greatness. Any clever fool can, as Miss Edgeworth's little boy, not at all foolishly, says, "call his hat Cadwallader," but it takes more or less of a genius to select the best epithet *de tout le monde* for a particular hat in a particular context.

From more than one side the objections were justified. By far the greater part of the *Œuvres Premières* had no value except for a curiosity which, in the better class of readers, probably felt a little ashamed of itself. Not that there was anything discreditable in the work: it was simply an obvious failure. Much of it had the extravagant *diablerie*, horror, griminess, etc., which was the wrong hallmark, as we may call it, of the earlier Romanticism of the lower class like Janin's *Âne Mort* and Borel's *Champavert*, with which Flaubert's own stuff was nearly contemporary. Almost all of it, to a reader who was not a child or a fool, was quite evidently that half-done work which proverbially ought not to be shown or told to children and fools themselves, and from which even those who are not children or fools can derive only a sort of pseudo-scientific, not an honestly æsthetic, pleasure. One does indeed see, from the first version of the *Éducation Sentimentale*, how he could improve things; and can at least guess how much he *would* have improved *Bouvard et Pécuchet*: but this was hardly *tanti*.

The comparison, however, of the earlier (1849-1856) versions of the *Tentation de Saint Antoine* with its final form in 1874 is an altogether different matter: and though probably only a few readers would care to have the complete texts side by side, as they ought to be for full critical appreciation

PREFACE

of the facts, it may be worth while, before taking account of the " definitive " form *as* definitive, to consider " the excellent differences "—a Shakespearean phrase which applies here itself excellently. It must be remembered that in this case there was actual or partial publication and republication; that instead of rejection there was simply amelioration. Of course there have been the usual eccentrics—perhaps occasionally sincere but much more often not—who have pretended to prefer the first form. If you only take the good old *Respice finem* for guide that matter ought to be easily settled. All ending—all real ending—should be quiet, by whatever disquiet it is preceded. This is managed consummately in the latest form: it is not so in the first. I hardly know anything of the kind finer than the conclusion as we now have it. Sun-rise and silent prayer, the terrors of the night having vanished and the face of Christ dominating all. To use a homely parallel the ingredients of the early version are not thoroughly mixed and, though not uncooked, not thoroughly cooked: there is still a sort of rawness about them.

It was, of course, necessary to read the two versions together carefully while preparing this Preface to the later one, and to give full weight to what M. Louis Bertrand's editorial care did for the earlier some twenty years ago before Flaubert's still earlier attempts were released or dug up, whichever phrase may be preferred. His chief argument—true in its facts though questionable in its effect—is that this earlier one—some fragments of which had always been known as having appeared in the *Artiste* under Gautier's editorship—had more pure Early Romanticism in it than the later. It certainly has, and in fact was certain to have. But it has also much more of the faults of 1830, as it was also certain to have: and it has a good deal of one of the worst of those faults—the attempt to reach the great Romantic vague by a sort of higgledy-piggledy disorder. It seems, from a most interesting pair of quotations from Flaubert's manuscripts, one original, the other copied from his friend, George Sand's *Mlle. la Quintinie*, that he had (at least at first) intended to depict a general tone *d'abrutissement, d'idiotisme et de fatigue* in the Saint, on which George Sand comments and which she explains George-Sandically. Now something of this undoubtedly suits the situation of Anthony, being confronted with all these mysteries and terrors in the first place with the Devil among and behind them; and with "the awful rose of Dawn" and God Himself in it, behind and over all. But in the earlier version this situation and this attitude have not got "disembroiled" enough. The incidents and the personification are in the hands of the group of Seven Deadly Sins, *plus* Logic, and in some way stage-managed by the Devil; the Saint is in a state of undignified fussiness too often; his pig, though a relief, seems generally superfluous, and at least once

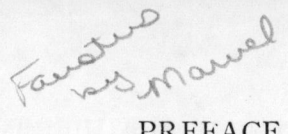

PREFACE 5

makes a plusquam-piggish and merely nasty speech; while the episode of Apollonius and Damis, which even in the final form one may think a little overdone, seems more disproportionate and out of place than ever.

Above all, there is no Hilarion.

Now it is no extravagance to say that it is worth while to read this first version if for nothing else than because you cannot perceive the full importance of this character unless you know that he is a *new* character, and can appreciate not merely what he *is* but what he *does*. It is, of course, possible that Flaubert might have found some other ways of getting rid of the defects of 1849-56: but he could hardly have found a better. The part supplies a sort of concatenation or mortar to the other parts. Anthony's supposed familiarity with the person (a former disciple of his) steadies the Saint, and gives, if a dangerous, a useful mouthpiece for the treacherous and ungodly suggestions which come much better from the other than from those chattering Deadlies and that most illogical Logic. As a scholar and a divine he serves as a special excuse for all the Heresiarchs and their crews who in the earlier version turn up rather too promiscuously. But more of him presently.

On the other hand the abolition of " Science " who appears in the earlier version as a separate *persona*, is, though a less constant gain, a considerable one. She is quite out of place in such a scene, such a company and such a time: nor is she, as perhaps by some *tour de force* she might have been, adjusted to all three. All through, moreover, there are touches of what I believe it is fashionable now to call architectonic—which certainly had not been achieved in '49, but which were delightfully visible in '74. I have always thought the *Tentation* by far Flaubert's greatest work: but I certainly should not have thought so if it had been only represented by the earlier version. Indeed the *Artiste* fragments— that about Nebuchadnezzar and others—would, if they had stood by themselves, have given a false impression. They might have made one think the rest of the *Tentation* better than it was, but then they could hardly have suggested that the author would make that rest so triumphantly good as it actually is.

Of course the use of such a word as " triumphantly " will shock or disgust or amuse people who agree with M. Faguet as to Gautier's *La Morte Amoureuse* being a *diablerie puérile*; with our Modernists as to the supernatural element in Religion being merely " magic," and so on; but of them and with them we do not reason. It is permissible as a certain ancient saying has it, for Dorians to speak Doric: and Literature, which is a somewhat supernatural thing itself, has proved long ago in a decidedly triumphant fashion that it is permissible for it to speak of the supernatural. But it must, by the same general tenor of law, speak of the supernatural, as of everything else, in a literary manner—that manner involving the observance of certain principles and methods, some at least of which have been discovered and set forth by persons from Aristotle of Stagira down to men of the present day : but many of which are not quite formulable, and are rather to be recognized by and in their results than indicated *a priori*.

Besides the great improvement of the introduction of Hilarion, the later version enjoys a much larger imparting of the elaborate stage-direction.

I have not the least idea whether Mr. Hardy derived from Flaubert any suggestion of the magnificent things of this kind in *The Dynasts* : but I know no third example of anything like such success in the use of a device which might be simply a bore; which might also be made a mere substitute for something else; but which can be and is here made to support and as it were present that "something else" with fullest dramatic effect. I can conceive objection being taken to the length of the Saint's preliminary discourse : but it seems to me essentially right. He has got to survey his life : and the reader or spectator (for there are not many actual dramas which present what is presented by them so forcibly as this) has to have it surveyed for him in order that the cause of the *Tentation*—that mixture of tedium of life and regret for it which gives the Devil standpoint and grip-hold—may arise. It arises : the passages chosen as *Sortes Biblicæ* being cunningly adjusted to fit the danger.

In the earlier version the temptations had been immediate and direct: they are here less so and are preceded by a sort of dream which shows him that the life, as to the actual course of which he had been half grumbling, half regretting, might have been one of splendour in Church and State. He has seen a vision of Nebuchadnezzar in pomp, but he wakes and, as a form of penitence, flogs himself. This ambiguous process results in the first personal temptation—no less than the appearance of the Queen of Sheba. The sign of the cross saves him, but only just: and Balkis departs with a mixture of sigh and sneer. But she leaves—Hilarion.

The way in which the Tempter (for such the old disciple really is) insinuates himself after a slightly uncanny overture which sustains the uncanniness of the whole atmosphere, is admirable. He is familiar with the Saint's ways; they have talked of all these things before; he can edge in doubts, *aporias*,[1] simple questions, quite naturally. And so the ghostly congregation and procession of the Heresiarchs comes on the stage quite appropriately, though the figures vary from personages who hardly deserve to be called Christians at all, like Manes and the wilder Gnostics, to " Fathers " by something more than courtesy, but obviously questionable on points, like Tertullian and Origen. Gymnosophists, Simon

---

[1] We want an English word for this. " Difficulty " is thus meant but is not quite good enough. " Poser " is near but undignified.

PREFACE

Magus and his " Ennoia "[1] (pretended successor of Helen), follow and are followed by Apollonius of Tyana and his faithful Damis. I have, I think, said before that Apollonius does not so much appeal to me: but only the cross itself, embraced, and not merely signed for, saves Anthony; and his reflections after the Tyanian disappears are rather doubtful. He admits indeed that the splendours of Nebuchadnezzar had not dazzled him, nor the charms of Balkis allured him so much. He begins to speculate on various forms and notions of Divinity: and this lets Hilarion in again.

The reader will hardly want much guide or comment along the way in which he, who is now almost declaredly Hilarion-Satanas, avails himself of this dangerous mood by displaying *all* religions from the clumsiest idols to Buddha (the fiend occasionally making Mephistophelian suggestions of Christian parallels) through Oannes, Belus, Ormuzd, the Ephesian Diana, Cybele, Isis, and so to Olympus itself—for a moment in all its glory, attracting Anthony's admiration. But Hilarion makes the mistake of too open propaganda: and the Saint with a sort of wrench, though sighing at each clause, pronounces the Lord's Prayer. Whereat the cross throws its shadow on the sky and there follows a *Götterdämmerung* which I have always liked to compare with Heine's (not the poem under that title, but the one specially called *Die Götter Griechenlands*)

[1] Thought personified—very much personified.

in the *Buch der Lieder*. Minor Divinities follow and even the special deity of the Jews as the "Lord of Hosts" is made to pass, in order probably to give an entrance to the Devil himself *as* the Devil, but in his archangelic form. He carries the Saint through space, shows him its vastness and only at last, when all other hope of safety seems gone, makes the demand for Adoration of himself, and denial or blasphemy of God. But Anthony does not comply; and, apparently abandoned in the Void, wakes to find himself in front of his own cave—alive but exhausted and by no means even yet in a hallowed state of mind. I suppose that it is at this point that a certain kind of criticism finds most fault with the *Tentation* as we have it. The refusal of Adoration should have settled the matter and given a satisfactory "curtain." As a matter of fact it does not do so: there are two scenes to come before the great if almost eventless close which has been spoken of above. The first, which one might think something of a repetition, is a last and concentrated effort on the part of the two temptresses, Suicide and Voluptuousness, to get Anthony, one or the other, for their prey. It is very powerfully done and can be pleaded for. He has seen all worlds, all faiths, all philosophies. They are all vanity. Why not finish with it all? or, if not, be content with that sensual pleasure which whatever may be said against it, and whatever payment for itself it may exact, is at any rate *something?*

PREFACE

But he succumbs to neither; and they finally wrestle with and defeat each other, leaving him rather proud than anything else. (In the earlier version Pride appears constantly throughout as the chief tempter.) They are succeeded by another quaint duel of the Sphinx and a Chimera (negation and delusion) half fighting, half making love: while these in turn give place to phantasmagoria of less important and famous monsters from pygmies and Cynocephali through Basilisks and Griffins to the Catoblepas and the Martichoras (I always liked the spelling Mantichora better), who figure in the furthest Fauna of Fancy. These appearances of animals change to birds, fishes, even vegetables, if not bacilli, and Anthony seems to recover animation at the presence (if with a sort of pan-theistical suggestion) of life even in a bewildering multitude of infinitesimal forms descending to the lowest. Then and not till then comes the end, glanced at before, the Saint returning, with the light and under the face of Christ, to the quiet prayer to which at first and throughout he has been unable to resign himself. In comparison with this the end of the earlier version where the Devil, though acknowledging himself beaten for the time, departs with jeers and threats to return, seems distinctly inferior: and that not merely on the strength of preference for a "happy ending." There are some interesting fragments of the first draft: or rather there are some passages which M. Bertrand thought best not to incorporate in but add to the presentation of that draft or series of drafts which he gave. And some people may regret the expulsion of the pig, specially when he wakes and feels the sun and says, " What a jolly sun! I was in such a funk to-night." But the thing could never have been brought off as a mystery-farce: and it *has* been at last brought off as a mystery-romance.

In passing from the *Tentation* to the *Trois Contes* there is a point which, though it can seldom have been missed by careful readers of Flaubert, should perhaps be put before beginners in the reading of him. These three small stories are—whether intentionally or not—curiously like miniatures of his three larger ones, leaving out *L'Éducation Sentimentale* which, as noticed elsewhere, was itself a shorter story expanded. It might, of course, be—and probably has been—contended that this indicates the kind of limitation of genius which is also elsewhere glanced at, and which, by people who like the sort of thing, may be connected further with speculations about what they themselves would doubtless call the author's mentality. For us that does not matter. But the fact remains that the Legend of St. Julian connects in the closest way with the *Tentation* itself, that *Hérodias* is almost as closely connected with *Salammbô*, and that though Madame Bovary is a thoroughly bad and worthless woman, while Félicité is a saint if ever there was one, both are essentially of the lower class of French countrywomen and the surroundings of both were the French country-side. Flaubert has chosen to show how, if he

PREFACE

had used the usual condiments of French novel-writing there, he could do without them here. And he has done it.

It is difficult to think of any other example so audaciously successful, of the pure art of tale-telling as the first. There is almost what is called in theology a *kenosis*, an emptying out, of all that is usually called "interest." As has often been pointed out elsewhere, France had shown the short story as such to be indigenous for many a century: and quite late in the preceding one Marmontel had made it clear that neither naughtiness nor the supernatural, nor high comedy, nor strong tragedy, nor exciting events and eccentric characters of any kind were necessary to success in it. Flaubert's own "realist" contemporaries and juniors were at any rate pretending to be real; but almost always tending to the uglier sides of reality, and endeavouring to set this off with more or less elaborate style. In *Un Cœur Simple* Flaubert is more absolutely commonplace in subject than the most "ordinary" phase of Marmontel: and never for one moment suggests either Edmond de Goncourt's strictly monopolized epithets nor Paul de Saint-Victor's (it is true that this was not intended for tale-telling) alleged habit of dotting down lovely words all over a sheet of paper and then just filling up the spaces with some sort of context. Take the most tempting passage in *A Simple Heart* for contrast with these, and further compare it with M. Zola's one, and in part not dissimilar, effort in " propriety " *Le Rêve*. Take the death (or afterdeath) scene of Virginie here and if you have any critical faculty the difference will give you some occupation and, I hope, much pleasure. You will find the scene presented (though the phrase may seem indecorous) " to the life ": but without the very slightest sign of effort in its portrayal, or attempt to deck it up with ornament. The mother sobbing at the foot of the bed *qu'elle tenait dans les bras* is a good sample. There is scarcely one writer in a hundred who could have refrained from adding something to this scarce half-dozen words which would not have spoilt or weakened them—an adverb to *tenait*, an adjective to *couche* at the very least.

It would perhaps be absurd to deny, and not very wise to overlook some designed and deliberate contrast between the substances of the first and second of these *Contes*. The first is, from its own first to its last, photographic; its objects and subjects, its incidents and characters are those of every place and every day with only localities of colour in place and tone in time allowed for. The substance of the second is mediæval legend. But there is hardly the least attempt to clothe this substance with what has been called in English " Wardour Street " language to suit. The final paragraph in the original—*Alors le Lépreux l'étreignait*, and the rest—is, if a foreigner may with due humility give his opinion on such a point, one of the very finest known to him in modern

French literature, for suiting of sound to sense, for rhythm, for selection of vocabulary: yet there is not a single word in it which is not quite an ordinary word by itself, or which is put in any startling collocation of phrase. A wonderful picture with a wonderful music attending and assisting its exhibition: but with as little "apparatus" about it as well could be. And all that has come before, though less worked up, is worked up in the same way. The grim irony of the last hunt, the useless and ineffectual slaughter which at once satirizes the hunter's former practice and irritates his present mood so as to make him more likely to commit the crime-error that is to follow—might easily have been made farcical or overdone in the other direction: but it is kept just right. The peculiar *gravity* which Flaubert maintains in both those stories is not quite like anything else. He has managed to keep all affectation out of it, and even to forgo, what the very greatest have not always forgone, a single flash, or one or two flashes, from behind the curtain to enliven or reassure the audience: yet he is never, in clause or in page, dull.

Hérodias, like its elder, less historical but more elaborately storied sister *Salammbô*, though not quite to the same extent, has been scarcely so great a favourite as some others of its author's works, and certainly less popular than its two companions in the same volume. *They* are almost invulnerable: you can pick holes in *it*. The curious Romantic fancy (perhaps a revenge for Boileau's condemnation of harmless Frankish names) for oddly spelt appellations—the fancy which made Gautier himself remark of Leconte de Lisle's transliterations of Hellenic names that "it would be simpler to write in Greek"—is rather too prominent. Saint John Baptist need not object to being called, as he is on Oxford class-lists, "Di. Joh. Bap," but one does not think he would like "Iaokanan"—at any rate it looks very ugly in French or English. The introduction of Aulus Vitellius—long before he became Emperor, but when his manners and morals were already bad and his customs disgusting—has no relevance whatever. Herodias (whom one fancies as a less fascinating, but hardly less fatal Cleopatra) is quite without charm: and Salome is almost a "super" except for her actual dance, and quite a *muta persona* except for the fatal demand. The Saint himself is for the most part hidden in his dungeon. There is indeed in Antipas the making—the "bones"—of a considerable character in novel if not in drama: but there is no place or scope for him as that. Perhaps the most striking thing in the whole is the last touch when after the Tetrarch has stared for hours through the night at the severed head with which he has been left alone, it is carried off by sympathizers who, "as it is very heavy, carry it by turns." And even this is one of those "asides" which, as was noted above, appear to be deliberately avoided in the other two stories. Indeed there are grounds for believing that as Flaubert intended contrast of subject but agreement in manner to be shown in these others, he meant *Hérodias* to differ in substance and in handling as well.

Even in this, appears however, to an extraordinary extent, and in the other two and the *Tentation* consummately, the "greatness as a writer" (*comme écrivain*) which even M. Scherer admitted. It is difficult to say whether that acute but prejudiced and perhaps rather narrow-sighted critic hated Romantics or Realists most: and without deciding between those who claim Flaubert as either, the mere fact of the double claim shows that there must have been something of both in him. Yet there was, as must be seen, from what has just been said, enough of something *else* in him, in the eyes of perhaps the most uncompromising censor of his time taking France and England together, not perhaps to "make up," but to be allowed in his favour. The present writer would, of course, allow much more, or rather hardly proceed by the way of allowances at all. From the opportunities of comparison with his first drafts we see that Flaubert practically got rid of all that was bad on the Romantic side, and that he never *published* anything inexcusably bad on the Realist. It is indeed probable, though one need not accept *L'Éducation Sentimentale* as a sufficient proof of it, that his range was not very wide; that it did not extend at all to sheer and cheerful comedy; and that intricacies of character were beyond it. People like

King Alfonso el Sabio (they say it is rather unfair to translate that " wise " and that it is only claims " learning "), who think that the Creator might now and then have taken a hint with advantage,[1] might themselves have made Flaubert rather a poet than a novelist, and rather a painter than either. I am, I confess, quite content with him as he is. And though perhaps *Madame Bovary* ought to be known lest his range should be thought even more limited than it is, I do not think he is quite so much at the top of his own artistic and literary power there as here.

GEORGE SAINTSBURY.

BATH, 1928.

[1] Apologists I believe also say that Carlyle exaggerates here in his " chaff " of the King.

CONTENTS

	PAGE
PREFACE	1
A SIMPLE HEART	23
THE LEGEND OF ST. JULIAN THE HOSPITALLER	73
HERODIAS	113
THE TEMPTATION OF ST. ANTHONY	157

A SIMPLE HEART

(*Un Cœur Simple*)

A SIMPLE HEART

(*Un Cœur Simple*)

I

For fifty years the good folk of Pont-l'Évêque had been coveting Mme. Aubain's servant Félicité.

For a hundred francs a year she did the cooking and the general work of the house, the sewing, the washing and the ironing. She could bridle a horse, fatten poultry, and churn butter, and she was faithful to her mistress, who was by no means easy to get on with.

Mme. Aubain had married a good-looking young fellow, who had no money and who died at the beginning of 1809, leaving her with two small children and a quantity of debts. She sold all her property except the farms of Toucques and Geffosses, which, at most, brought her in five thousand francs per annum, and left her house in Saint-Melaine for a less expensive one, which had belonged to her forbears and was situated behind the market.

This house had a slate roof, and stood between an arcade and a narrow street which ran down to the river. There was an unevenness in the level of the floors which made a visitor stumble. A narrow entrance hall divided the kitchen from the principal living-room, in which Mme. Aubain sat in a wicker chair near the window all day long. Eight mahogany chairs were placed in a row against the white panelled walls of the room. A heap of wooden and cardboard boxes was piled up like a pyramid upon the top of an old piano which stood under a barometer. On either side of the chimney-piece, which was in yellow marble and Louis XV period, with a clock in the middle in the form of a temple of Vesta, there was a stuffed armchair. The whole room smelt rather musty, for the floor was below the level of the garden.

On the first floor was "Madame's" room. It was very large, with a wallpaper of faded flowers and a portrait of "Monsieur" in the costume of a dandy of those days. It opened into a smaller room, in which were two cots, without mattresses. Next was the drawing-room, which was always kept closed, and which was filled with furniture covered with sheets. A passage led to a study; books and odds and ends of papers filled the shelves of a bookcase, in the centre of whose three wings there stood a big writing-table of dark wood. The two panels at the end of the room were covered with pen-and-ink drawings, landscapes in water-colour, and engravings by Audran, relics of better days and bygone luxury. On the second floor a high window, looking over the fields, gave light to Félicité's garret.

Félicité rose at dawn, so as not to miss Mass, and worked till the evening without stopping. Then, dinner over and the plates and dishes put away, and the door carefully locked, she buried a log in the embers of the dying fire and went to sleep in front

A SIMPLE HEART

of the hearth, with her rosary in her hand. Of all the hagglers in the market-place she was the most obstinate, and as for cleanness, the polish on her pots and pans was the despair of other servants. Thrifty in her habits, she ate slowly, gathering up the crumbs of her loaf off the table—a twelve-pound loaf baked specially for her and lasting three weeks.

All the year round she wore a printed calico handkerchief, attached to her back with a pin, a bonnet into which her hair was tucked, grey stockings, a red skirt, and a bibbed apron, such as hospital nurses wear, over her jacket. Her voice was sharp and her face thin, and at twenty-five she would have been taken for forty. From fifty onwards she looked any age. Always silent, straight of figure, and little given to unnecessary gesticulation, she looked like a wooden doll which moves by clock-work.

II

Like many others, she had had a love-story. Her father, who was a mason, was killed by a fall from a scaffold. Then her mother died, her sisters went their own ways, and a farmer took her in while she was still quite small, and gave her charge of the cows out in the fields. She was in rags and shivered with cold; she lapped up water out of ponds, was beaten for no reason whatever, and, finally, was turned out of the house for stealing thirty sous, a theft of which she was innocent. She went to another farm, where she looked after the poultry, and, as her employers were pleased with her, the other servants were jealous.

One evening in August—she was then eighteen—they took her to a fête at Colleville. She was at once bewildered and upset by the noise of the fiddling, the lamps hung in the trees, the medley of costumes with their lace and their jewelry, and the great crowd of people all dancing at the same time. She was standing aloof, shyly, when a smart young fellow, who was smoking his pipe as he leant on the shaft of a cart, came up to her and asked her to dance with him. He treated her to cider, coffee, cakes, and a silk handkerchief, and, fancying that she knew what he was after, offered to see her home. When they got to a cornfield he roughly threw her down. She, terrified, shouted for help, and he decamped.

Another evening, when she was on the Beaumont road, she wanted to get past a great cart laden with hay, which was going slowly along, and, as she brushed against the wheels, she recognized Théodore.

He came up to her and told her quite coolly that she ought to forgive him for his behaviour, which had been due to drink.

She did not know what to say, and had a strong desire to run away.

He at once began to talk about the crops and the principal people in the village, saying that his father had left Colleville for the farm at Les Écots, so they were now neighbours. "Indeed," she said. He added that his people wanted to get him married, but he was in no particular hurry and was waiting for a wife to suit his own taste. She dropped her eyes. Then he asked her whether she was thinking of getting married. She replied, with a smile, that it was not fair of him to tease her. He warmly assured

A SIMPLE HEART

her that he was not doing so, and passed his arm round her waist. She walked on, clasped to his side, and gradually they slackened their pace. The wind blew softly, the stars were shining, the huge cart loaded with hay was swinging in front of them, and the four horses raised dust as they dragged on their weary way. Then, without any order from Théodore, they turned to the right. He kissed her once more and she disappeared into the darkness.

The following week he got her to consent to make appointments with him.

They used to meet behind a wall, under some solitary tree, at the bottom of a farmyard. She was not a little innocent girl like a young lady in good society, for the ways of animals had taught her things, but her commonsense and the instinct of her honour saved her from going wrong. This opposition inflamed Théodore's passion to such an extent that, in order to satisfy it, or, perhaps, for more simple reasons, he offered to marry her. She could hardly believe him, but he avowed his love most heatedly.

Shortly afterwards he said that he had something tiresome to tell her: the year before, his parents had bought him a substitute for his military service, but he might now be taken again any day, and the thought of doing his service frightened him. This cowardice seemed to Félicité a proof of his affection, and it redoubled hers. She stole away at night to meet him as arranged, when he worried her with his anxiety and his entreaties.

In the end he told her that he would go himself to the Prefecture to get news, which he would give her between eleven and midnight the following Sunday.

She hastened to meet her lover at the appointed hour.

Instead of him, she found one of his friends.

He told her that she could not see Théodore again. To save himself from conscription, he had married Mme. Lehoussais, of Toucques, a very rich old woman.

There was a wild burst of grief. She threw herself down, screaming and appealing to God, and lay, moaning in the field, till daylight. Then she went back to the farm and announced her intention of leaving. At the end of the month, when she had received her wages, she tied up her small personal belongings in a handkerchief and went to Pont-l'Évêque.

In front of the inn there, she put some questions to a woman in a widow's bonnet, who, as luck would have it, happened to be looking out for a cook. The girl did not know much about cooking, but she seemed so willing and so unexacting in her demands that Mme. Aubain ended by saying, " Very well, I will take you."

A quarter of an hour afterwards Félicité was settled in her house.

At first she lived in a kind of panic at " the style of the house " and the memory of " Monsieur," which brooded over all. Paul and Virginie, aged seven and four respectively, seemed to her to be fashioned out of some precious substance. She carried them about pick-a-back, and was upset because Mme. Aubain forbade her to kiss them

A SIMPLE HEART

every minute. Nevertheless she was happy. Her pleasant surroundings had made her grief disappear.

Every Thursday some regular visitors came in to play Boston, and Félicité put out the cards and foot-warmers in good time. They came punctually at eight, and departed before the clock struck eleven.

Every Monday morning the second-hand dealer in old iron, who lived in the arcade, set out his wares. Then there was a great stir in the town, the buzzing of voices mingled with the neighing of horses, the bleating of lambs, the grunting of pigs, and the sharp rattle of carts in the streets.

About noon, when marketing was in full swing, there would be seen a tall old peasant, with cap on the back of his head, and hooked nose. This was Robelin, the farmer of Geffosses. A little later came Liébard, the farmer from Toucques, a small, red-faced, fat fellow, in a grey jacket and leggings with spurs.

Both had fowls or cheeses to put before their landlady. Félicité was invariably up to all their tricks, and they went away filled with respect for her.

From time to time Mme. Aubain had a visit from one of her uncles, the Marquis de Gremanville, whose health had been ruined by fast living and who was now living on the last remaining scrap of his property at Falaise. He always came at the luncheon hour, accompanied by a horrible poodle, whose paws left their dirty mark on the furniture. In spite of his efforts to appear well-bred—and he even went so far as to raise his hat every time he said, "My late father"—his habits usually got the better of him, for he filled his glass again and again and indulged in remarks which were ill-fitted for genteel society.

Félicité used to get him out of the house, saying politely, " You have had enough, Monsieur de Gremanville: good-bye till next time! " and she shut the door.

She used to open it with pleasure to M. Bourais, a retired lawyer. His white tie and his bald head, his frilled shirt-front and his roomy brown coat, his way of rounding his arm as he took snuff, the stamp of a marked individuality on everything he did, all made an impression such as we feel when we meet someone out of the common.

As he looked after " Madame's " property, he used to remain shut up with her in " Monsieur's " study for hours, though he was always afraid of being compromised. He had a great respect for the powers that be, and pretended to some knowledge of Latin.

To make the children's lessons more pleasant, he gave them a geography book with illustrations. These showed various scenes all over the world, such as cannibals with head-dresses of feathers, a monkey carrying off a young lady, Bedouins in the desert, the harpooning of a whale, and so on. Paul used to explain these pictures to Félicité, and that, indeed, was all the education she ever got. The education of the children was undertaken by Guyot, a poor creature employed at the town hall, who was well known for his beautiful handwriting, and who used to sharpen his pen-knife on his boots.

When the weather was bright, the entire household used to start early for a day at the Geffosses farm. Its courtyard is on a slope, with the farmhouse in the middle, and, in the distance, the sea like a grey streak on the horizon.

Félicité would bring slices of meat out of her basket, and they would take their lunch in a room opening out of the dairy. It was the last remnant of a country-house, now no more. The tattered wall-paper quivered in the draughts. Mme. Aubain would sit with bowed head, overcome by memories of the past. The children were half afraid to talk. " Why don't you go and play ? " she would say, and they quickly left the room.

Paul went up into the barn, caught birds, played at ducks and drakes over the pond, or hammered on the great casks with a stick like a drummer. Virginie fed the rabbits, or scampered off to pick corn-flowers, in her swift movement displaying her little embroidered knickers.

One autumn evening they went home by the fields. The moon in its first quarter lit up part of the sky, and a mist floated like a scarf over the winding Toucques. Cattle, lying out in the middle of the fields, looked placidly at the four as they passed by. In the third meadow some of them got up, and made a half circle in front of them.

" There's nothing to be afraid of," said Félicité, and, crooning softly, she stroked the back of the nearest beast; he wheeled round, and the others did the same. But when they crossed the next field, a dreadful bellowing was heard. It came from a bull, which had been hidden from them by the mist, and which came towards the two women.

Mme. Aubain started to run. " No! No! don't go so fast! " They hurried on, however, hearing behind them a loud breathing which came nearer and nearer. Its hoofs were like hammers as they beat upon the turf. "Look, he is galloping now!" Félicité turned round and tore up some clods, which she hurled into its eyes. It lowered its muzzle, shook its great horned head with rage, and bellowed horribly. Mme. Aubain, at the end of the field with her two children, looked distractedly for a gap in the high bank.

Félicité continued to retreat before the bull, throwing clods of earth, which blinded it, and crying out, "Be quick! Be quick!"

Mme. Aubain got down into the ditch, pushed Virginie first and then Paul, fell back several times as she tried to climb up the steep bank, but managed it at last with a plucky effort.

The bull had driven Félicité with her back against a fence; its slaver was being blown into her face, and, in another second, she would have been gored. She had just time to slip through, and the great brute stopped short in amazement.

This affair was talked about in Pont-l'Évêque for many a year, but Félicité was not in the least proud of what she had done, as she did not think for a moment that she had been a real heroine.

Virginie was her sole care, for, as a result of her fright, the little girl had become very nervous, and M. Poupart, the doctor, advised sea-bathing at Trouville. In those days it had not many visitors. Mme. Aubain collected particulars, consulted Bourais, and made preparations as though for a long journey.

She sent off her luggage the day before her own

departure in Liébard's cart. Next day he brought round two horses, one of which had a woman's saddle with a velvet back, while on the back of the other a sort of seat was made with a rolled-up cloak. Mme. Aubain rode on this one, with Félicité looking after Virginie on the horse in front of her. Paul was on M. Lechaptois's donkey, which had been lent on condition that great care was taken of it.

The road was so bad that two hours were taken to get over eight kilometres. The horses sank in the mud up to their pasterns, and floundered about in their attempts to get out; sometimes they stumbled in the ruts, or had to jump. In some places Liébard's mare stopped abruptly. He waited patiently until she went on again, talking about the people who had estates along the road, and adding moral reflections on their various stories.

For instance, when they were passing a house covered with nasturtiums in Toucques, he shrugged his shoulders and said: " A Mme. Lehoussais lives there. Instead of taking a young man, she . . ." Félicité did not hear the rest. The horses trotted and the donkey galloped. They all turned down a by-path, a gate was swung open, two boys appeared, and they dismounted in front of a manure-heap immediately outside the door of the house.

When Mme. Liébard saw her mistress, she showed her delight in no small measure. She served up a lunch of a sirloin of beef, tripe, pudding, a fricassee of chicken, sparkling cider, a fruit tart, and brandied plums, garnishing it with compliments to Madame, who seemed to be in better health, to Mademoiselle, who was now " splendid," and to Monsieur Paul, who had " grown considerably." Nor did she forget their defunct grandparents whom the Liébards knew, as they had been in the service of the family for several generations. Like them, the farm had an ancient look. The beams of the ceiling were worm-eaten, the walls black with smoke, the window-panes grey with dust. On an oak dresser were all sorts of oddments—jugs, plates, pewter bowls, wolf-traps, sheep-shears, and a huge syringe, which made the children laugh. Every tree in the three courtyards had mushrooms at its base or a bit of mistletoe in its branches. Several had been thrown down by the wind, and had taken root again at the middle; all were bending under their great weight of apples. The thatched roofs, like brown velvet and of varying thickness, weathered the heaviest squalls, but the cart-shed was tumbling down. Mme. Aubain said that she would see to it, and ordered the horses to be saddled again.

Another half-hour passed before they reached Trouville. The little cavalcade dismounted to pass the Écores, a cliff overhanging boats on the sea below, and three minutes later they were at the end of the quay and entered the courtyard of the Golden Lamb, the inn kept by the excellent Mme. David.

From the very first days of their stay, the change of air and the sea-baths brought strength to Virginie. As she had no bathing-dress, she went into the sea in her chemise, and Félicité dressed her afterwards in a coast-guard's cabin which was used by bathers.

In the afternoons they used to go off with the donkey beyond the Black Rocks, in the direction of Hennequeville. The path at first went uphill and

A SIMPLE HEART

down dale across ground with the sward of a park, and then came out on a plateau, where green fields and plough-land were lying side by side. At the edge of the road holly stood up stiffly out of masses of briars, and here and there the zigzag branches of a great dead tree were silhouetted against the blue sky.

They nearly always rested in a meadow, with Deauville on their left, Havre on their right, and the open sea in front of them. It shimmered in the sunshine, smooth as a mirror, and so still that its murmur could scarcely be heard; unseen sparrows twittered, and the sky covered all as with a huge arch. Mme. Aubain did her needlework, Virginie plaited rushes, Félicité gathered lavender, and Paul, very much bored, wanted to go home.

Other days they crossed the Toucques in a boat and looked for shells. When the tide was out, sea-urchins, star-fish, and jelly-fish were left stranded, and the children ran after the foam-flakes tossed hither and thither by the wind. The sleepy waves, breaking on the sand, spent themselves all along the beach. It stretched away out of sight, bounded on the landside by the dunes which came between it and the Marsh, a broad meadow in the shape of an arena. As they came home that way, Trouville, on the slope of the hill in the background, grew bigger at every step, and seemed to be spread out before them in a bright medley with its houses of every variety of size and shape and colour.

When it was hot, they did not leave their room. Streaks of light from the dazzling sun poured through the blinds. Not a sound was to be heard in the village: not a soul was to be seen in the streets. The prevailing quiet was increased by the silence. In the distance men were caulking and hammering on their boats, and the smell of tar was wafted along by the heavy, warm breeze.

The principal amusement was seeing the return of the fishing-boats. As soon as they had passed the buoys, they began to tack. The sails were lowered about two-thirds down the masts, and with their foresails swelling out like balloons, they glided through the splashing waves to the middle of the harbour, where they suddenly dropped their anchors. Then the crew moored their boats to the quay and began to throw ashore their cargoes of quivering fish. A line of carts was awaiting them, and women in cotton bonnets hurried out to take the baskets and kiss their husbands.

One of these women came up to Félicité one day, and a little while afterwards she went home very happy indeed, for she had found a long-lost sister.

Nastasie Barette, the wife of one Leroux, followed her to the house, carrying a baby in her arms, while one child was holding on to her right hand and a little cabin-boy, his arms akimbo and his cap cocked over his ear, walked on her other side.

After a quarter of an hour Mme. Aubain sent them off. They were always to be seen in the neighbourhood of the kitchen or when the family took their walks abroad, but the husband never appeared.

Félicité became very fond of them. She bought them a blanket, some shirts and a stove; it looked as if they were doing very well out of her.

Mme. Aubain was disgusted by this weakness, and

A SIMPLE HEART

she did not like the familiarity of the nephew for he said " thee " and " thou " to Paul. And so, as Virginie was coughing and the weather was not good, the family went back to Pont-l'Évêque.

M. Bourais gave her some information on the choice of a college: Caen was considered the best, and Paul was sent there. He said good-bye bravely, being quite happy to go to live in a place where he would have play-fellows.

Mme. Aubain resigned herself to the absence of her boy, knowing that it was inevitable: Virginie soon got over it. Félicité missed the noise he used to make, but she found a new occupation to distract her thoughts: from Christmas onwards she took the little girl to church for religious instruction every day.

III

After making a genuflexion at the door she walked up the lofty nave between the double row of chairs, opened the door of Mme. Aubain's pew, sat down, and began to look about her. The choir-stalls were occupied by boys on the right and girls on the left, and the curé stood at the lectern. In a stained-glass window in the apse the Holy Ghost looked down upon the Virgin: in another window she was seen kneeling before the infant Jesus, and behind the shrine on the altar a group carved in wood depicted St. Michael destroying the dragon.

The priest began with a short sketch of sacred history. As she listened, Félicité imagined before her the Garden of Eden, the Flood, the Tower of

Babel, cities in flames, dying nations, overthrown idols, and in this bewildering vision she clung steadfastly to her veneration for the Most High and to her fear of His wrath. Then she wept as she listened to the story of the Passion. Why had they crucified Him, Who loved children, Who healed the blind, Who fed the multitudes, and Who had wished, in His meekness, to be born among the poor on the dung-heap of a stable? The sowings, the harvestings, the wine-presses, all those familiar things of which the Gospels speak, were ordinary, everyday occurrences to her. The passing of God had made them holy, and she loved the lambs more tenderly because of her love for the Lamb, and the doves because of the Holy Ghost.

She found it difficult to imagine the Holy Ghost in person, for it was not only a bird but a fire as well, and, at times, a breath. She thought that it might be its light, which flits about over the edge of marshes at night-time, its breath, which makes the clouds race across the sky, its voice, which gives sweet music to the bells, and she sat in a state of adoration, enjoying the coolness and the quiet of the church.

Of dogmas she neither understood nor attempted to understand anything. The curé discoursed, the children read aloud their lessons, and she finally went to sleep, waking up suddenly at the sound of their little wooden shoes clattering over the flag-stones as they left the church.

It was thus that, by being obliged to hear it, she learned the catechism, her education in religious matters having been neglected in her youth. From that time she imitated Virginie in all her observances, fasting when she fasted, and going to confession with her. On the festival of Corpus Christi they made an altar of repose together.

Virginie's first communion gave her much preliminary anxiety. She worried over her shoes, the rosary, the book, the gloves. How she trembled as she helped Mme. Aubain to dress the child!

All through the Mass she was in a state of feverish excitement. One side of the choir was hidden from her by M. Bourais, but opposite to her was the flock of maidens, with their white crowns above their hanging veils, making, as it were, a field of snow, and she recognized her dear little one in the distance by her dainty neck and reverential attitude. The bell tinkled. The heads bowed low, and there was silence. With the pealing of the organ, choir and congregation joined in singing the *Agnus Dei*. Then the procession of the boys began, and after them the girls rose from their seats. Step by step, their hands clasped in prayer, they approached the lighted altar, knelt on the first step, received the sacrament in turn, and came back in the same order to their seats. When Virginie's turn came, Félicité leant forward to see her, and, with the imaginativeness born of deep affection, it seemed to her that she, herself, was that child: Virginie's face became hers, she was wearing the child's dress, the child's heart was beating in her breast. As, with eyes closed in reverence, she opened her mouth as if to receive the sacred wafer, she nearly fainted with emotion. Early next day she went to the sacristy to receive the sacrament from Monsieur the curé. She took it with reverence, but did not experience the same joy.

Mme. Aubain wanted to give her child a perfect education, so, as Guyot could not teach her English or music, she decided to send her to the Ursuline Convent at Honfleur as a boarder. The child had no objection. Félicité thought that her mistress was unfeeling, and sighed. Then she thought that, perhaps, she was right: such matters were rather beyond her.

So, one day, an old cart stopped at their door, and a nun, who had come to fetch the young lady, got down from it. Félicité hoisted the luggage up beside the driver, to whom she gave some parting instructions: she had put six pots of jam and a dozen pears, as well as a bunch of violets, in the child's trunk.

At the last moment Virginie was seized with a violent fit of sobbing. She threw her arms round her mother, who kissed her on the forehead, saying, "Come, come! Be brave, be brave!" The steps were taken away, and the cart drove off.

Then Mme. Aubain's strength gave way. In the evening all her friends, the Lormeau family, Mme. Lechaptois, those dreadful spinsters, the Rochefeuilles, M. de Houppeville, and Bourais, came in to console her.

At first she missed her daughter very greatly indeed, but she had a letter from her three times a week, and wrote to her the other days, walked in her garden, read a little, and thus passed the weary hours.

Every morning, as usual, Félicité went into Virginie's room, and looked at the walls. She felt very dull at not having her hair to comb, her boots to lace up, and her little body to tuck into bed, and not to see her sweet face every day and all day, and

A SIMPLE HEART

hold her hand when they went out together. For lack of other occupation she tried to make lace, but her fingers were clumsy and broke the threads. She could not settle to anything, lost her sleep, and, to use her own phrase, was quite worn through.

To " amuse herself," she asked leave to have visits from her nephew Victor. He would come on a Sunday after Mass, his cheeks rosy, his chest bare, and exhaling a smell of the country he had walked through. She set a place at the table for him, and they lunched together. Herself eating as little as possible, to save expense, she would stuff him so much that he would fall asleep. At the first stroke of the bell for vespers, she would wake him up, brush down his trousers, tie his tie, and go off to church, leaning on his arm with all the pride of a mother.

His parents always told him to get something out of her—a packet of brown sugar, some soap, brandy, or even money from time to time. He brought his clothes for her to mend, and she gladly did the work, thankful for anything that would bring him there again.

In August his father took him off on a coasting trip. This was the month of the children's holidays, and their home-coming made up for the absence of her nephew. But Paul was becoming capricious and Virginie was getting too old for the familiar " thee " and " thou "; this made things a little uncomfortable and put a barrier, as it were, between her and the children.

Victor went to Morlaix, Dunkirk, and Brighton, in succession, and brought her a present after every trip. The first time, it was a box made of shells, then a coffee cup, and then, again, a big man made out of gingerbread. He was growing very good-looking, with his slim figure, his little moustache, his good, candid eyes, and his little leather cap, stuck on the back of his head like a pilot's. He amused her by telling her stories, in which there was a jumble of nautical expressions.

One Monday, July 14th, 1819, a date which she never forgot, he told her that he had been taken on for a long voyage, and on the following night but one he would go on board the Honfleur boat, to join his schooner, which was to leave Havre very shortly. He would, perhaps, be away for two years.

The prospect of such a long absence upset Félicité very much, and so, to bid him one more farewell on the Wednesday evening, when Madame's dinner was over, she put on her clogs and quickly covered the four leagues between Pont-l'Évêque and Honfleur.

When she reached the Calvary, she took the turn to the left instead of to the right, got lost in the timber-yards, and retraced her steps. Some people to whom she spoke advised her to hurry. She went right round the harbour, which was full of ships, and tripped over hawsers. Then the ground sunk under her feet, lights flashed across each other, and she thought she was going mad, for she saw horses in the sky. On the edge of the quay others were neighing, frightened by the sea. They were hoisted up with ropes and dropped into a boat, in which passengers were elbowing each other in the midst of casks of cider, baskets of cheese, and sacks of corn, while chickens were cackling and the captain was swearing, and a cabin-boy, indifferent to it all, leant over the cat-head. Félicité, who had not recognized him, cried " Victor ! " and he raised his head. She rushed forward, but at that very moment the gangway was pulled ashore.

The Honfleur packet, women singing as they hauled it, passed out of the harbour, its ribs creaking as the heavy waves lashed its bow. The mainsails swung round, and no one could now be seen on board : out on the sea, shimmering like silver in the light of the moon, it was but a black speck which grew ever fainter and fainter, sank, and was gone.

As Félicité passed by the Calvary, she had a desire to commend to God's mercy what she cherished most, and she stood, her face bathed in tears, praying for a long time, her eyes gazing at the clouds. The town was asleep, coast-guards were walking to and fro, and water poured unceasingly through the holes in the sluice, with the noise of a torrent. The clocks struck two.

The convent parlour would not be open before daybreak, and if she were late, Madame would be annoyed, so, in spite of her desire to kiss the other child, she went home. The maids at the inn were just waking up as she reached Pont-l'Évêque.

So the poor little fellow was going to be tossed by the waves for months and months. His previous voyages had not frightened her. People came back from England and Brittany, but America, the Colonies, the Islands, were all lost in unknown parts, at the other end of the world.

From that time Félicité thought only of her nephew. On sunny days she was tortured with thirst; when there was a storm she was afraid that he would be struck by lightning. As she listened to the wind howling in the chimney or dislodging slates, she saw him buffeted by this same tempest, on the very top of a broken mast, with his body thrown backwards under a sheet of foam; or, again —and this was a reminiscence of her illustrated geography-books — he was being devoured by savages, captured by monkeys in a forest, or dying on some desert shore. But she never spoke of her anxiety.

Mme. Aubain had anxieties of her own about her daughter. The kind nuns said that she was an affectionate child, but a delicate one. The slightest emotion unnerved her. She had to give up the piano.

Her mother insisted on regular reports from the convent. One morning, when the postman did not call, she lost patience, and walked up and down in the room, from her chair to the window. It was really extraordinary that there had been no letter for four days!

To console her by her own example, Félicité said: " As for me, Madame, it is six months since I had a letter ! "

" From whom, indeed ? "

The servant answered gently: " Why—from my nephew ! "

" Ah ! your nephew." And Mme. Aubain shrugged her shoulders and resumed her walk, as if to say: " I was not thinking of him, and, what is more, I don't care one little bit about him, a cabin-boy, a young rascal—what does it matter about him ? whereas my daughter . . . why, just think ! "

Félicité, although she had been brought up amid rough folk, was indignant with Madame, but soon forgot. It seemed to her quite easy to lose one's head when the little girl was concerned. For her, the two children were of equal importance, they were both united in her heart by one bond, and their destinies must be the same.

The chemist told her that Victor's ship had reached Havanna: he had read this bit of news in a paper.

To her Havanna meant cigars, and so she imagined it as a place where nobody did anything but smoke, with Victor walking about among the niggers in a cloud of smoke. Could one, "in case it was absolutely necessary," come back over-land? How far was it from Pont-l'Évêque?

To get such information, she put questions to M. Bourais. He got out his atlas and then began explaining the longitudes. Félicité's bewilderment made the pedant smile broadly. Finally, he made a very tiny black mark with his pencil in a circle on the map, saying, "Here it is!" She bent over the map: this network of coloured lines tired her eyes, and she learnt nothing from it. So, when Bourais kindly asked her to tell him what was worrying her, she begged him to show her the house where Victor was living. He threw up his hands, sneezed, and went into fits of laughter: such simplicity was real joy to him. And Félicité could not make out what he was laughing at; how could she, when probably she expected to see the actual portrait of her nephew, so limited was her intelligence!

A fortnight afterwards Liébard came into the

kitchen at market-time, as was his wont, and gave her a letter from her brother-in-law. As neither of them could read, she sought help from her mistress.

Mme. Aubain, who was counting the stitches in her knitting, put her work down and broke the seal of the letter. She shuddered, and said in a low voice with an impressive look: " They have bad news to tell you . . . your nephew . . ."

He was dead. That was all they had to say.

Félicité fell on to a chair with her head against the wall, and closed her eyelids, which suddenly became pink. Then, with bent forehead, hands hanging down, and staring eyes, she repeated at intervals: " Poor little chap! Poor little chap! "

Liébard watched her and sighed. Mme. Aubain trembled a little. She suggested that she should go to see her sister at Trouville. Félicité replied, with a shake of her head that there was no necessity to do so. There was a silence. The excellent Liébard thought it a good opportunity to withdraw.

Then Félicité said: " It is nothing to them—nothing in the least! "

Her head fell forward again, and at little intervals, and quite mechanically, she picked up the knitting-needles on the work-table.

Some women passed across the yard with a barrow of dripping linen. As she saw them through the window, she remembered her washing: she had left it to soak the day before, and to-day she must wring it out, and she left the room. Her board and her tub were at the edge of the Toucques. She threw a heap of chemises on to the bank, rolled up her sleeves, and took her wooden beater, with which she smote so hard

A SIMPLE HEART

that the noise of the blows could be heard in the neighbouring gardens. The fields were empty, the river moved gently in the wind: down below, long grasses waved to and fro like the hair of corpses floating in the water. She kept her grief to herself, and was very brave until the evening; but in her own room she gave way to it utterly, lying on her bed with her face buried in the pillow and her clenched hands against her temples.

Much later, she heard the circumstances of Victor's death from the captain himself. They had bled him too much at the hospital for yellow fever. Four doctors held him at once. He died in a moment, and the chief doctor said: "Good! There goes another one!"

His parents had always treated him very cruelly. She preferred not to see them again, and they made no advances, either because they forgot all about her, or because they were hard in their wretched state.

Virginie grew weaker. Tightness of the chest, coughing, recurrent fever, and the marble paleness of her cheeks showed that she had some deep-seated complaint. M. Poupart had advised a stay in Provence. Mme. Aubain decided on it, and, but for the air of Pont-l'Évêque, would have brought her daughter home at once. She made an arrangement with a job-master, to drive her to the convent every Tuesday. There is a terrace in the garden from which one can see the Seine. Virginie, on her arm, took her walks there over the fallen vine-leaves. Sometimes the sunlight coming through the clouds made her blink, as she looked out on the sails in the distance and the horizon stretched before her, from the château of Tancarville to the lighthouses of Havre. Afterwards they rested in the arbour. Her mother had procured a little cask of excellent Malaga, and laughing at the idea of getting tipsy, she used to drink a thimble-full, but no more.

Her strength returned. Autumn slipped quickly away. Félicité reassured Mme. Aubain, but one evening, when she returned from a walk in the neighbourhood, she found M. Poupart's gig at the door. He was in the hall and Mme. Aubain was tying on her bonnet.

"Give me my foot-warmer, my purse, my gloves. Do be quick about it!"

Virginie had congestion of the lungs, and, perhaps, was dangerously ill.

"Not yet!" said the doctor, and they both got into the carriage as whirling snow-flakes began to fall. Night was coming on, and it was very cold.

Félicité hurried into the church to light a taper. Then she ran after the carriage, which she caught up in an hour, jumped lightly up behind, and hung on to the fringes of the seat. Then she had a sudden thought: "The courtyard has not been shut up. What if robbers got in!" And she jumped down.

At dawn next day she went to the doctor's. He had come in and started for the country again. Then she waited in the inn, thinking that somebody or other would bring her a letter. Finally, as it was growing dark, she got into the Lisieux omnibus.

The convent was at the end of a steep lane. When she was half-way through it, she heard strange sounds, the tolling of a bell. " It's for someone else," she thought, and she pulled the knocker violently.

After some minutes, she heard somebody shuffling down to the door: it was opened ajar, and a nun appeared.

The good sister with an air of compunction said that " she had just passed away." At that very moment the bell of St. Leonard's was tolled with renewed vigour.

Félicité went up to the second floor. From the threshold of the room she saw Virginie lying on her back, her hands clasped, her mouth open, and her head thrown back under a black crucifix that leant over her, between curtains that were absolutely still and less white than her face. Mme. Aubain, at the foot of the bed which she was clasping with her arms, was uttering agonizing sounds. The mother-superior was standing on the right. Three candlesticks on the chest of drawers made spots of red, and through the windows could be seen a white fog. Some nuns led Mme. Aubain away.

For two nights Félicité never left the dead girl. She said the same prayers over and over again, sprinkled the sheets with holy water, sat down again, and watched her. At the end of her first vigil, she observed that the child's face had become yellow, her lips had turned blue, her nose seemed sharper, and her eyes had sunk in. She kissed them several times, and she would not have been very much astonished if Virginie had opened them again: to minds like hers the supernatural is quite simple.

She made the girl's toilette, wrapped her in her shroud, put her in her coffin, placed a wreath upon her body, and loosened her hair. It was fair and amazingly long for a child of her age. Félicité cut off a big lock, half of which she slipped into her bosom, determined never to part with it.

The body was taken back to Pont-l'Évêque, in accordance with the wishes of Mme. Aubain, who followed the hearse in a closed carriage.

After the Mass, it took another three-quarters of an hour to reach the cemetery. Paul walked in front, sobbing. M. Bourais was behind, and, behind him, again, were the principal people of Pont-l'Évêque, the women wearing black mantles, and Félicité. She thought of her nephew; and, as she had not been able to pay this tribute of love to him, her grief was all the greater, just as if she were burying him with Virginie.

Mme. Aubain's despair was boundless. She rebelled against God first of all, deeming it unjust of Him to have taken her daughter from her—she had never done any harm, and her conscience was so clean! Ah, no! She ought to have taken Virginie to the south. Other doctors would have saved her. She accused herself, wished to join her child, and cried in distress in the middle of her dreams. One dream, especially, never seemed to leave off haunting her. Her husband, dressed like a sailor, came back from a long voyage, and told her as he wept that he had received orders to carry off Virginie. Then they took counsel together how to hide her somewhere.

On one occasion she came in from the garden quite

A SIMPLE HEART

upset. A little while ago—and she pointed out the spot—the father and daughter had appeared to her side by side: they did nothing, but they looked at her.

For several months she remained in her room, showing no interest in anything. Félicité lectured her gently: she must take care of herself for her son's sake, and for the other, in remembrance of " her."

" Her? " answered Mme. Aubain, as though she were waking from a sleep. " Yes, yes! You do not forget it! " This was an allusion to the cemetery, to which she was strictly forbidden to go.

Félicité used to go there every day. Precisely at four, she would skirt the houses, climb the hill, pass through the gate, and come to Virginie's grave. It was a little column of pink marble with a stone at the foot and a little garden enclosed by chains. The beds were hidden by a carpet of flowers. She watered their leaves, freshened up the sand, going down on her knees so that she might tidy everything up more easily. When Mme. Aubain was able to come there she felt a relief and some sort of consolation.

Then years slipped gently by, one very much like another, and nothing happened in them but the recurrence of the great festivals: Easter, the Assumption, All Saint's Day. Household events marked dates that were remembered afterwards. In 1825, for instance, two glaziers white-washed the hall: in 1827 a piece of the roof fell into the courtyard and nearly killed a man: in the summer of 1828 it was

Madame's turn to offer the sacred bread: about that time, Bourais went away mysteriously: and one by one the old acquaintances departed—Guyot, Liébard, Mme. Lechaptois, Robelin, and Uncle Gremanville, who had been paralysed for a long time.

One night the guard of the mail-coach announced the Revolution of July in Pont-l'Évêque. A few days later, a new sub-prefect was appointed. This was Baron de Larsonnière, formerly consul in America, who brought with him, in addition to his wife, his sister-in-law and three young ladies who were already quite tall. They were to be seen on his lawn, dressed in light drapery, and they had a negro servant and a parrot. Mme. Aubain received a visit from them which she did not fail to return. Félicité hastened to tell her as soon as they were seen in the distance.

But only one thing could really rouse her interest, and that was letters from her son. He was quite unable to make a career for himself, as he was a haunter of taverns. She paid his debts and he made new ones. Mme. Aubain's sighs, as she knitted by the window, reached the ears of Félicité spinning in the kitchen.

The two used to stroll together along the fruit-wall, and they always talked of Virginie, wondering whether this or that thing would have given her pleasure, or what she would have said on such or such an occasion.

All her little belongings filled a cupboard in the room with its two beds. Mme. Aubain went through them as seldom as she could.

One summer day she reluctantly decided to do so,

A SIMPLE HEART

and moths flew out of the cupboard when she opened the door.

Virginie's frocks were in a row underneath a shelf on which were three dolls, some hoops, some little pots and pans, and the basin which she had used. They took out her petticoats as well, her stockings, and her handkerchiefs, and spread them out on the two beds before folding them up again. The sunshine streamed in upon these poor little things, bringing out their stains and the creases made by the child's movements. The air was warm and the sky was blue, a blackbird warbled, and a deep peace seemed to reign over every living thing. They came across a little plush hat, with some long chestnut-coloured fur round it, but moths had quite ruined it. Félicité begged for it. They gazed at each other, and their eyes filled with tears. Then the mistress opened her arms, and the servant threw herself into them. They clasped each other in a warm embrace, satisfying their grief in a kiss which made them equal.

This was the first time that such a thing had happened in their lives, for Mme. Aubain was not expansive by nature.

Félicité was as grateful as if she had received some great favour, and from that day cherished her with dog-like devotion and religious veneration.

The kindness of her heart increased more and more.

When she heard the drums of a regiment marching down the street, she stood at the door with a pitcher of cider and invited the soldiers to drink. She looked after cholera patients. She protected

Polish refugees, one of whom announced his desire to marry her. But they fell out, for, on her return from the Angelus one morning, she found he had got into the kitchen, and was quietly eating a dish of meat seasoned with vinegar.

After the Poles it was old Colmiche, an ancient person who was supposed to have committed atrocities in '93. He lived by the side of the river in the ruins of a pig-sty. The little ragamuffins peered at him through the cracks of the walls and threw pebbles at him as he lay on his mattress, constantly shaken by catarrh. His hair was very long, his eyes inflamed, and on his arm there was a swelling as big as his head. Félicité brought him some linen, tried to clean out his filthy den, and thought of getting him to live in the bake-house, if it did not annoy Madame. When the tumour burst, she dressed it every day: sometimes she brought him cake and would set him out in the sun on a truss of straw. The poor old fellow, slobbering and trembling, would thank her in faint accents, fearful to lose her, stretching forth his hands as he saw her going away.

He died, and she had a Mass said for the repose of his soul.

That very day a great piece of happiness came her way. Just at dinner-time, Mme. de Larsonnière's negro appeared with the parrot in its cage, with perch, chain, and padlock. The Baroness told Mme. Aubain in a little note that, her husband having been promoted to a Prefecture, they were leaving that evening. She begged her to accept the bird as a remembrance and mark of her regard.

A SIMPLE HEART

For a long time this parrot had had a place in Félicité's thoughts, for it came from America, and that name brought back Victor to her, so much so that she put questions to the negro about it. She had once even said, " How happy Madame would be to have it ! "

The negro reported the conversation to his mistress, who, not being able to take the bird with her, got rid of it in this way.

IV

His name was Loulou. His body was green, the tips of his wings were pink, his forehead was blue, and his throat golden.

He had a tiresome mania for biting his perch, tearing out feathers, scattering dirt about, and upsetting the water of his bath. He bored Mme. Aubain, and she made a present of him to Félicité.

Félicité undertook his training. Soon he repeated, " Nice boy! Your servant, sir! How are you, Marie? " He was placed beside the door, and surprised many people by not answering to the name of Jacquot, for all parrots were called Jacquot. They likened him to a turkey or a faggot, and thereby Félicité felt great stabs. Loulou was curiously obstinate, for he would not talk when he was looked at !

None the less he enjoyed having people about him. On Sundays when those dreadful Rochefeuille spinsters, M. de Houppeville, and some new friends —Onfroy the apothecary, M. Varin, and Captain

Mathieu, were playing their game of cards, he beat the windows with his wings, and threw himself about so furiously that it was impossible to hear oneself speak.

Bourais's face undoubtedly struck him as very funny, for as soon as he saw him he started laughing with all his might. His shrieks rang through the courtyard and were repeated by the echo. The neighbours came to their windows and laughed too. M. Bourais, in order to escape the bird's eye, would slip along under the wall, hiding his face in his hat, get to the river, and come into the house by the garden gate, and the looks he cast at the bird were by no means affectionate!

Loulou had been cuffed by the butcher boy for having dared to put his head into his basket. From that day he was always trying to give him a nip through his shirt. The boy threatened to wring his neck, although he was not cruel, in spite of his tattooed arms and big whiskers. Very much the contrary! He had a sneaking liking for the parrot, so much so, indeed, that, being in a merry humour, he wanted to teach him to swear.

Félicité, alarmed at such proceedings, put the bird in the kitchen. His little chain was removed and he wandered about the house.

When he came downstairs he used to lean on the steps with his beak and then raise his feet alternately. Félicité was frightened lest such gymnastic performances should make him giddy. He fell ill and could not talk or eat any longer. There was a thickening under his tongue, such as fowls have sometimes. She cured him by pulling out the little bit of skin with her finger-nails. One day M. Paul stupidly blew the smoke of his cigar into his face, and on another occasion Mme. Lormeau teased him with the point of her umbrella, which he got hold of with his beak. Finally he got lost.

Félicité had put him down on the grass for some fresh air. She went away for a minute, and, when she came back, there was no parrot!

At first she hunted for him among the shrubs, by the river, and on the roofs of the houses, without listening to her mistress's cries of "Take care! You are surely mad!" Then she went through all the gardens in Pont-l'Évêque, and stopped passers-by, saying, "You don't happen to have seen my parrot by any chance?" She described him to those who did not already know him. Suddenly she thought that she made out something green that was fluttering behind the mills at the foot of the hill. But on the top of the hill there was nothing. A peddler assured her that he had come across the bird a little while before in old Mother Simonne's shop at Saint-Melaine. She hastened there; they had no idea what she meant. At last she came home, worn out, her slippers in rags, and death in her soul. As she sat beside Madame on the garden-seat and told her all her adventures, something light dropped on her shoulder—it was Loulou! What on earth had he been up to? Perhaps he had been out for a walk in the neighbourhood!

She had some trouble in getting over this, or, rather, she never did really get over it.

Following a chill, she had some throat-trouble, and, soon afterwards, ear-ache. Three years later she was deaf, and she spoke very loud, even in church. Although her sins could have been proclaimed in every corner of the diocese without dishonour to her or the upsetting of people in general, the curé thought it would be better if he heard her confession in the sacristy only.

Then her misfortunes were added to by imaginary buzzings in her head. Often her mistress would say, " Good heavens, how stupid you are ! " and she would reply, " Yes, Madame ! " as she looked about for something.

Her little circle of ideas grew narrower and narrower, and the pealing of church bells and the lowing of cattle no longer meant anything to her. Human beings did their appointed tasks in ghostly silence. Only one sound reached her ears now— the voice of the parrot.

As though to amuse her, he would reproduce the ticking of the spit, the piercing cry of a hawker of fish, and the noise of the joiner's saw in the house opposite, and, when the bell rang, he would imitate Mme. Aubain's " Félicité ! the door, the door ! "

They used to carry on conversations together, he reciting, *ad nauseam*, the three phrases in his repertory, she replying in phrases which were just as disconnected, though they came from the bottom of her heart. In her isolated state Loulou was almost a son and a lover to her. He would climb up her fingers, nibble at her lips, and hold tightly to her little shawl, and when she bent her forehead and shook her head, as nurses do, the great wings of her bonnet and the wings of the bird quivered together.

When clouds gathered and the thunder growled,

A SIMPLE HEART

he would utter piercing shrieks, no doubt remembering the downpours in his native forests. The streaming rain would drive him nearly mad. He used to fly wildly about, dash up to the ceiling, upset everything, and, going through the window, splash about in the garden. But he would soon come back to one of his perches, and, as he hopped about to dry his feathers, he would show his beak and his tail in turn.

One morning in the terrible winter of 1837, when she had put him in front of the fire because of the cold, she found him dead, in the middle of his cage, head downwards, his claws in the bars. No doubt a clot of blood had killed him, but she jumped to the conclusion that he had been poisoned with parsley, and, in spite of the absence of any proof, her suspicions fell on Fabu.

She wept so much that her mistress said, " Very well, have him stuffed! "

Félicité asked the chemist's advice, who had always been kind to the parrot. He wrote to Havre, and a man called Fellacher undertook the job, but as parcels sometimes went a-missing in the mail-coach, she decided to take the parrot as far as Honfleur herself.

Along the roadside were endless apple trees which had lost their leaves, and there was ice on the ditches. Dogs barked round the farms; and Félicité, with her hands under her cloak and her little black sabots and her basket, walked quickly along the middle of the road. She went through the forest, passed Le Haut-Chêne, and came to Saint-Gatien. Behind her in a cloud of dust, and with gathering speed caused by a hill, a mail-coach rushed down at full gallop like a hurricane. Seeing this woman, who did not trouble to get out of the way, the guard raised himself up over the hood, and the postilion shouted, too, while his four horses which he could not hold in increased their speed. The two leaders grazed her, but he jerked them to one side. In a wild fury he raised his long whip as he passed, and gave her such a lash from head to waist that she fell on her back.

When she recovered consciousness the first thing she did was to open her basket. Fortunately, nothing had happened to Loulou. She felt her right cheek burning, and when she put her fingers on it they were red; the blood was flowing.

She sat down on a heap of stones and bandaged her face with her handkerchief. Then she ate a crust which she had taken the precaution to put in her basket, and made light of her wound in gazing at the bird.

When she reached the crest of Ecquemauville, she saw the lights of Honfleur shining out in the night like a host of stars; in the distance the sea was spread dimly before her. Then a feeling of faintness prevented her going on. The misery of her childhood, the cruel shattering of her first love, the going away of her nephew, the death of Virginie, all came back to her at once, like the waves of an inrushing tide, and rising to her throat, choked her.

Afterwards she made a point of speaking to the captain of the boat, and, without telling him what was in it, asked him to take special care of her parcel.

A SIMPLE HEART

Fellacher kept the parrot for a long time. He was always promising to send it off the following week. After six months he announced that a box was on its way, and then nothing more was heard of it. It seemed most unlikely that Loulou would ever come back, and Félicité said to herself, "They have stolen him!"

At last he arrived, and looking perfectly splendid, too! He stood on a branch which was screwed into a mahogany socket, with one foot in the air and his head on one side, biting at a nut, which the bird-stuffer, with a love for the really magnificent, had gilded.

Félicité shut him up in her room. This place, to which very few people were ever admitted, contained such a quantity of religious objects and miscellaneous oddments that it looked like a chapel and a bazaar all in one.

A big wardrobe prevented you opening the door wide. Opposite the window overlooking the garden a little round one gave a glimpse of the courtyard. Beside the turn-up bedstead there was a table, with a water-jug, two combs, and a cube of blue soap in a chipped plate. On the walls there were rosaries, medals, several benign Virgins, and a holy-water dish made out of a coconut. On the chest of drawers, which was covered with a cloth like an altar, were the shell box that Victor had given her, a watering-can and a toy-balloon, copy-books, the geography book with the plates, and a pair of little boots. And, fastened by its ribbons to the nail of the looking-glass, was the little plush hat. Félicité even carried her idea of respect to such an extreme as to preserve one of Monsieur's frock-coats. All the old odds and ends which Mme. Aubain had done with she carried off to her room. Thus there were some artificial flowers along the edge of the chest of drawers and a portrait of the Comte d'Artois in the window-recess.

With the aid of a bracket Loulou was fixed on the smoke-stack which jutted out into the room. Every morning when she awakened, she saw him there in the light of dawn, and she recalled days that were no more, and the smallest details of smallest acts, without pain, with a feeling of absolute peacefulness.

Having no intercourse with anybody, she lived in the dull state of a sleep-walker. The Corpus Christi processions roused her again. Then she went about begging for candlesticks and mats from her neighbours, to decorate the altar which they set up in the street.

In church she was always gazing at the window with the representation of the Holy Ghost, and observed that it had a certain resemblance to the parrot. This resemblance seemed to her still more striking in a picture by d'Épinal of the baptism of Our Lord. With its purple wings and its emerald-green body, the dove therein was a perfect likeness of Loulou.

She bought it and hung it in the place of the Comte d'Artois, so that she could see them both together in one glance. They were associated together in her thoughts, the parrot being consecrated by this connection with the Holy Ghost, which became more vivid to her eye and more intelligible

A SIMPLE HEART

to her mind. The Father could not have chosen to express Himself through a dove, for those birds cannot speak, but rather through one of Loulou's ancestors. Although Félicité used to say her prayers with her eyes on the picture, she gave a glance from time to time to the parrot.

She had a strong desire to join the Ladies of the Virgin, but Mme. Aubain dissuaded her from doing so.

Then a great event loomed into sight—Paul's marriage.

He had been, in turn, a lawyer's clerk, in business, in the Customs, the Inland Revenue, and had even made efforts to get into the Department of Woods and Rivers, when, at the age of thirty-six, by an inspiration from heaven, he suddenly discovered his real line—the Registrar's office. There he showed such great capability that an inspector offered him his daughter in marriage and promised him his influence.

So Paul, grown serious, brought his bride to his mother's house.

The young lady criticized severely the ways of the people of Pont-l'Évêque, gave herself all the airs of a very high and mighty person, and wounded Félicité's feelings.

Mme. Aubain felt relief at her departure.

The following week came news of the death of M. Bourais in an inn in Lower Brittany. The rumours of his suicide were confirmed and doubts as to his honesty arose. Mme. Aubain went into his accounts and was very soon acquainted with the long list of his misdeeds—embezzled arrears of payments due, secret sales of wood, forged receipts, etc. Besides all this, he had had an illegitimate child and "relations with a person at Dozulé."

These misdeeds upset her very much. In the month of March, 1853, she was seized with a pain in her chest; her tongue seemed to be covered with film, and leeches had no beneficial effect on her difficult breathing. She died on the ninth evening of her illness, being just seventy-two.

She was considered younger, thanks to the bands of brown hair in which her pale, pock-marked face was set. There were few friends to regret her, for she had a certain disdainful manner which kept people at a distance.

But Félicité mourned for her as servants seldom mourn for their masters. That Madame should die before her upset her ideas, seemed contrary to the natural order of things, was unthinkable and monstrous.

Ten days afterwards, which was the time spent on a hurried journey from Besançon, the heirs arrived. The daughter-in-law ransacked the drawers, chose some furniture and sold the rest; and then they went back to their Registrar's business.

Madame's armchair, her small round table, her foot-warmer, the eight chairs, were all gone. Yellow patches in the middle of the panels showed where the engravings had hung. They had carried off the two little beds with their mattresses, and all Virginie's belongings had disappeared from the cupboard. Félicité went from room to room almost reeling under the weight of her sorrow.

Next day there was a notice on the door, and the

A SIMPLE HEART

apothecary shouted in her ear that the house was to be sold.

She staggered, and was obliged to sit down. What distressed her most of all was the giving up of her room, which was so suitable for poor Loulou. Enveloping him in a look of anguish as she made supplications to the Holy Ghost, she formed the idolatrous habit of kneeling in front of the parrot when she prayed. Sometimes the sun came through the little window and caught his glass eye, when a great luminous ray would shoot out from it, and she would be in ecstasies.

Her mistress left her an income of three hundred and eighty francs a year. The garden kept her in vegetables, and, as for clothes, she had enough to last her till the end of her days, and she used as few candles as possible by going to bed at dusk.

She rarely went out, as she did not wish to go near the dealer's shop, in which some of the old furniture was exposed for sale. Since her fit of giddiness, she had been dragging one leg, and as her strength was failing, old Mother Simonne, whose grocery shop had been a failure, came in every morning to chop wood and pump water for her.

Her eyes grew weak. The shutters were no longer opened. Many years rolled by, and the house was neither let nor sold.

As she was afraid of being evicted, she never asked for it to be repaired. The boards of the roof rotted; her bolster was never dry all through one winter. After Easter she spat blood.

Then Mother Simonne called in a doctor. Félicité wanted to know what was the matter with her. Too

deaf to hear, the only word that reached her was
"pneumonia," a word with which she was
acquainted. She answered gently, "Ah! like
Madame!" thinking it natural that she should follow
her mistress.

The time of Corpus Christi was drawing near.

The first altar was always at the bottom of the hill,
the second in front of the post office, and the third
about the middle of the street. There was some little
rivalry in the matter of this one, and, in the end,
the women of the parish chose Mme. Aubain's
courtyard.

The hard breathing and fever increased. Félicité
was vexed at not being able to do anything for the
altar. If only she could have put something on it!
Then she thought of the parrot. The neighbours
protested that it would not be decent, but the curé
granted his permission, which gave her such joy that
she begged him to accept Loulou, her only precious
possession, when she died.

From Tuesday to Saturday, the eve of the Festival,
she coughed more often. By the evening her face
had shrivelled up, her lips stuck to her gums, and
she had fits of sickness. Very early next morning,
feeling very low, she sent for a priest.

Three kindly women were beside her during the
extreme unction. Then she said that she had to
speak to Fabu. He came in his Sunday clothes,
very ill at ease in the lugubrious atmosphere.

"Forgive me," she said, making an effort to
stretch out her arms, "I thought it was you who
killed him!"

What did she mean by such rubbishy talk? She

A SIMPLE HEART 67

had suspected him of murder—a man such as he! He got very angry and was going to make a row.

"Can't you see," said the woman, "that she is no longer in her right mind?"

From time to time Félicité talked to the shadows round about her. The women went away, and Mother Simonne had her lunch.

A little later she brought Loulou close to Félicité, saying, "Come, now, say good-bye to him!"

Although the parrot was not a corpse, worms had been devouring him; one of his wings was broken, and the stuffing was coming out of his stomach. But she was blind now, and she kissed him on the forehead and held him tight to her cheek. Mother Simonne took him away from her to put him on the altar.

V

The scents of summer were rising from the fields, flies were buzzing, the sun was making the river shine, and was warming the houses. Mother Simonne came back into the room and fell softly asleep. The noise of church bells awakened her, as people came out from vespers. Félicité's delirium subsided, and as she thought of the procession she saw it as if she had been taking part in it.

All the school-children, the choirs, and the firemen walked on the pavement, while in the middle of the road there marched the verger carrying his halberd, the beadle with a great cross, the schoolmaster, watching the behaviour of the little boys, the nun, uneasy about her little girls, of whom three of the sweetest, with angelic curls, were throwing rose-petals into the air; the deacon conducted the band with outstretched hand, and two thurifers turned back at every step towards the Holy Sacrament which was borne by Monsieur the curé, wearing his beautiful chasuble, under a canopy of deep-red velvet held at each corner by a churchwarden. A wave of people surged on behind between the white drapings covering the walls of the houses, and they reached the bottom of the hill.

A cold sweat moistened Félicité's temples. Mother Simonne sponged it with a piece of linen, saying to herself that one day she would have to go that way, too.

The hum of the crowd increased, was very loud for a moment, and then went farther away.

A fusillade shook the windows. It was the postilions saluting the monstrance. Félicité turned her eyes round and said as loud as she could, " Is he all right? " She was worried by the thought of the parrot.

Her death agony began. A rattling in her throat became more and more rapid and made her sides heave. Bubbles of froth were on the corners of her mouth, and her whole body trembled.

Soon the booming of the ophicleides, the high voices of the children, and the deep voices of the men were heard in the distance. At intervals all was silent, and the tramping of feet, deadened by the carpet of flowers, sounded like a flock moving across a field of grass.

The clergy appeared in the courtyard. Mother

Simonne climbed on to a chair to reach the little window, and so looked down on the altar. Green garlands hung down over it, and it was decked with a flounce of English lace. In its centre was a small frame in which relics were set. There were two orange-trees at the corners, and on its whole length there stood silver candlesticks and china vases, which held sunflowers, lilies, peonies, foxgloves, and tufts of hortensia. This mass of brilliant colour descended from the altar itself to the carpet at its foot which was spread well over the pavement. Some rare objects caught one's eye: a silver-gilt sugar-caster with a crown of violets, pendants of Alençon stones sparkling on beds of moss, and two Chinese screens with landscapes. Loulou, hidden under roses, showed nothing but his blue forehead, like a plaque of lapis lazuli.

The churchwardens, the choirs, the children took up positions on the three sides of the courtyard. The priest went slowly up the steps and placed upon the lace covering of the altar his great golden sun, which shone forth upon them all. They all knelt. There was a great silence. The censers were swung at the full length of their little chains.

An azure vapour came up into Félicité's room. She opened her nostrils wide and inhaled it sensuously, mystically. She closed her eyes. Her lips smiled. The beat of her heart grew slower and slower, more fleeting each instant, more gentle, as a fountain sinks, an echo vanishes. And when she drew her last breath, she believed that she saw in the half-opened heavens a gigantic parrot hovering above her head.

THE LEGEND OF ST. JULIAN THE HOSPITALLER

(*La Légende de Saint Julien L'Hospitalier*)

THE LEGEND OF ST. JULIAN THE HOSPITALLER

(*La Légende de Saint Julien L'Hospitalier*)

I

Julian's father and mother lived in a castle in the middle of a wood, on the slope of a hill.

The four towers at its corners had pointed roofs covered with scales of lead, and the base of the walls rested on masses of rock which fell steeply to the bottom of the enclosure below. The pavement of the courtyard was clean as the flagstones of a church. Long gutter-spouts in the form of dragons looking downwards spat the rain-water into the cistern, and on the window-ledges of each story a basil or a heliotrope flowered in painted earthenware pots.

A second enclosure made with stakes held an orchard first of all, and then a garden in which combinations of flowers formed figures, and then, again, a trellis walk in which you took the air, and a court for the pages to play mall. On the other side were the kennels, the stables, the bake-house, the wine-presses, and the barns. All round this there spread a green meadow, which was enclosed by a strong thorn-hedge.

They had been living in peace for so long that the portcullis was never lowered; the moats were full of water; swallows nested in the cracks of the battlements; and the archer who marched up and down the ramparts all day long, retired to his watch-tower when the sun beat down too strongly, and slept like a monk.

Inside, iron-work shone brightly everywhere; tapestries covered the walls to keep out the cold; cupboards were filled to overflowing with linen; casks of wine were piled up in the cellars, oaken chests were bursting with the weight of bags of money. In the armoury, between standards and wild beasts' heads, were to be seen weapons of every age and every nation, from the slings of the Amalekites and the javelins of the Garamantes to the short swords of the Saracens and the coats of mail of the Normans. The chief spit in the kitchen could roast an ox. The chapel was as magnificent as the oratory of a king. There was even, in a secluded spot, a Roman vapour-bath, but the good lord made no use of it, holding that it was a practice of heathens.

Wrapped always in a cloak of foxes' skins he walked about his castle, administering the law to his vassals and settling the quarrels of his neighbours. In winter he watched the snowflakes falling, or had stories read to him. When the first fine days came, he rode out upon his mule along the by-ways beside the corn which was turning green, chatting with and giving advice to the peasants. After many adventures he had taken a lady of high degree as his wife.

She was very fair of skin, and somewhat proud and serious. The horns of her coif brushed against the lintels of the doors, the train of her cloth dress trailed

THE LEGEND OF ST. JULIAN

three yards behind her. Her household was ordered like the inside of a monastery. Every morning she allotted to her servants their appointed tasks, inspected the preserves and the unguents, span at her distaff, or embroidered altar-cloths. By much praying to God a son was born to her.

Then there were great rejoicings, with a banquet which lasted three days and four nights, torch-light illuminations, music by harp-players, and much strewing of green branches. They ate of the choicest spices and fowls as large as sheep; to amuse the guests a dwarf came out of a pasty, and with the crowd ever growing the supply of drinking-cups was insufficient, and they were obliged to drink out of horns and helmets.

The lady who had just been made a mother took no part in these festivities. She remained quietly in bed.

One night she awoke, and it seemed to her that she saw a shadow moving under the light of the moon which came through her window. It was an old man in a robe of rough cloth, with his beads at his side, a wallet on his shoulder, looking very like a hermit. He came near her pillow and said to her, without opening his lips: " Rejoice, O mother, thy son shall be a saint!"

She was about to cry out, but he glided over the streak of moonlight, rose gently into the air, and vanished. The songs at the banquet burst forth more loudly. She heard the voices of angels, and her head fell back upon the pillow, over which was hanging the bone of a martyr in a setting of garnets.

Next day all the servants were questioned, and they

said that they had seen no hermit. Dream or reality, it must have been a communication from heaven, but she was careful to say nothing about it, fearing lest she should be accused of pride.

The guests departed early that day, and Julian's father happened to be outside the postern gate, to which he had just escorted the last of them, when suddenly a beggar rose up before him in the mists. He was a gipsy, with plaited beard, rings on his arms, and flaming eyes. As one inspired, he stammered out these disjointed words: " Ah! Ah! thy son! Much blood! Much glory! Always happy! The family of an emperor!"

And, stooping to pick up his alms, he was lost in the grass and disappeared.

The good lord looked right and left and called with all his might. No one! The wind whistled, the morning-mists flew away. He attributed this vision to a weary head, from having slept too little. " If I talk about it, they will make a laughing-stock of me," said he to himself. But the destined glory of his son dazzled him, although the promise was not clear, and he doubted even whether he had heard it.

Husband and wife kept their secrets. But they both cherished their son with an equal love, and, treating him with the deference due to one distinguished by God, they paid infinite attention to his person. His cradle was stuffed with the finest down. A lamp in the form of a dove burned continually above it; three nurses rocked him. In his swaddling clothes, with his pink face and blue eyes, his mantle of brocade and his cap covered with

THE LEGEND OF ST. JULIAN

pearls, he looked like an infant Jesus. He teethed without once crying.

When he was seven, his mother taught him to sing. To make him brave, his father set him on a big horse. The child smiled with pleasure, and was not long in learning all about chargers.

A very learned old monk taught him Holy Writ, the Arabic way of counting, the Latin letters, and how to paint miniatures on vellum. They used to work together high up in a turret, far from all noise. The lesson over, they would go down into the garden where they studied the flowers as they walked slowly backwards and forwards.

Sometimes there was to be seen passing through the valley below a string of laden animals led by a man on foot, garbed in Eastern fashion. The lord, who recognized a merchant in the fellow, would send a servant out to him, and the stranger would turn from his direct road without fear. Conducted into the reception-hall, he would bring out of his chests pieces of velvet and silk, jewels, perfumes, and curious things of unknown use, and by and by the fellow would take his departure, having taken a big profit and suffered no bodily harm.

On other occasions a band of pilgrims would come knocking at the gate. Their damp garments would steam in front of the fire, and when they had had a big meal they would tell stories of their travels: the wanderings of their ships over stormy seas, marches across burning sands, the ferocity of the heathen, the caves of Syria, the Manger and the Sepulchre. Then they would give the young lord scallop-shells from off their cloaks.

Often the lord feasted his old companions-in-arms. As they drank they would call to mind their wars, the storming of fortresses, and the crashing noise of engines of war, and their great wounds. Julian, who listened to them, uttered cries, and then his father had no doubt that one day he would be a conqueror. Yet of an evening, as he came out of the chapel after the Angelus and passed through rows of poor people bowing before him, he would dip into his purse with such modesty and so noble an air, that his mother was convinced that she would assuredly see him an archbishop before his days were ended.

His seat in the chapel was beside his parents, and, however long the service might be, he remained on his knees on his stool, his cap on the floor and his hands clasped in prayer.

One day, while Mass was being said, he raised his head and saw a little white mouse coming out of a hole in the wall. It trotted along the first step of the altar, and, after turning right and left two or three times, fled by the way it had come. The following Sunday he was disturbed by the thought that he might see it again. It came back, and every Sunday he expected to see it, was annoyed with it, took a violent dislike to it and determined to rid himself of it.

So, having closed the door and sprinkled some crumbs on the steps of the altar, he took up a position in front of the hole with a switch in his hand. After a very long time a pink nose appeared followed by the rest of the mouse. He gave it a light blow, and stood amazed over the little body which made not the least movement. A drop of blood made a

THE LEGEND OF ST. JULIAN

stain upon the pavement. He quickly wiped it off with his sleeve, threw the mouse outside, and said nothing about it to anybody.

There were all sorts of birds pecking at the seeds in the garden. He thought it a good idea to put peas in a hollow reed. When he heard twittering in a tree he came up softly, raised his pipe, and blew out his cheeks. The little creatures rained down upon his shoulders in such abundance that he could not help laughing and rejoicing over his trick.

One morning, as he was coming home by the rampart, he saw a fat pigeon preening itself in the sunshine on the top of the wall. He stopped to look at it, and as there was a breach in this part of the wall a bit of stone was handy. He swung his arm, and the stone brought down the bird, which fell like a lump into the moat. He dashed down, tearing himself in the briars and groping about everywhere, more nimble than a young dog. The pigeon was hanging, quivering with broken wings, in the branches of a privet. Its obstinate clinging to life irritated the child. He set to work to wring its neck, and the bird's convulsions made his heart beat, filling him with a savage, unbridled lust for blood. When at last it stiffened in death, he felt that he would swoon.

That evening during supper, his father declared that at his age he should begin to learn the art of the chase, and he went to look for an old notebook in which was contained in the form of questions and answers everything connected with sport. A master showed in it to his pupil the art of training dogs, taming falcons, and setting snares: how to recognize the stag by its droppings, the fox by its footmarks, the wolf by the place where it has scratched the ground: the right way to know their tracks, the manner of starting them, where their lairs are generally to be found, the most favourable winds, and a list of calls and rules for the quarry.

When Julian could repeat all this by heart, his father got together a pack of hounds for him.

First to be noticed were twenty-four greyhounds from Barbary, swifter than gazelles but prone to run wild; then seventeen couples of Breton dogs, with red coats and white spots, of incredible endurance, strong of chest, and of far-resounding voice. To oppose the boar and its dangerous doublings, there were forty hounds, as shaggy as bears. Some mastiffs from Tartary, nearly as tall as asses, flame-coloured, broad-backed, and straight-legged, were intended for hunting the bison. The black coats of the spaniels shone like satin; the yapping of the talbots rivalled the chorus of the beagles. In a yard by themselves, shaking their chains and rolling their eyes, were eight Alain dogs, formidable brutes which fly at the belly of a horseman and are not afraid of lions.

All of them had sonorous names, ate wheaten bread, and drank out of stone troughs.

The falconry, perhaps, excelled the pack of hounds. The good lord at very considerable expense, had obtained tercels from the Caucasus, sakers from Babylon, gerfalcons from Germany, and peregrines captured on cliffs by icy seas in distant climes. They were housed in a big shed covered with thatch, and chained to perches according to their size, and in front

THE LEGEND OF ST. JULIAN

of them was a bit of turf, on which from time to time they were placed to unstiffen their limbs.

Purse-nets, hooks, wolf-traps, and every kind of apparatus for hunting were in readiness.

Often they took out setters into the country who quickly gave notice of the presence of game. Then huntsmen, advancing slowly, cautiously, spread a huge net over their motionless bodies. At a word of command they started barking; quails rose on the wing, and ladies of the neighbourhood invited with their husbands, their children and their handmaids to the sport, all threw themselves on the birds and easily caught them.

On other occasions a drum would be beaten to start hares; foxes would fall into pits, or the springing of a trap would catch a wolf by its paw.

But Julian despised these handy devices and preferred to hunt far away from the crowd with his horse and his falcon. This was almost always a great Scythian tercel, white as snow. Its leathern hood was topped with a plume, and golden bells quivered on its blue feet; and it stood firmly on its master's arm, as his horse galloped and the plains unrolled before them. Julian, loosening the jesses, would suddenly let it go, and the daring bird would fly up into the air straight as an arrow. Then were to be seen two specks of unequal size circling and meeting, and finally disappearing in the blue skies above. The falcon would soon come down, tearing to pieces some bird, and would return to perch upon the gauntlet, its wings quivering. In this fashion Julian chased herons, kites, rooks, and vultures.

He loved to blow his horn and follow his hounds

as they ran along the slopes of the hills, jumped the streams, and climbed to the woods again, and when the stag began to groan under their bites, he slaughtered it cleverly and was delighted by the fury of the mastiffs as they devoured it, cut in pieces on its reeking hide.

When the days were misty, he hid in a marsh in quest of geese, otters, and young wild-duck.

Three squires used to wait for him from dawn at the foot of the steps, and though the old monk, leaning out of his window, might make signs to call him back, he would not return. He would go out in the blazing sun, in rain, and in storms, drinking water from the springs out of his hand and eating wild apples as his horse trotted along, and resting under an oak when tired; and he would return in the middle of the night, covered with gore and mud, with thorns in his hair and impregnated with the odour of wild beasts. He became like them. When his mother embraced him, he took it coldly, as if he were dreaming of things of great importance.

He killed bears with his knife, bulls with his axe, and boars with his pike; and once, even, having no weapon but a stick, he defended himself against some wolves which were gnawing corpses at the foot of a gibbet.

One morning he went off before dawn, well equipped for the chase, with a cross-bow on his shoulder and a quiver full of arrows at his saddle-bow.

His Danish jennet, followed by two bassets, moved sedately along, making the ground ring under its hooves. Drops of rime stuck to his cloak and a

THE LEGEND OF ST. JULIAN 83

stiff breeze was blowing. A bit of the sky cleared, and in the pale dawning light he saw rabbits hopping about at the edge of their burrows. The two bassets at once sprang upon them and quickly broke their backs one after the other.

Shortly afterwards he entered a wood. At the end of a branch, a grouse was sleeping, numbed by the cold, its head under its wing. With a back-stroke of his sword, Julian cut off its feet, and, without picking it up, continued his ride.

Three hours later he found himself on the peak of a mountain, which was so high that the sky seemed almost black. Before him a rock like a long wall ran downwards and hung over a precipice; at its farther end two wild goats were looking into the abyss beneath. As he had no arrows with him, for he had left his horse behind, he thought that he would go right down to them. Crouching low and with bare feet, he at last reached the first of them and stuck his dagger deep into its side. The other, seized with panic, leapt into the abyss. Julian rushed forward to stab it, and, as his right foot slipped, fell on the first carcass, with his head hanging over the precipice and his arms spread out.

Going down into the plain again he followed the course of a river which was lined with willows. From time to time cranes, flying very low, passed over his head. He killed them with his whip, without missing one.

Meanwhile the air had grown milder and had melted the hoar frost, and the sun appeared through the belts of mist. In the distance he saw a lake shimmering with unruffled surface like a sheet of lead. In the middle of it was an animal which Julian did not know, a beaver with a black muzzle. In spite of the distance he killed it with an arrow and was exceedingly annoyed that he could not carry off its skin.

Then he went on through an avenue of great trees whose tops made a kind of triumphal arch at the entrance to a forest. A roe-deer bounded out of a thicket, a fallow-deer showed itself at a crossing, a badger came out of a hole, a peacock spread its tail on the grass; and, when he had slain them all, yet more roe-deer and fallow-deer, and badgers, and peacocks, and blackbirds, jays, polecats, foxes, hedgehogs, lynxes—an infinite number of beasts and birds appeared and became more numerous at every step. They circled round him, all trembling, gazing at him with gentle, supplicating looks. But Julian did not tire of killing, by turns using his cross-bow, unsheathing his sword, and thrusting with his knife, thinking of nothing, and remembering nothing at all. He only knew from the mere fact of his being alive that he had been hunting in some country or other, through hours or days which he could not count, and that everything had happened with the ease of dreams.

An extraordinary sight gave him pause. Stags were crowding into a valley shaped like an arena, and pressing close together were warming each other with their breath, which could be seen steaming in the mist.

For a few minutes the hope of such a slaughter took his breath away for pleasure. Then he dismounted, rolled up his sleeves, and began to shoot.

THE LEGEND OF ST. JULIAN

At the whistle of the first arrow all the stags at once turned their heads. There were gaps in their serried ranks, plaintive cries rose, and a great commotion shook the herd.

The brim of the valley was too high to climb. They leaped about in this enclosure, trying to escape. Julian took aim and shot, and arrows fell like shafts of rain in a storm. The infuriated stags fought, reared, climbed on each others' backs, and their bodies with their entangled antlers made a broad mound which crumbled as it shifted about.

At last they died and lay prone upon the sand, froth on their nostrils, their entrails gushing out, and their bellies gradually ceasing to heave. Then all was motionless. Night was approaching, and in the spaces between the branches of the trees the sky was red as a sheet of blood.

Julian leant back against a tree. He gazed with wide-opened eyes at the huge massacre, unable to understand how he had perpetrated it.

On the other side of the valley, on the edge of the forest, he saw a stag, a hind, and its fawn.

The stag, which was black and of very great size, carried sixteen points, and had a white beard. The hind, which was pale as a dead leaf, was cropping the grass, and the spotted fawn was pulling at her dugs, without interfering with her movements.

Once more the cross-bow rang out. The fawn was killed at once. Then its mother, gazing upward to the skies, bellowed with a deep, heart-breaking, human voice. Julian, exasperated, stretched her on the ground with a shot full in the breast.

The great stag had seen him and made a bound.

Julian sped his last arrow at him; it hit the stag's forehead and remained sticking there.

The great stag did not seem to feel it. Striding over the dead bodies he came steadily forward, to fall upon him and disembowel him, and Julian retreated in unspeakable terror. The huge beast stopped, and with flaming eyes, solemn as a patriarch and as a judge, said three times, while a bell tinkled in the distance: "Accurst! accurst! accurst! One day, O ferocious heart, thou shalt murder thy father and thy mother!"

He bent his knees, closed his eyes gently, and died.

Julian was horror-stricken, and then suddenly crushed with fatigue; disgust and a very great feeling of sadness entered into his soul. With his face buried in his hands, he wept for a long time.

His horse was lost, his hounds had forsaken him, the solitude which encircled him seemed all full of threats of indefinable perils. Then, driven by fear, he made his way across country, and choosing a path at random, found himself almost immediately at the gates of the castle.

He could not sleep at night. By the swaying light of the hanging lamp he was always seeing the great black stag. He was obsessed by its prophecy, and he fought against it. "No! No! No! It is impossible for me to kill them!" Then he meditated: "But if I were to wish to kill them!" And he feared lest the Devil should inspire him with that desire.

For three months his mother prayed in anguish beside his pillow, and his father strode up and down

THE LEGEND OF ST. JULIAN

the corridors groaning. He sent for the most famous doctors, who prescribed quantities of drugs. Julian's illness, they said, came from some pestilential wind or from a love-desire. But the young man shook his head in reply to all questions.

Strength returned to him, and they took him out into the courtyard, the old monk and the good lord each supporting him with an arm.

When he had completely recovered, he utterly refused to hunt. His father, wishing to make him very happy, made him a present of a great Saracen sword. It hung with armour and other weapons at the top of a pillar, and to get it down a ladder was necessary. Julian went up. The sword was too heavy and slipped out of his grasp, and, as it fell, grazed the good lord so close that it cut his mantle. Julian believed that he had killed his father, and swooned.

From that time he dreaded weapons. The sight of a naked blade turned him pale. This weakness was an affliction for his parents, and at last the old monk ordered him in the name of God, of honour, and his ancestors, to take up once more the tasks and amusements of a man of gentle birth.

Every day the squires used to amuse themselves by practising with the javelin. Julian very quickly excelled in this. He would hurl his javelin into the neck of a bottle, would break the teeth of a weathercock, and hit the nails on a door a hundred paces off.

One summer evening, when things were growing indistinct in the rising mist, he was under the trellis in the garden and saw right at the bottom of it two white wings fluttering by the top of the low fruit-wall. He was certain that it was a stork, and he threw his javelin. A piercing shriek was heard.

It was his mother, whose headdress, with its long fringes, remained nailed to the wall.

Julian fled from the castle, and that place knew him no more.

II

He joined a band of adventurers which was passing by.

He became acquainted with hunger and thirst, fevers and vermin. He became accustomed to the hurly-burly of brawls and to the sight of men at the point of death. The wind tanned his skin. His limbs hardened with the constant wearing of armour, and as he was very strong, courageous, temperate, and wary, he soon became commander of a company.

When a fight began he would urge his men forward with a great flourish of his sword. With a knotted rope he would scale the walls of citadels at night, swinging to and fro in the gales, while burning fragments of Greek fire stuck to his cuirass and boiling resin and melted lead poured from the battlements. Often a stone crashing down broke his buckler to pieces. Bridges overladen with men gave way under him. Swinging his battle-axe he disposed of fourteen horsemen. In tournaments he overcame all challenges of his supremacy. More than a score of times he was left for dead.

Thanks to Providence he always escaped death, for he would protect priests, orphans, widows, and,

THE LEGEND OF ST. JULIAN

most of all, old men. When he saw one of them walking in front of him, he would call out to him to show his face, as if fearing to kill him by mistake.

Runaway slaves, peasants in revolt, fortuneless bastards, and every kind of dauntless fellow flocked to his flag, and he made an army of his own. It grew. He became famous. All the world wanted him.

He succoured in turn the Dauphin of France and the King of England, the Templars of Jerusalem, the Surena of the Parthians, the Negus of Abyssinia, and the Emperor of Calicut. He fought against Scandinavians covered with fish-scales, negroes with round shields of hippopotamus hide, mounted on red asses, and gold-coloured Indians, brandishing over their diadems great swords brighter than mirrors. He conquered the Troglodytes and the Anthropophagi. He went through such burning regions that men's hair caught fire like torches, under the blazing sun; and through others so freezing that their arms were loosened from their bodies and fell to the ground; and countries where there was so much fog that they marched surrounded by phantoms.

Republics in difficulty consulted him. At interviews with ambassadors he would obtain unhoped-for terms. Should a monarch behave too badly, Julian would arrive suddenly at his court and remonstrate with him. He set free peoples, and delivered queens from their prisons in towers. It was he, and no other, who slew the viper of Milan and the dragon of Oberbirbach.

Now the Emperor of Occitania, having triumphed

over the Spanish Moslems, had taken the sister of the Caliph of Cordova to himself as his concubine, and he kept a daughter of hers, whom he brought up to be a Christian. But the Caliph, pretending to seek conversion, visited him with a great escort, massacred his garrison, and threw him into an underground dungeon, treating him with great harshness, in order to extract large sums from him.

Julian rushed to his aid, destroyed the army of the infidels, besieged the town, killed the Caliph, cut off his head, and threw it over the ramparts like a ball. Then he liberated the Emperor from his prison and set him on his throne again in the presence of all his court.

As a reward for such great services, the Emperor presented him with many baskets of money. Julian would have none of them. Thinking that he desired yet more, the Emperor offered him three-quarters of his wealth. Again Julian refused. Then he offered to divide his kingdom with him, and Julian thanked him and declined. The Emperor was in tears with vexation, not knowing how to show his gratitude, when he tapped his forehead and whispered to a courtier. The curtains of a tapestry were drawn aside, and a young girl was seen.

Her large dark eyes shone like the light of two very soft lamps; her lips were parted in a delightful smile. The ringlets of her hair caught in the jewels of her half-open robe, and under the transparent tunic the youthfulness of her body could be discovered. In every way, with her slim figure she was dainty and good to look at.

THE LEGEND OF ST. JULIAN

Julian was dazzled with love, the more because he had led a very chaste life till then.

So he took the Emperor's daughter in marriage, with a castle which she held from her mother, and when the festivities were over, and countless mutual courtesies had been exchanged, they went their way.

It was a palace of white marble, in the Moorish style, built on a promontory in a grove of orange-trees. Flower-covered terraces sloped down to the edge of a bay, where pink shells crackled underfoot. Behind the castle stretched a forest in the shape of a fan. The sky was ever blue, and the trees swayed gently in the sea breeze or in the wind from the mountains, which closed the horizon in the far distance.

The rooms were full of shadow, but they were lighted up by the facing of their walls. Tall columns, slender as reeds, supported their domes, which were adorned by reliefs in imitation of stalactites in caves. There were fountains in the large rooms, mosaics in the courts, festooned partitions, countless daintinesses of architecture, and everywhere so great a silence that the rustling of a scarf or the echo of a sigh could be heard.

Julian no longer made war. He rested with a quiet people round him, and every day a crowd passed before him, bowing, and kissing his hand in the manner of the East.

Clothed in purple he would remain leaning in the embrasure of a window, calling back memories of his huntings in days gone by. He would have liked to race across the desert after the gazelle and the ostrich, to lie in ambush in the bamboos waiting for the leopard, to pass through forests swarming with rhinoceros, to climb the most inaccessible peaks to get a better shot at the eagle, and to fight the white bear on ice-floes.

Sometimes, in a dream, he would see himself like Adam, the father of us all, in the midst of Paradise, among the beasts. Stretching forth his arm, he would have them die. Or, again, they would pass before him, two by two, according to their size, from the elephants and the lions to the ermines and the ducks, as on the day when they entered Noah's ark. From the shade of a cave he would hurl javelins on them, and would never miss one: others would follow them, and there would be no end to the slaughter, and he would awake with wild eyes rolling.

Some princes among his friends invited him to hunt. He always refused, believing that, by penance of that kind, he would turn aside his evil fortune, for it seemed to him that the fate of his parents hung on the slaughter of animals. But it pained him inexpressibly that he could not see them, and his other great desire became most grievous to bear.

His wife sent for jugglers and dancers to amuse him. She would go out with him into the country in an open litter; at other times they would lie in a boat, watching the fishes darting hither and thither in water clear as the sky. Often she would throw flowers in his face, or, crouching at his feet, would draw melody from a three-stringed mandoline. Then, laying her two clasped hands upon his shoulder, she would say timidly: "What is amiss with you, dear lord?"

THE LEGEND OF ST. JULIAN

He would not answer, or would break into sobs. At last one day he confessed his horrible thought.

She fought against it, arguing very well: probably his father and mother were dead, but if he were ever to see them again, what chance, what purpose would ever bring him to commit so horrible a crime? Therefore there was no cause for his fears, and he should make up his mind to hunt again.

Julian smiled as he listened to her, but could not bring himself to satisfy her wish.

One evening in August when they were in their room, she had just lain down, and he was about to kneel down to pray, when he heard the barking of a fox and then some light footsteps under the window, and he saw indistinctly what he took to be the forms of animals. The temptation was too strong, and he unhooked his quiver from the wall.

She seemed surprised.

"I am going to obey you," he said, " I shall be back at sunrise."

Nevertheless she dreaded a gloomy end to the venture.

He reassured her and went out, marvelling at her inconsistent mood.

Soon afterwards a page came in to inform her that two strangers were demanding an instant audience of the lady, as they could not see the absent lord.

Thereupon there entered an old man and an old woman, bowed and dusty, dressed in linen, and each leaning on a stick.

They took courage, and told her that they were bringing Julian news of his parents. She leant forward to listen to them.

But having first taken counsel together with a look, they asked her whether he was still fond of them, and if he sometimes talked about them.

"Ah, yes!" she said.

Then they exclaimed, "Very well, then, we are they!" and they sat down, being very weary and spent with fatigue.

The young wife was by no means sure that her husband was their son, but they gave her proof by describing particular marks on his skin.

She jumped out of bed, called her page, and a repast was set before them.

Although they were extremely hungry, they could scarcely eat, and she noticed, aside, how their bony hands shook as they lifted the goblets. They asked innumerable questions about Julian, to all of which she had a reply, but she was careful not to speak of the gloomy fancy in which they were concerned.

As there was no sign of his returning, they had left their castle and they had been travelling for several years, following up faint clues without losing hope. So much money had been required for river-tolls and hostelries, the dues of princes, and the urgent demands of thieves, that they had nothing left in their purses, and they were now begging their way. But what did that matter, as they would soon be embracing their son? They extolled his happiness in having so charming a wife, and seemed never tired of gazing at her and kissing her.

The richness of the room greatly astonished them, and the old man, after examining the walls, asked why the coat-of-arms of the Emperor of Occitania was there.

THE LEGEND OF ST. JULIAN

" He is my father," she replied.

At that he started, remembering the gipsy's prophecy, and the old woman thought of the hermit's words. Doubtless their son's glory was but the dawn of eternal splendour, and both stood open-mouthed under the light of the candelabra on the table.

They must have been very handsome in their youth. The mother had still all her hair, which hung in fine plaits to the bottom of her cheeks, like snow-drifts, and the father, with his tall form and great beard, looked like a statue in a church.

Julian's wife advised them not to wait for him. She put them in her own bed, and then shut the window, and they fell asleep. A new day was about to begin, and little birds were singing outside.

Julian had crossed the park and was walking through the forest with light steps, enjoying the soft turf and the mildness of the air. The shadows of the trees stretched across the moss. From time to time the moon made white patches in the thin groves and he would hesitate before going on, believing that he saw a streak of water; or the surface of quiet ponds would be blended with the colour of the grass. Everywhere there was deep silence, and he came across none of the animals which a few minutes earlier had been wandering round his castle.

The wood grew thicker and the darkness became deeper. Puffs of warm air, charged with enervating scents, went by him. He sank in great heaps of dead leaves, and leaned against an oak to breathe a little.

Suddenly, from behind his back, a darker mass leapt forth. It was a wild boar. Julian had no time to catch hold of his bow, and was as mortified as if some misfortune had befallen him.

Then, when he had come out of the wood, he saw a wolf stealing along a hedge. He shot an arrow at it. The wolf stopped, turned its head to have a look at him, and went on its way again. It trotted on, always at the same distance, stopped from time to time, and, as soon as he aimed, continued its flight.

In this way Julian crossed an endless plain and then hillocks of sand, and at last he reached table-land which looked over a great tract of country. Flat stones lay scattered about upon it amongst vaults in ruins. He stumbled over the bones of dead men, and here and there worm-eaten crosses were leaning forward with a melancholy appearance. But forms moved in the fleeting shadows of the tombs, and hyenas rose out of them, scared and panting. Their claws scraping on the stones, they came up to him and sniffed at him, showing their gums as they yawned. He drew his sword and at once they went off in all directions, and did not pause in their headlong, limping gallop until they were lost in a cloud of dust in the distance.

An hour later he met a savage bull in a ravine, thrusting its horns forward and pawing the sand with its foot. Julian thrust his lance at it under its dewlap. The lance was shivered to pieces, as though the animal were of bronze, and he closed his eyes, expecting to be killed. When he opened them again, the bull had disappeared.

Then his very soul was weighed down with shame.

THE LEGEND OF ST. JULIAN

A higher power was making his strength of no avail, and he went back into the forest to return to his home.

The forest was a confused mass of entangling creepers. He was cutting a way through them with his sword when a marten suddenly glided between his legs, a panther made a bound over his shoulder, and a serpent wound its way up an ash tree.

Among the leaves there appeared a monster of a jackdaw which gazed at Julian, and here and there on the branches a multitude of great sparks shone out, as though the firmament had rained all its stars upon the forest. They were the eyes of animals—wild cats, squirrels, owls, parrots, monkeys.

Julian shot his arrows at them. The feathered shafts settled on the leaves like white butterflies. He threw stones at them, and the stones fell back without touching anything. He cursed, would have liked to fight, roared imprecations, and choked with rage.

And all the animals which he had hunted appeared before him and made a narrow ring round him. Some sat upon their haunches, others stood erect. He was in the middle of the ring, frozen with terror, unable to make the smallest movement. With a supreme effort of will, he advanced one step. Those in the trees opened their wings, those on the ground moved their limbs, and all went forward with him. The hyenas walked in front of him, the wolf and the wild-boar behind. The bull, on his right, was swaying its head, and on his left the serpent was winding through the grass, while the panther with arched back went forward with long velvet-footed strides. He walked as slowly as he could so as not to irritate them, and he saw porcupines, foxes, vipers, jackals and bears coming out of the depths of the thickets.

Julian started to run. They ran. The serpent hissed, and the stinking beasts slavered. The boar prodded his heels with its tusks, and the wolf rubbed the palms of his hands with its hairy muzzle. The monkeys made faces at him and pinched him, and the marten rolled over his feet. A bear, with a backhand blow of its paw, knocked his cap off, and the panther contemptuously dropped an arrow which it was carrying in its mouth.

There was biting irony in their sly movements. As they watched him out of the corner of their eyes they seemed to be thinking out a plan of revenge. Deafened by the buzzing of insects, flailed by the tails of birds, and choked by the breath of beasts, he walked with outstretched arms and closed eyes like a blind man, without even having strength to cry " Mercy! "

A cock's crow rang in the air and others answered. It was day, and he recognized the roof of his palace beyond the orange-trees.

Then, at the edge of a field, he saw, three yards away, some red partridges fluttering in the stubble. He unfastened his cloak and threw it over them like a net. When he uncovered them he only found one, and that long dead and rotten.

This trick exasperated him more than all the others. His thirst to butcher seized him again, and, failing beasts, he would have liked to slaughter men.

He climbed the three terraces and burst open the

THE LEGEND OF ST. JULIAN

door with a blow of his fist, but at the foot of the staircase the thought of his dear wife softened his heart. Doubtless she was asleep and he was going to take her by surprise.

Removing his sandals he turned the latch softly and went in.

The leaded window-panes made more dim the pale light of dawn. His feet caught in garments scattered about the floor, and, a little farther, he knocked against a side-table laden with dishes. She had probably had her supper here, he said to himself, and he went on towards the bed, hidden in the darkness at the far end of the room. He drew near, and, to kiss his wife, bent down over the pillow on which the two heads were lying side by side. Then he felt the touch of a beard against his mouth.

He started back, thinking that he was going mad, but came near the bed again, and, groping with his fingers, felt long tresses of hair. To convince himself that he was wrong, he passed his hand slowly over the pillow again. It was really a beard this time, and a man, a man lying with his wife!

Blazing out in boundless fury, he leapt upon them, stabbing with his dagger, stamping and foaming, roaring like a wild beast. Then he stopped. The dead, pierced to the heart, had not even stirred. He listened closely to their last groans as they died almost simultaneously, groans which, as they became weaker, were echoed in the far distance by another. Vague at first, this plaintive, long-drawn-out voice began to come nearer, swelled, and became horrible, and, terrified, he recognized the belling of the great black stag. And as he turned round, he thought that he saw the ghost of his wife, with a light in her hand, framed in the doorway.

The noise of the murder had drawn her there. With one wide glance she understood it all, and fled in horror, dropping her torch.

He picked it up.

His father and mother were before him, stretched on their backs, with deep wounds in their breasts. And their faces, in gentle majesty, looked as though they were keeping a secret for ever. There were splashes and pools of blood all over their fair skins, on the bedclothes and the floor, and on the ivory crucifix hanging in the alcove. The scarlet reflection from the window, struck at that moment by the sun, lit up these red splashes and made countless others all over the room. Julian walked towards the two bodies, telling himself, wishing to believe, that it could not be, that he was utterly mistaken, that sometimes one sees likenesses which cannot be explained. Finally he bent forward a little to look very closely at the old man, and he saw between the barely-closed eyelids a glazed eye which scorched him as with a flame. Then he went to the other side of the couch where lay the other body, its white hair covering part of its face. Julian passed his fingers under the plaits and raised the head. He looked at it, holding it at arm's length with one hand, while in the other he held up the torch. Drops of blood were oozing from the mattress and falling one by one upon the floor.

At the end of the day, he presented himself before his wife, and in a voice that was utterly unlike his own commanded her first of all not to answer him,

THE LEGEND OF ST. JULIAN

come near him, or even look at him, and, under pain of damnation, to execute all his orders, which were unalterable.

The funeral rites were to be performed in accordance with the instructions in writing which he had left on a *prie-Dieu* in the chamber of the dead. He made over to her his palace, his vassals, all his possessions, and he did not even keep his clothes or his sandals, which would be found at the head of the stairs.

She had obeyed God's will in furnishing cause for his crime, and she must pray for his soul, since from that day he ceased to exist.

The dead were regally buried in a church attached to a monastery three days' journey from the castle. A monk whose cowl was drawn over his face followed the procession far apart from the others, and none dared to speak to him. During the Mass he remained lying face downwards in the middle of the porch, his arms stretched out in the form of a cross, and his forehead in the dust.

After the burial he was seen to take the road leading to the mountains. He turned to look round several times and finally disappeared.

III

He went on his way, begging for his daily bread throughout the world. He would hold out his hand to those who rode on the high-roads, and approach the reapers with bended knee, or he would stand motionless before the gates of courtyards, and so sad was his face that never was he refused alms.

In a spirit of humility he would tell his story, and then all would fly from him, making the sign of the cross. In the villages which he had passed through before, as soon as he was recognized, they would shut their doors in his face, threaten him shrilly, and cast stones at him. The most charitable of them would place a bowl upon their window-sills, and would then close the shutters so as not to see him.

Repulsed everywhere, he shunned mankind, and fed on roots, plants, wild fruits, and shell-fish which he looked for on beaches.

Sometimes on rounding a hill he would have under his eyes a jumble of houses crowded together, with stone spires, bridges, towers, and dark streets crossing each other, from which there rose a ceaseless hum.

The need to mingle with the life of others would force him to go down into the city, but the brutish faces of the men, the noises of their trades, and the petty nature of their conversation froze his heart. On high days and holidays when the clanging of cathedral bells set the whole populace a-laughing from daybreak, he would watch them coming out of their houses, their dancing in public spaces, the beer-fountains at the crossways, the damask hanging over the balconies of princes, and, when evening came, through the lower windows, the long family tables and little children sitting on their grandparents' knees. Sobs choked him, and he would go back to the open country again.

He would watch with thrills of love colts in the meadows, birds in their nests, insects on the flowers. All, at his approach, would run farther away, would

THE LEGEND OF ST. JULIAN 103

hide in terror, or would fly off swiftly. He sought lonely out-of-the-way places. But the wind would bring to his ears murmurs as of death-agonies. Dewdrops falling to the ground would recall other, heavier drops. Every evening the sun would spread bloodred splashes across the sky, and each night in his dreams he would see his murder of his parents again.

He made himself a hair shirt with iron spikes. He climbed on his knees every hill that had a chapel at the top. But pitiless memory would dim the brilliance of shrines and add fresh torture to the mortification of the flesh of the penitent.

He did not rebel against God for having afflicted him with this deed, and yet the thought that he could have committed it made him despair.

His own person was so abominable to him, that in the hope of obtaining release from it, he risked it in perilous enterprises. He saved the paralysed from fires and children from the depths of chasms. The abyss cast him up; the flames spared him. Time did not lessen his suffering. It became intolerable, and he resolved to die.

And one day when he was by a spring, as he was leaning over it to judge the depth of the water, there appeared before him an old man. Very emaciated, with a white beard and so mournful a face that Julian could not restrain his tears. The other also wept. Without recognizing the likeness, Julian had a vague recollection of having seen his face. He uttered a cry; it was his father; and he thought no more of killing himself.

So with the burden of his recollections he travelled through many countries, and he came to a river which was dangerous to cross, by reason of its swift current and a great stretch of slime along its banks. No one for a long time had dared to try to cross it.

An old boat, its stern buried in the mud, raised its bow among the reeds. Julian examined it and found a pair of oars, and the thought came to him to make use of his life in the service of others.

He began by making on the bank a sort of roadway which would enable people to come down to the channel of the river. He broke his nails in moving huge stones, propped them against his waist to carry them, slipped in the mud, sank in it, and nearly perished several times. Then he mended the boat with bits of wreckage and made a hut for himself with clay and trunks of trees.

News of the ferry having spread, travellers appeared. They waved flags and called him from the other side, and Julian quickly jumped into his boat. It was very heavy, and they overloaded it with all sorts of baggage and packages, without counting beasts of burden, which added to the crowding together by kicking in their alarm. He asked for nothing for his labour; some gave him remnants of food out of their wallets or worn-out clothes for which they had no further use. Some brutes would shout blasphemies at him. Julian would gently reprove them, and they replied with insults. He was content to bless them.

A little table, a stool, a bed of dry leaves, and three clay cups—that was the whole of his furniture. Two holes in the walls served for windows. On one side there stretched, as far as the eye could see,

THE LEGEND OF ST. JULIAN

barren plains, with dim ponds here and there; and in front of him there rolled on the great river with its greenish waters. In spring there came from the damp earth an odour of decay. Then a riotous wind would raise clouds of dust. Everywhere it entered, muddying the water and grating in the mouth. A little later came clouds of mosquitoes, which never stopped buzzing and stinging from morning till night and from night till morning. And then came horrible frosts which made everything as hard as stone and roused a wild desire to eat meat.

Months would roll by in which Julian saw no one. Often he would close his eyes and try to regain his youth in memory. The courtyard of a castle would appear before him, with greyhounds on the steps, grooms in the armoury, and a fair-haired youth under a vine-covered trellis, between an old man clothed in furs and a lady with a great coif. Suddenly, the two corpses were there. He would throw himself face downwards on his bed and say again and again through his tears: "Ah, poor father! Poor mother, poor mother!" And he would fall into a drowsiness through which the mournful visions still went on.

While he was sleeping one night, he thought he heard someone calling him. He strained his ears but made out nothing but the roar of the waters of the river.

But once more the same voice cried, "Julian!" It came from the farther bank, which seemed to him extraordinary, considering the breadth of the river.

A third time he was called: "Julian!"

And this high-pitched voice had the sound of a church bell.

Lighting his lantern, Julian went out of his hut. A wild hurricane was raging through the night. The darkness was profound, broken occasionally by the whiteness of the leaping waves.

After a moment's hesitation Julian let slip his moorings. At once the water became calm, and the boat glided over it to the other bank, where a man was waiting.

He was wrapped in a ragged cloth, his face like a mask of plaster, and his two eyes redder than coals. Holding the lantern close up to him, Julian saw that he was covered with a hideous leprosy, but, nevertheless, there was something of a royal majesty in his bearing.

As soon as he entered the boat, it sank amazingly, overwhelmed by his weight; it rose again with a shudder and Julian began to row.

At every stroke the surf made its bow rise high out of the water. The water, blacker than ink, rushed furiously past on either side. It hollowed into gulfs and rose mountains high, and the boat leapt upwards and then down into the depths, where it spun round, tossed by the wind.

Julian bent his body, stretched his arms to their fullest extent, and, using his feet as a support, swung himself round to get more power. The hail lashed his hands, the rain ran in streams down his back, the violence of the wind choked him, he stopped. Then the boat drifted quickly and was carried down the river. But with the knowledge that this was a matter of the very greatest importance, an order

THE LEGEND OF ST. JULIAN 107

which he must on no account disobey, he took up his oars again, and the rattle of the thole-pins cut through the clamour of the tempest.

The little lantern burned in front of him. Some birds, fluttering past, hid it from time to time. But ever he saw the eyes of the Leper, who stood in the stern, motionless as a pillar.

And that went on for a very, very long time.

When they reached the hut, Julian closed the door, and he saw the Leper sitting on the stool. The sort of shroud which covered him had fallen to his hips, and his shoulders, his chest, his shrunken arms were hidden by the scaly pustules plastered all over them. Immense wrinkles furrowed his brow. He had a hole in place of a nose, like a skeleton, and from his bluish lips there came breath, thick and nauseous as a fog.

" I am hungry ! " he said.

Julian gave him what he had: an old piece of bacon and the crust of a black loaf. When he had devoured them, the table, the bowl, and the handle of the knife bore the same spots that could be seen on his body.

Then he said : " I am thirsty ! "

Julian went to get his pitcher, and, as he took it, there came from it an aroma which enlarged his heart and his nostrils. It was wine. What a find !

But the Leper stretched out his hand and emptied the whole pitcher at one draught.

Then he said : " I am cold ! "

Julian, with his candle, set light to a pile of bracken in the middle of the hut.

The Leper came to warm himself, and as he squatted on his heels, he trembled all over and grew weaker. His eyes no longer gleamed, his sores ran, and in an almost lifeless voice he murmured: "Thy bed!"

Julian helped him gently to drag himself there, and, to cover him, even stretched the sail of his boat over him.

The Leper groaned. His teeth showed at the corners of his mouth, a faster rattle shook his breast, and at every breath his stomach hollowed even to his backbone. Then he closed his eyes.

"My bones are like ice! Come close to me!"

And Julian, lifting the cloth, lay down on the dead leaves side by side with him.

The Leper turned his head. "Take off thy clothes, that I may have the warmth of thy body!"

Julian took off his clothes, and then, naked as on the day that he was born, he lay down on the bed again. And he felt against his thigh the skin of the Leper, colder than a serpent and rough as a file.

He tried to hearten him, and the other answered in gasps: "Ah, I am dying! Come closer to me, warm me! Not with thy hands; no, with thy whole body!"

Julian stretched himself completely over him, mouth to mouth, breast to breast.

Then the Leper clasped him. And suddenly his eyes assumed the brightness of stars, his hair lengthened out like the rays of the sun, the breath of his nostrils had the sweetness of roses. A cloud of incense rose from the hearth, the river began to sing.

Meanwhile an abundance of delight, a superhuman joy descended like a flood upon Julian's soul as he lay there in a swoon, and he who still clasped him

THE LEGEND OF ST. JULIAN

in his arms grew taller and yet taller, touching with his head and his feet the two walls of the hut.

The roof flew off, the firmament unrolled—and Julian ascended towards the blue expanse, face to face with Our Lord Jesus, who bore him to Heaven.

And that is the story of St. Julian the Hospitaller, more or less as it is to be found on a church window in the land where I live.

HERODIAS

(Hérodias)

HERODIAS

(*Hérodias*)

I

THE citadel of Machærus rose east of the Dead Sea on a basalt peak in the shape of a cone. It was surrounded by four deep valleys, two on either of its sides, one in front, and another behind. Houses were crowded together against its base, encircled by a wall which wound in and out over the broken ground; and, by a road which made a gash in the rock, the town was connected with the fortress whose walls were a hundred and twenty cubits high, with many angles, battlements along the edge, and, here and there, towers, which seemed like jewels sparkling in this crown of stone suspended over the abyss.

Within the citadel was a palace ornamented with porticoes, and roofed with a terrace which was enclosed by a balustrade of sycamore wood, with poles arranged to support an awning.

Before daybreak one morning, the Tetrarch Herod Antipas came out to lean on it and look round him.

Immediately beneath his gaze, the mountains were beginning to unveil their crests, while most of their bulk was still hidden in the depths below. A mist was floating: it divided, and the outline of the Dead Sea was seen. The dawn, rising behind Machærus, spread forth in rosy hues. Soon it lit up the sands of the shore, the hills, the desert, and, farther away, all the mountains of Judæa, dipping into their rugged, grey, exposed parts. In the middle was drawn the dark line of Engedi, and in the recess was the dome-like form of Hebron. Eschol was there with its pomegranates, Sorek with its vines, Carmel with its fields of sesame, and, looking down on Jerusalem, there rose the huge tower of Antony in the shape of a cube.

The Tetrarch looked away from it to gaze at the palm trees of Jericho on his right, and he thought of the other towns in his Galilee—Capernaum, Endor, Nazareth, Tiberias—which, perhaps, he would never see again.

And the Jordan flowed on across the arid plain, which, all white, glistened like a sheet of snow. The lake now had the appearance of an expanse of lapis lazuli. At its southern point, in the direction of Yemen, Antipas recognized something that he was afraid to see. Brown tents were scattered about, men with lances were moving among their horses, and dying fires shone like sparks on the flat ground.

They were the troops of the King of the Arabs, whose daughter he had put away to take Herodias, the wife of one of his brothers who was living in Italy and who made no claim to power.

Antipas was waiting for help from the Romans, and was devoured with anxiety, for Vitellius, Governor of Syria, was slow in coming.

HERODIAS

No doubt, he said to himself, Agrippa had destroyed his prospects with the Emperor. His third brother Philip, ruler of Batanea, was arming secretly. The Jews had had enough of his idolatrous ways, and everyone else of his government, and so he was hesitating between two schemes: either to conciliate the Arabs, or to make an alliance with the Parthians. On the pretext of celebrating his birthday, he had invited the commanders of his troops, the stewards of his lands, and the chief men of Galilee to a great feast that very day.

He searched all the roads with his piercing eye. They were empty. Eagles flew above his head, and the soldiers along the ramparts were asleep against the walls; nothing stirred within the castle.

On a sudden, a voice in the distance, coming, apparently, out of the depths of the earth, made the Tetrarch turn pale. He bent down to listen; it had ceased. It rose once more. Clapping his hands, he called loudly, " Mannaëi! Mannaëi! "

A man appeared, naked to the waist like the masseurs at baths. He was enormously tall, old, very lean, and he wore a sword in a bronze sheath at his thigh. His hair, caught up by a comb, made his forehead seem longer than it really was. Sleepiness dulled his eyes, but his teeth shone, and he trod lightly on the pavement, the suppleness of a monkey in his body, his face impassive as a mummy's.

" Where is he? " asked the Tetrarch.

Mannaëi, pointing with his thumb to an object behind them, answered, " Still there! "

" I thought I heard him! "

And Antipas, breathing more freely, inquired

about Iaokanan, the same whom the Latins call St. John the Baptist. Had those two men been seen again, who as a favour had been admitted to his cell a month or so before, and had the reason for their visit been discovered since?

Mannaëi replied: "They had some mysterious words with him, like thieves when they meet at cross-roads in the evening. Then they went off in the direction of Upper Galilee, declaring that they would bring great tidings."

Antipas bowed his head, and then exclaimed with all the appearance of terror: "Guard him! Guard him! And let no one enter! Keep the door fast closed! Fill in the pit! They must not even suspect that he is alive!"

Mannaëi had executed these commands before they were issued, for Iaokanan was a Jew, and, like all Samaritans, he abominated Jews. Their temple at Gerizim, which Moses had intended to be the centre of Israel, was dead and gone since the reign of Hyrcanus, and the Temple at Jerusalem roused them to fury, as an outrage and an ever-present injustice.

Mannaëi had entered it secretly, to pollute the altar with dead men's bones. His companions, less swift than he in their departure, had been beheaded.

He saw it in the gap between two hills. The white marble of its walls and the sheets of gold on its roof shone brightly in the sun. It was like a luminous mountain, some superhuman thing, crushing everything with its opulence and its arrogance.

Then he stretched out his arms towards Sion, and, with body erect, his head thrown back, his fists

HERODIAS

clenched, he hurled a curse at it, believing there was efficacy in his words.

Antipas listened, without appearing shocked.

The Samaritan spoke again: " At times he is restless and would like to escape: he hopes to be set free. Other times, he is quiet like a sick animal. Other times, again, I see him walking up and down in the darkness, repeating, ' What matters it? That He may increase, I must decrease.' "

Antipas and Mannaëi looked at each other. But the Tetrarch was weary of reflection.

All these mountains round him, like great waves petrified in layers, the black chasms in the sides of the cliffs, the immense blue sky, the violent brilliance of the morning light, the depths of the abysses, troubled him, and a wave of depression swept over him as he gazed at the desert, with its disarray of amphitheatres and palaces tumbling in ruin. The hot wind swept upwards with a smell of sulphur, like an exhalation from the accursed cities, buried deep beneath the banks of heavy waters.

These marks of an eternal anger gave terror to his thoughts, and he stayed there, his elbows on the balustrade, his eyes staring, and his forehead in his hands. Somebody touched him. He turned round. Herodias was before him.

She was wrapped to her feet in a long thin purple robe. She had left her chamber in a hurry, and was wearing neither necklaces nor ear-rings; a tress of her black hair fell down over one arm, and the end of it was buried between her breasts. Her nostrils, which were too prominent, were quivering; all the joy of a victory was shining in her face, and with a great voice which shook the Tetrarch, she said: "Cæsar is friendly towards us! Agrippa is in prison!"

"Who has told thee?"

"I know it!"

And she went on: "It is because he wished Caius to be Emperor!"

All the time that he was living on their charity, Agrippa had been scheming to get the title of king, for which they had the same overweening desire as himself. But in future there would be no more fears. "The dungeons of Tiberius are hard to open, and existence within them is sometimes far from safe!"

Antipas understood her, and although she was Agrippa's sister, her horrible intent seemed to him justified. Murders such as these were a natural consequence of things—a fatality in royal houses. In Herod's, men had stopped counting them.

Then she set forth all that she had done: Agrippa's clients bought, his letters opened, spies in every doorway, and how she had managed to seduce Eutyches the informer.

"It cost me nothing! And for thee, have I not done more? I have given up my daughter!"

She had left that child in Rome after her divorce, greatly hoping to have others by the Tetrarch. She never spoke of her, and he wondered now at this sudden display of tender feeling.

The awning had been spread and big cushions promptly put beside them. Herodias sank back in them, and, turning her back to him, began to weep. Then she passed her hand over her eyes, saying that she did not want to think of it any more, and that

HERODIAS

she was quite happy. And she reminded him of their talks there in the atrium, meetings at the baths, walks along the Via Sacra, and nights in the great villas, with their murmuring fountains and arches of flowers, and the Roman Campagna spread out before their eyes. She gazed at him, as in days gone by, rubbing herself gently against his breast, with little coaxing gestures.

He pushed her away. The love which she was trying to revive was so far away now! And all his misfortunes came from it, for war had been going on now for nearly twelve years. She had aged the Tetrarch. His shoulders were bent with cares beneath his dark toga with its violet edge, his white hair mingled, unkempt, with his beard, and the sunshine which came through the awning lit up a brow wrinkled with troubles. Herodias's brow was wrinkled, too. As they sat face to face, they looked at each other in the manner of wild beasts.

The mountain roads began to show signs of life. Herdsmen drove oxen forward with their goads, children pulled at donkeys, grooms led horses. Those who came down from the heights beyond Machærus disappeared behind the castle; others climbed the ravine in front and unloaded their baggage in courtyards when they reached the town. These were the Tetrarch's purveyors, and servants sent on ahead by his guests.

But, at the end of the terrace, to the left, there appeared an Essene, white-robed and barefoot, with the aspect of a stoic.

Mannaëi rushed forward from the right with raised sword.

Herodias cried out to him: "Kill him!"

"Halt!" said the Tetrarch.

He stopped, on the instant, as did the other. They then withdrew backwards by different staircases, watching each other intently.

"I know him," said Herodias. "His name is Phanuel, and he is trying to see Iaokanan, whom in your blindness you are keeping alive."

Antipas pleaded that he might be of use some day. His attacks on Jerusalem were bringing the rest of the Jews over to their side.

"No!" she replied. "They accept any master, and are incapable of making a country for themselves." As for the man who was stirring up the people with hopes cherished since the days of Nehemiah, the best policy was to suppress him.

It was not a matter of urgency, thought the Tetrarch, and as for Iaokanan being a source of danger—what nonsense! And he pretended to laugh at the idea.

"Be silent!" And once more she told him how she had been humiliated when she was going out one day in the direction of Gilead to gather balsam. "Some people were putting on their clothes by the side of the river. On a mound near them a man was speaking. He was wearing a camel-skin about his loins and his head was like the head of a lion. As soon as he saw me he spat at me all the curses of the prophets. His eyes flamed, his voice roared. He raised his arms as though to call down thunderbolts upon me. It was impossible for me to get away from him; my chariot-wheels were up to their axles in the sand, and I moved off slowly, cowering beneath my

HERODIAS

cloak, frozen by those insults which were falling like storms of rain."

With Iaokanan still alive, there could be no life for her. When he was seized and bound with cords, the soldiers had orders to stab him if he resisted. He was submissive. Serpents had been put into his prison; they died.

The futility of these ruses exasperated Herodias. Besides, why was he warring against her? In whose interest was he plaguing her? The discourses which he had addressed to multitudes had spread abroad and were circulating. She was hearing them wherever she went; they were filling the whole air. Against legions she would have been brave enough, but this elusive force was more harmful than swords, and it dumbfounded her. White with rage, she paced up and down the terrace, lacking words to express her choking thoughts.

She thought, too, that the Tetrarch would give in to public opinion and consider the advisability of casting her off. Then all would be lost! From the days of her childhood she had cherished the dream of a great empire. It was to gain it, that she had left her first husband and thrown in her lot with this one, who, as she thought, had duped her.

"I received fine support when I came into thy family!"

"It is as good as thine," said the Tetrarch simply.

Herodias felt the blood of priests and of kings, her ancestors, boiling in her veins. "Why, thy grandfather was a sweeper in the Temple of Ascalon! The rest were shepherds, robbers, drivers of caravans, a horde, paying tribute to Judah from the days of King David onwards. All my ancestors have vanquished thine. The first of the Maccabees drove thine out of Hebron, and Hyrcanus compelled them to be circumcised." And, breathing the contempt of the patrician for the plebeian, the hatred of Jacob against Edom, she reproached him for his indifference to insults, his gentleness towards the Pharisees who were betraying him, his cowardice in the face of the people who detested him. "Thou art as they are—admit it. And thou art yearning for the Arab girl who goes from one house to another with her dances. Take her back, then! Go and live with her in her tent, devour the bread she has baked under the ashes, swallow the curdled milk of her sheep, kiss her blue cheeks, and forget me!"

The Tetrarch was no longer listening to her. He was looking at a house with a flat roof, on which there were a girl and an old woman, who held a parasol with a red handle as long as a fisherman's rod. In the middle of the carpet a big travelling basket lay open; girdles, veils, gold and silver pendants overflowed from it in confusion. Occasionally the girl bent over these things and shook them in the air. She was dressed like Roman girls, in a tunic which curled up at the edges, with a peplum with emerald tassels; blue bands kept back her hair, which, no doubt, was over-heavy, for from time to time she lifted her hand to it. The shadow of the parasol was moving over her and half concealed her. Two or three times Antipas had a glimpse of her delicate neck, the turn of an eye, the corner of a little mouth. But he could see the whole of her figure, from her hips to her neck, bending in

HERODIAS

its suppleness and rising to its full height again. He looked out for the repetition of that movement, and his breathing became more rapid; a flame shone in his eyes. Herodias was watching him.

He asked, "Who is it?"

She replied that she had no idea, and went away, suddenly grown calm.

Some Galileans were waiting under the porticoes for the Tetrarch—the chief Scribe, the overseer of the pastures, the manager of the salt-pits, and a Babylonian Jew, commander of his horsemen. All saluted him with one voice, and he disappeared towards the inner rooms.

Phanuel rose up before him at the corner of a corridor.

"Ah, thou again! Thou art come to see Iaokanan, no doubt?"

"And to see thee! I have a weighty thing to tell thee!"

Without losing sight of Antipas, he followed him into a dimly-lighted room. Light came from outside through a grating which extended the entire length of the cornice. The walls were painted a deep red colour, almost black. At the end of the room stretched an ebony bed, with ox-hide straps. A golden shield above it shone like a sun. Antipas went from one end of the great room to the other, and lay down upon the bed.

Phanuel remained standing. Raising his arm, he said as one inspired, "The Most High sends from time to time one of His sons. Iaokanan is one of these. If thou treatest him ill, thou wilt be punished!"

"It is he who persecutes me!" cried Antipas. "He asked me to do that which was impossible, and since that time he has been rending me in pieces. And I was not harsh to begin with! He has even sent men from Machærus who are turning my provinces upside down. Woe unto his life! As he attacks me, I am defending myself!"

"His bursts of rage are too violent," Phanuel answered, "but no matter, thou must set him free!"

"One does not set savage beasts free," said the Tetrarch.

The Essene replied: "Have no more anxiety! He will go to the Arabs, Gauls, and Scythians. His work has to spread to the ends of the earth!"

Antipas seemed lost in a vision. "His power is very great. I like him in spite of myself!"

"Then thou wilt set him free?"

The Tetrarch shook his head. He was afraid of Herodias, Mannaëi, and the unknown.

Phanuel tried to persuade him, promising, as a guarantee of his plans, that the Essenes would make their submission to the kings. People respected these poor men, clothed in flax, unsubdued by torture, who read the future in the stars.

Antipas remembered something that Phanuel had said just before.

"What is this affair which thou hast told me was important?"

A negro came in suddenly. His body was white with dust, his voice rattled, and he could only say:

"Vitellius!"

"What? He is on his way?"

HERODIAS

" I have seen him. Before three hours have passed, he will be here ! "

The curtains of the corridors were shaken as by the wind. A great hubbub arose in the castle, a din of people hurrying about, furniture dragged here and there, and plates clattering. And from the tops of the towers trumpets sounded to warn the scattered slaves.

II

The ramparts were thronged with people when Vitellius entered the courtyard. He was leaning on the arm of his interpreter, and he wore the toga, laticlave, and laced boots of a consul, and round him was a group of lictors. A large red litter adorned with plumes and mirrors was borne in after him.

The lictors planted their twelve bundles of rods, with a hatchet in the middle and fastened by a thong, against the gate. Then the assembled crowd trembled before the majesty of the Roman people.

The litter which eight men were bearing came to a stop. There stepped out of it a youth with a big stomach, a blotched face, and rows of pearls upon his fingers. They offered him a cup full of wine and spices. He drank it and called for another.

The Tetrarch had fallen at the Proconsul's knees, saying how distressed he was that the favour of his presence had not been announced to him sooner. Otherwise he would have ordered that all the honours due to the Vitellii should be paid to him on his journey. They were descendants of the goddess Vitellia, and a road from the Janiculum to the sea still bore their name. There were quæstors and consuls without number in their house, and to Lucius, who was now his guest, thanks were due as conqueror of the Clites and father of this young Aulus, who might be described as returning to his own country, for the East was the home of the gods. These extravagances were uttered in Latin, and Vitellius received them impassively.

He replied that Herod the Great was himself enough to make the glory of a nation. The Athenians had made him supervisor of the Olympian games. He had built temples in honour of Augustus, and he had been patient, shrewd, formidable, and always loyal to the Cæsars.

Between the pillars with their bronze capitals Herodias was seen coming forward with the bearing of an empress, surrounded by women and eunuchs carrying lighted perfumes on silver-gilt dishes.

The Proconsul took three steps to meet her, and she saluted him with an inclination of her head. "How fortunate it is," she exclaimed, "that, henceforth, Agrippa, the enemy of Tiberius, cannot possibly do harm!"

Vitellius was unaware of what had happened, and she seemed to him a dangerous woman; and, as Antipas swore that he would do everything for the Emperor, he observed, "Even if others were injured thereby?"

He had taken hostages from the King of the Parthians, but the Emperor had forgotten it, for Antipas, who had been present at the conference and had wanted to show his value, had sent off news of it at once. Hence the deep hatred of Vitellius,

HERODIAS 127

and his delay in sending Herod the assistance he needed.

The Tetrarch stammered, but Aulus said with a laugh, " Be calm, I am protecting you ! "

The Proconsul pretended not to have heard. The future of the father was dependent on the defilement of the son, and this flower from the mud of Capreæ procured him such immense advantages that he paid very special attention to him, though he was distrustful of him, as of any poisonous flower.

A tumult rose below the gate. A string of white mules was led in, on which were personages in the dress of priests. They were Sadducees and Pharisees whom the same ambition drove to Machærus, the former wanting to obtain the right to perform sacrifices, and the latter to keep it. Their faces were gloomy, especially those of the Pharisees, enemies of Rome and of the Tetrarch. The skirts of their tunics got in their way in the throng, and their tiaras slipped about on their foreheads above the little slips of parchment with their Holy Writ.

Almost at the same time came in soldiers of the advance-guard. They had put their shields into sacks, to save them from the dust, and behind them was Marcellus, the Proconsul's lieutenant, with some publicans, who gripped wooden tablets under their arms.

Antipas presented the principal men round him—Tolmaï, Kanthera, Sehon, Ammonius of Alexandria, who bought asphalt for him, Naaman, captain of his light infantry, and Iacim the Babylonian.

Vitellius had noticed Mannaëi. " That fellow there, what is he ? "

The Tetrarch with a gesture informed him that he was the executioner.

Then he introduced the Sadducees. Jonathas, a little man of easy manners, who spoke Greek, begged the master to honour them with a visit to Jerusalem. He replied that he would probably go there. Eleazar, with a hooked nose and long beard, begged on behalf of the Pharisees for the return of the high priest's cloak, detained by the civil authority in the tower of Antony. After them, the Galileans denounced Pontius Pilate: on an occasion when a lunatic had been hunting for David's golden vases in a cave near Samaria he had killed some of the inhabitants. They all spoke at once, Mannaëi more violently than any of them. Vitellius declared that the guilty would be punished.

Cries broke out in front of a portico, where the soldiers had hung their shields. Now that the coverings had been taken off, the effigy of Cæsar could be seen on the bosses. This, to the Jews, was idolatry. Antipas harangued them, while Vitellius, who was on a raised seat in the colonnade, became more and more astonished at their fury. Tiberius had been right when he banished four hundred of them to Sardinia. But in their own country they were strong; and he gave orders to take down the shields.

Then they surrounded the Proconsul, begging for the redress of injustices, for privileges, for charity. Clothes were torn, they trampled on each other, and slaves with sticks hit out right and left to make room. Those nearest the gate went down into the road, others came up it, and they flowed backwards

HERODIAS

and forwards, two streams crossing each other in this swaying crowd, penned in by the enclosure of the walls.

Vitellius asked why there was such a crowd. Antipas told him the reason, his birthday, and he pointed to some of his servants, who were leaning over the battlements and hauling up huge baskets of meat, fruit, and vegetables, antelopes and storks, great azure-coloured fish, grapes, water-melons, and pomegranates, heaped up in pyramids. It was too much for Aulus, who, carried away by that gluttony which was to astonish the whole world, rushed off to the kitchens. As he passed a cellar, he noticed some pots that were like breast-plates. Vitellius came and looked at them, and insisted on having the underground rooms in the fortress opened.

These were cut in high vaults out of the rock, with pillars at regular distances. The first contained old armour, but the second was filled to overflowing with pikes, whose points peeped out of a forest of feathers. The third looked as if it were carpeted with reed mats, so straight and close together lay the slim arrows. Scimitar blades covered the walls of the fourth. In the middle of the fifth were rows of helmets, whose crests looked like a regiment of red serpents. In the sixth, only quivers were to be seen, and in the seventh, greaves; in the eighth, were arm-plates; and in the others were forks, grappling-irons, ladders, ropes, even poles for catapults and bells for the chests of dromedaries! And, as the hill extended farther, widening out to its base, and hollowed out inside like a beehive, there were still more numerous and deeper rooms under these.

Vitellius, Phineas, his interpreter, and Sisenna, the chief publican, went through them by the light of torches, borne by three eunuchs. In the gloom they made out hideous objects invented by the barbarians: maces studded with nails, poisoned javelins, pincers like crocodiles' jaws. In short, the Tetrarch had sufficient war-material in Machærus to equip forty thousand men.

He had collected it in case his enemies should make alliances together against him. But the Proconsul might believe, or say, that it was to fight the Romans, and he began to think how he could explain. They were not his: much of it was necessary for self-protection against brigands: some of it, too, against the Arabs: or else, the whole collection had belonged to his father. And, instead of walking behind the Proconsul he went in front with rapid strides. Then he placed himself against the wall, which he screened with his toga by extending his arms; but above his head was the top of a door. Vitellius saw it, and wanted to know what was behind it.

The Babylonian alone could open it.

" Call the Babylonian ! "

They waited for him. His father had come from the banks of the Euphrates to offer himself and five hundred horsemen to Herod, for the defence of the eastern frontiers. When the kingdom was divided up, Iacim had remained with Philip and was now in the service of Antipas.

He came forward, with a bow at his shoulder and a whip in his hand. Many-coloured cords were wound tightly round his crooked legs; his rough

HERODIAS

arms emerged from a sleeveless tunic, and a fur cap shaded his face; his beard was curled in ringlets. At first he seemed not to understand the interpreter, but Vitellius threw a look at Antipas, who at once repeated his order. Then Iacim placed both his hands against the door, and it slid into the wall.

A breath of hot air came out of the darkness. A winding passage led downwards; they followed it and reached the threshold of a cavern, which was larger than the other subterranean chambers. At the end of it an arcade opened out upon the precipice, which defended the citadel on that side. A honeysuckle clinging to the roof let its flowers fall down full in the light. A thread of water was murmuring as it crossed the level floor.

White horses were there, a hundred, perhaps, eating barley from a shelf which was level with their mouths. All their manes were painted blue, they had their hooves wrapped in coverings of esparto grass, and the hair between their ears was puffed over their foreheads like a wig. They whisked their very long tails gently against their legs. The Proconsul stood before them mute with admiration.

They were marvellous beasts, supple as serpents, light as birds. They were off as swiftly as their rider's arrow, and they would tumble men over and bite them in the stomach. They would get themselves out of the difficulties of rocky ground, leap across chasms, and keep up their headlong gallop on the plains for a whole day; a word would stop them. As soon as Iacim went in they came to him, like sheep when a shepherd approaches them, and, stretching out their necks, they looked at him uneasily with child-like eyes. From force of habit he gave a deep, hoarse cry, which put them in good spirits, and they reared up, hungry for wide expanses, begging for a gallop.

Antipas, fearing that Vitellius might carry them off, had shut them up in this place, which was kept for animals in times of siege.

"It is a bad stable," said the Proconsul, "and thou art in danger of losing them. Make an inventory, Sisenna!"

The publican drew tablets from his girdle, counted the horses, and set down the number. The agents of the tax companies were in the habit of corrupting the governors, in order to ransack the provinces. This man with his weasel jaw and blinking eyes was sniffing about everywhere.

Finally they went up into the courtyard again.

There were round bronze plates here and there in the centre of the pavement, covering the cisterns. Vitellius noticed one which was larger than the others and which did not ring underfoot as they did. He struck them all, one after another, and then shouted, as he stamped, "I have it! I have it! Herod's treasure is here!"

Hunting for Herod's treasure was a mania with the Romans. The Tetrarch swore that they did not exist. What, then, was underneath?

"Nothing! A man, a prisoner."

"Show him," said Vitellius.

The Tetrarch did not obey. The Jews would have found out his secret. His aversion to lifting the cover made Vitellius impatient.

HERODIAS

"Break it in!" he cried to the lictors.

Mannaëi had guessed what was in their thoughts. When he saw the axe, he thought that Iaokanan was going to be beheaded, and he stopped the lictor at the first blow on the plate, and inserted a sort of hook between it and the paving-stones; then, stiffening his long thin arms, he raised it gently, and it fell back, while everyone admired the old man's strength. Under the double cover of wood was a trap-door of the same size, which fell apart in two pieces at a blow from his fist. Then was seen a hole, a huge pit, round which there wound a stairway without a rail, and those who leant over the edge saw at the bottom something incomprehensible and terrifying.

A human being lay on the ground, covered with long hair which was tangled with the beast's hair in which he was clothed. He got up. His forehead touched a grating fixed horizontally across the pit, and from time to time he went back into the depths of his lair.

The crests of the tiaras were glittering in the sun, the hilts of the swords were shining, and the pavement was unbearably hot; doves were flying out of the cornices and wheeling over the courtyard. It was the time when Mannaëi usually threw grain to them. He was crouching in front of the Tetrarch, who stood near Vitellius. The Galileans, priests, and soldiers made a ring behind, and all were silent, in anxious expectation of what would happen next.

First, in a sepulchral voice, there came a great sigh. Herodias heard it at the other end of the palace. Irresistibly attracted thither, she went through the crowd and bent forward to listen, with one hand on Mannaëi's shoulder.

The voice rose. "Woe unto you, Pharisees and Sadducees, brood of vipers, swollen wineskins, tinkling cymbals!"

They recognized the voice of Iaokanan. His name went round, and more people hastened up to listen.

"Woe unto thee, O people! Woe to the traitors of Judah and the drunkards of Ephraim, and to those who dwell in the fat valley and reel with the fumes of wine! May they pass away as running water, as the slug that melteth in its going, as the child killed in the womb that does not see the sun! Then must thou, Moab, flee into the cypresses like the sparrows, and into the caves like the jerboas. The gates of the fortresses shall be broken faster than nut-shells, the walls shall crumble, the towns shall burn, and the scourge of the Eternal shall not cease. It shall turn your limbs over in your blood, as wool in a dyer's vat. It shall tear you as a new harrow; it shall scatter upon the mountains all the scraps of your flesh!"

Of what conqueror was he speaking? Was it Vitellius? Only the Romans could exterminate like that. Murmurs began to rise from those standing round, "Enough, enough! Let him cease!"

He went on in a louder voice: "The little children shall drag themselves over ashes by the corpses of their mothers. Men shall go by night in peril of the sword to seek their bread among the ruins. Jackals shall snatch bones in the public places where the old men used to converse in the evening. The virgins, swallowing their tears, shall play the lute at banquets of strangers, and the bravest of thy sons shall bend low their backs, flayed by burdens too heavy to bear!"

The people saw once more before their eyes the days of their exile and all the calamities of their history. These were the words of the prophets of olden times. Iaokanan was hurling them forth, one after another, like mighty blows.

But the voice became gentle and sang out melodiously. He told of a freeing of peoples and wonders in the sky: the new-born Child would put his arm into the lair of the dragon, there would be gold in place of clay, the desert would blossom as a rose. "That which is now valued at sixty kissars shall not cost one obol. Fountains of milk shall gush forth from the rocks, men shall fall asleep in the wine-presses with full bellies. When comest Thou, O Thou for whose advent I am hoping? In expectation of Thy coming, let all the people kneel, and Thy dominion shall be eternal, O Son of David!"

The Tetrarch flung himself back. The existence of a Son of David was an insult and a menace to him.

Iaokanan railed at his kingship: "There is none other king but the Eternal!" And at his gardens, his statues, his furniture of ivory—he was like the ungodly Ahab.

Antipas broke the little cord by which the seal hung on his breast, and threw it into the pit, commanding him to be silent.

The voice replied: "I will howl like a bear, like a wild ass, like a woman in travail. Thy incest is already punished, for God is afflicting thee with the barrenness of a mule!"

And laughter, like the noise of splashing waves, came up out of the pit.

Vitellius persisted in staying there. The interpreter with an unmoved voice repeated in the language of the Romans all the insults which Iaokanan was roaring out in his own. The Tetrarch and Herodias were forced to endure them twice over. He was panting, and she was staring, open-mouthed, at the bottom of the pit.

The awful man turned his head upwards, and, clutching the bars, glued to them a face, which was like a mass of briars in which two blazing coals were shining.

"Ah! It is thou, Jezebel! Thou hast taken his heart with the creaking of thy slipper. Thou wast neighing like a mare. Thou hast set up thy bed upon the mountains to perform thy sacrifices! The Lord shall tear off thy ear-rings, thy purple robes, thy linen veils, the bracelets from thine arms, the rings from thy feet, and the little golden crescents that quiver on thy brow, thy silver mirrors, thy fans of ostrich feathers, the soles of mother-of-pearl that increase thy stature, the arrogance of thy diamonds, the scents of thy hair, the painting on thy nails, all the artifices of thy languorous ease, and there shall not be pebbles enough for the stoning of this adulterous woman!"

She looked about her for a defender. The Pharisees hypocritically lowered their eyes; the Sadducees looked the other way, fearing to offend the Proconsul. Antipas looked as if he would die upon the spot.

The voice swelled out louder and ever louder, like

HERODIAS

the rolling and roar of claps of thunder, and, as the echo in the mountains bore it back, it burst over Machærus in peals innumerable.

"Stretch thyself in the dust, O daughter of Babylon! Make them grind flour! Take off thy girdle, unloose thy shoes, turn up thy garments, cross the rivers! Thy shame shall be discovered, thine infamy shall be seen, thy sobs shall break thy teeth! The Eternal abhors the stench of thy crimes! Accursed one! Accursed one! Die like a dog!"

The trap-door was closed and the cover fell back upon it. Mannaëi would fain have strangled Iaokanan.

Herodias disappeared. The Pharisees were scandalized. Antipas in their midst was trying to justify himself.

"Doubtless a man must marry his brother's wife," replied Eleazar, "but Herodias was not a widow, and, besides, she had a child, which made the affair abominable."

"There you are entirely wrong," objected Jonathas, the Sadducee. "The Law condemns these marriages, but does not proscribe them absolutely."

"It matters not," said Antipas. "People are very unjust to me, for, when all is said and done, Absalom used to sleep with the wives of his father, Judah with his daughter-in-law, Ammon with his sister, Lot with his daughters."

Aulus, who had been asleep, reappeared at that moment. When the matter had been put before him, he sided with the Tetrarch.

Nobody, said he, should be upset by such nonsense, and he laughed uproariously at the censure of the priests and at Iaokanan's fury.

Herodias, standing in the middle of the palace steps, turned round towards him, saying, "Thou art wrong, O Master! He is ordering the people to refuse to pay taxes."

"Is that true?" asked the publican promptly.

The replies were affirmative, on the whole, and the Tetrarch gave them his support.

Vitellius thought the prisoner might escape, and as the behaviour of Antipas seemed questionable, he posted sentinels at the gates, along the walls, and in the courtyard. Then he went off towards his rooms, accompanied by the deputations of priests. Each of these set before him its grievances, without touching on the question of the high priesthood. As they all besieged him at the same time, he dismissed them.

Jonathas was just leaving him when he saw Antipas, in an embrasure, talking with a long-haired man dressed in white—an Essene—and he was sorry that he had taken his side.

There was one reflection which had consoled the Tetrarch: he had no further concern with Iaokanan, for the Romans had taken over the charge of him. What a relief that was!

At that moment Phanuel was walking on the road round the walls. He called him, and, pointing to the soldiers, said: "They are the strongest! I cannot set him free! It is no fault of mine!"

The courtyard was empty; the slaves were resting. Against the red sky which set the horizon in a blaze, the smallest upright objects stood out black.

Antipas made out the salt-pits at the other end of the Dead Sea, but could no longer see the tents of the Arabs. No doubt, they had gone off. The moon was rising, and a feeling of peace came down upon his soul.

Phanuel, his chin sunk upon his breast, was in great tribulation. At last he set forth what he had to say.

Ever since the beginning of the month he had been studying the sky before dawn, when the constellation of Perseus was at its zenith. Agala was barely visible, Algol was less brilliant, Mira Ceti had disappeared. From this he augured the death of a man of importance, in Machærus, that very night.

Who was it to be? Vitellius was too well guarded. They would not execute Iaokanan. "It must, then, be I," thought the Tetrarch.

Perhaps the Arabs were coming back? Perhaps the Proconsul would find out his dealings with the Parthians? Assassins from Jerusalem formed the escort of the priests, and they had daggers concealed in their clothing. The Tetrarch had no doubts concerning Phanuel's science.

He thought of having recourse to Herodias, whom, all the same, he hated. But she would give him courage, and all the bonds of the sorcery, to which, once upon a time, he had yielded, were not broken.

When he entered her room, cinnamon was smoking in a porphyry basin, and powders, unguents, stuffs as thin as clouds, embroideries lighter than feathers, were scattered about. He said nothing of Phanuel's prediction, nor of his fear of the Jews and the Arabs; she would have accused him of being a coward. He merely spoke of the Romans: Vitellius had told him nothing, even in confidence, of his military plans, and he, Antipas, suspected he was a friend of Caius, Agrippa's constant companion. So he would be exiled, or perhaps he would have his throat cut.

Herodias, tolerant yet contemptuous, endeavoured to reassure him and finally took out of a little box a curious medal, embellished with the head of Tiberius in profile. That would be sufficient to make the lictors turn pale and accusations melt away.

Antipas, moved and grateful, asked how she had got it.

" It was given to me ! " she answered.

From under a curtain in front of them a bare arm was stretched forth—a delightful young arm such as Polycletus might have chiselled in ivory. Rather awkwardly, and yet gracefully, it groped about in the air to pick up a tunic left behind on a stool near the wall. An old woman pulled back the curtain and passed the garment gently in.

A vague memory which he could not exactly fix, came across the Tetrarch's mind.

" Is that slave thine ? "

" What does it matter to thee ? " replied Herodias.

III

The guests filled the banqueting-hall to overflowing. It had three aisles like a basilica, divided by pillars of algum wood, with bronze capitals ornamented with carvings. There were two balconies with open-work in front, and a third in golden

HERODIAS

filigree projected in a curve from the back, facing a huge arch at the other end of the hall.

Candelabra, which burned on tables set in rows the whole length of the chamber, made sheaves of fire among the cups of painted earthenware and the copper dishes, the cubes of snow and the piles of grapes, but owing to the loftiness of the roof their red glow seemed to become gradually smaller and smaller, and points of light shone as stars do through branches of trees at night. Through the opening of the great bay, torches could be seen on the terraces of houses, for Antipas was feasting his friends, his people, and all those who came to his palace.

Slaves, alert as dogs, moved about in felt slippers, carrying dishes. The Proconsul's table was placed on a dais with flooring of sycamore underneath the gilded balcony. It was enclosed by Babylonian tapestries to form a kind of pavilion. Three ivory couches, one facing the hall and two at the sides, were occupied by Vitellius, his son, and Antipas, the Proconsul being on the left, near the door, Aulus on the right, and the Tetrarch in the centre.

He wore a heavy black cloak whose material was invisible under the colours imposed upon it, rouge upon his cheeks, his beard in the shape of a fan, and blue-powdered hair clasped by a diadem of jewels. Vitellius kept on his purple shoulder-belt, which crossed his linen toga diagonally. Aulus had had the sleeves of his robe tied behind him: it was of violet silk with silver plaques. His hair, with its pads, rose in tiers, and a sapphire necklace sparkled on his breast, which was plump and white like a woman's. Near him on a mat a very beautiful boy was sitting, cross-legged and always smiling. Aulus had seen him in the kitchens, and could not do without him. As he could not keep his Chaldean name in his head, he called him simply "the Asiatic." From time to time he stretched himself upon his couch, and then his bare feet dominated the gathering.

On his side were the priests and the Tetrarch's officers, some residents from Jerusalem, and the chief men from the Greek towns. Below the Proconsul were Marcellus and the publicans, some friends of the Tetrarch, and notable people from Cana, Ptolemaïs and Jericho. Then in a confused throng were to be seen mountaineers from the Lebanon, and old soldiers of Herod; twelve Thracians, a Gaul, two Germans, gazelle hunters, shepherds of Edom, the Sultan of Palmyra, sailors from Ezion-Geber. Each had in front of him a cake of soft paste to wipe his fingers on, and, with arms stretched out like vultures' necks, they took olives, pistachio nuts, and almonds. All had merry faces under their garlands of flowers.

The Pharisees had spurned these as a Roman indecency. They shivered when they were sprinkled with galbanum and incense, a mixture reserved for the services in the Temple. Aulus rubbed his armpits with it, and Antipas promised him a whole consignment, together with three hampers of the very balm which had made Cleopatra covetous of Palestine.

A captain from his garrison at Tiberias, who had just come in, had placed himself behind Antipas to inform him of some extraordinary occurrences, but the Tetrarch's attention was divided between the Proconsul and what was being said at the neighbouring tables. They were talking of Iaokanan and people of his kind: Simon of Gittoi cleansed sins with fire, and a certain Jesus . . .

" The worst of them all! " cried Eleazar. " What an infamous mountebank! "

Behind the Tetrarch a man rose, pale as the hem of his chlamys. He came down from the dais and, interrupting the Pharisees, exclaimed: " That is a lie! Jesus works miracles! "

Antipas wanted to see some. " You ought to have brought Him with you! Tell us something about them! "

Then he told how he, Jacob, having a sick daughter, had gone to Capernaum to entreat the Master to come and to heal her. The Master had replied, " Go back to thy home, thy daughter is healed." And he had found her on the threshold of his house, she having left her bed when the palace dial marked the third hour, the very moment when he was approaching Jesus.

Certainly, argued the Pharisees, potent herbs and practices did exist. Here even at Machærus was to be found sometimes the baaras which makes men invulnerable. But to heal without either seeing or touching the sick was impossible, unless Jesus made use of demons.

And the friends of Antipas, the chief men of Galilee, shook their heads and said: " Demons, evidently."

Jacob, standing between their table and the table of the priests, was haughtily yet gently silent.

They called on him to speak. "Justify His power!"

He bowed his shoulders, and then in a low voice, slowly, as if he were afraid of himself, said: "You know not then that He is the Messiah?"

All the priests looked at each other, and Vitellius asked the meaning of the word. His interpreter waited a minute before answering.

They gave that name to a liberator who would bring them the enjoyment of all the wealth of the earth and dominion over all peoples. Some even held that two were to be looked for. The first would be vanquished by Gog and Magog, Demons of the North, but the other would exterminate the Prince of Evil, and for centuries they had been expecting him to come at any moment.

The priests having consulted together, Eleazar spoke. To begin with, he said the Messiah would be David's son and not a carpenter's. He would confirm the Law: this Nazarene was attacking it. And here was a stronger argument: he should be preceded by the coming of Elias.

"But Elias has come!" replied Jacob.

"Elias! Elias!" repeated the crowd down to the far end of the hall. All in their imagination saw an old man with ravens flying over his head, lightning setting fire to an altar, and idolatrous chief-priests being thrown into raging torrents; and women in the tribunes thought of the widow of Sarepta.

Jacob went on repeating till he was exhausted that he knew him. He had seen him, and the people had seen him, too.

"His name?"

Then he cried with all his strength, "Iaokanan!"

Antipas fell back as if he had been struck full in the chest. The Sadducees leapt upon Jacob. Eleazar went on shouting—trying to be heard. When silence was established, he threw his cloak about him and put questions like a judge.

"Seeing that the prophet is dead . . ."

Murmurs interrupted him. It was believed that Elias had only disappeared.

He turned furiously on the crowd, and then went on with his inquiries: "Thou thinkest that he has come to life again?"

"Why not?" said Jacob.

The Sadducees shrugged their shoulders. Jonathas opened his little eyes wide, and tried to laugh inanely. Nothing could be sillier than the body's claim to everlasting life. And he recited for the benefit of the Proconsul this line from a contemporary poet:

"*Nec crescit, nec post mortem durare videtur.*"

At that moment Aulus bent over the edge of his couch, his brow in a sweat, his face green, his hands clenched on his stomach. The Sadducees feigned great emotion—next day the high priesthood was restored to them. Antipas paraded his despair. Vitellius remained immovable. His anxiety was, nevertheless, very keen, for with his son vanished his fortune. Aulus had not finished vomiting before he wanted to begin eating again.

"Give me some marble dust, scraped rock of Naxos, sea-water, anything. Suppose I took a bath?"

He chewed some snow, and then, after wavering between a pasty of Commagene and some pink ouzels, he decided on pumpkins and honey. The Asiatic gazed at him: this capacity for gorging marked him as a wonderful being, sprung from a superior race.

They served ox-kidneys, dormice, nightingales, mince-meat in vine leaves, and the priests discussed the question of resurrection. Ammonius, pupil of Philo the Platonist, thought them stupid people, and said so to some Greeks who were jeering at oracles. Marcellus and Jacob had come together. The former was telling the latter of the happiness he had experienced on being baptized into Mithras, and Jacob was urging him to follow Jesus. Palm and tamarisk wines, wines of Safet and Byblos flowed from jars into bowls, from bowls into cups, from cups down throats; men chattered and opened their hearts to each other. Iacim, although a Jew, no longer concealed his worship of the planets. A merchant from Aphaka amazed the nomads by his description of the marvels of the temple of Hierapolis, and they asked him how much the pilgrimage would cost. Others clung to the religion of their birth. A German who was nearly blind sang a hymn in praise of the promontory in Scandinavia on which the gods appear with haloes round their faces, and people from Shechem would not eat turtle-doves, out of respect for the dove Azima.

Several stood as they talked in the middle of the hall, and the steam of their breath mingling with the smoke from the candelabra made a fog in the air. Phanuel passed along the wall. He had just been studying the heavens again, but he did not go up to the Tetrarch as he was afraid of being smeared with oil, which is a great pollution for the Essenes.

Knockings at the gate of the castle resounded through the hall. It was now known that Iaokanan was kept prisoner there. Men with torches were climbing up the path, a dark crowd was swarming in the ravine, and from time to time they shouted, " Iaokanan! Iaokanan! "

" He is upsetting everything! " said Jonathas.

" There will be no more money, if he goes on," the Pharisees added.

And recriminations were heard on all sides: " Protect us "—" Make an end of him "—" Thou art deserting religion "—" Ungodly as the Herods."

" Less so than you," retorted Antipas. " My father built your Temple."

Then the Pharisees, the sons of the proscribed, and the partisans of Mattathias charged the Tetrarch with the crimes of his family. They had egg-shaped heads, matted beards, weak and evil-looking hands, or snub-nosed faces, big round eyes, and the appearance of bull-dogs. A dozen of them, scribes and attendants on the priests, who fed themselves on the leavings of the burnt-offerings, made a rush to the edge of the dais and began to threaten Antipas with their knives. He harangued them, while the Sadducees defended him mildly. He caught sight of Mannaëi and gave him a signal to go away, for Vitellius was showing by his looks that these affairs concerned him not at all.

Those of the Pharisees who had remained on their couches worked themselves into a state of demoniacal fury. They smashed the plates before them. They had been served with a stew of wild ass, a great favourite of Mæcenas, which was an unclean food. Aulus chaffed them about the ass's head which, it was said, they revered, and poured forth other sarcasms on their aversion to the hog. No doubt it was because that great beast had killed their Bacchus, and they were much too fond of wine, as was shown by the discovery of a golden vine in the Temple!

The priests did not understand what he was saying. Phineas, by origin a Galilean, refused to translate it. Then he began to rage furiously, especially because the Asiatic had disappeared, being terrified, and the food was not to his liking; the various dishes were commonplace and the sauces were tasteless. He calmed down, however, when he saw sheep-tails from Syria, which are bundles of fat.

The Jewish character seemed hideous to Vitellius. Their God could quite well be Moloch, whose altars he had come across on the road, and sacrifices of children and the story of the man who was mysteriously fattened up came back to his mind. He, a Latin, was nauseated by their intolerance, their iconoclastic fury, their brutish failings. He wanted to leave the hall, but Aulus refused. With his robe pushed down to his thighs, he was lying behind a great heap of food, too gorged to eat more, but obstinately refusing to leave it.

The people's mood became more excited. They gave themselves up to thoughts of independence. They recalled the glory of Israel: every conqueror had been chastised—Antigonus, Crassus, Varus.

HERODIAS

"Wretches!" said the Proconsul, for he understood Syriac, and his interpreter was only useful in giving him his own time to answer.

Antipas very quickly drew out the Emperor's medal, and, looking at it trembling with fear, put it before Vitellius with the image and superscription upmost.

Suddenly the golden panels of the tribune were folded back, and in the brilliancy of blazing tapers, and in the midst of slaves and garlands of anemones, Herodias appeared. She bore upon her head an Assyrian mitre, which was held in its place by a chinstrap: her hair spread in ringlets over a scarlet peplum, which was slit down the length of the sleeves. With two stone monsters, like those of the treasure house of the Atrides, standing erect on either side of the door, she had the appearance of Cybele with her lions at her side. With a bowl in her hand, she cried out from the top of the balcony above Antipas, "Long life to Cæsar!"

This homage was echoed by Vitellius, Antipas, and the priests. Then there arose from the extreme end of the hall a hum of surprise and admiration. A young girl had just entered. Under a bluish veil which concealed her head and her breast, could be made out the arch of her eyes, the milky-whiteness of her ears, and the exceeding fairness of her skin. A square of shot silk covered her shoulders and was fastened to her loins by a jewelled girdle. Her black drawers were bespangled with mandrakes, and she lazily clattered little slippers of humming-birds' down.

Going up on to the dais, she drew aside her veil.

It was Herodias, just as she used to be in the days of her youth. Then she began to dance. To a measure played by a flute and a pair of castanets, her feet moved, one in front of the other. Her rounded arms seemed to be calling for someone who was ever fleeing away. She ran after him, lighter than a butterfly, like an inquiring Psyche, a wandering soul, and seemed on the point of fluttering away.

The castanets gave place to the mournful notes of a trumpet. Hope had been followed by utter dejection. Her poses gave the impression of sighs, and there was such a languor in all her body that one could not tell whether she were weeping for a god or dying in rapture in his embrace. Her eyes were half closed, her body twisted and turned, her breasts quivered, though her face remained expressionless and her little feet did not cease moving.

Vitellius compared her to Mnester, the mime. Aulus was still vomiting. The Tetrarch was lost in a dream, and was no longer thinking of Herodias. He fancied that he saw her by the Sadducees. The phantom moved away.

It was no phantom. She had had Salome, her daughter, taught far away from Machærus, so that the Tetrarch should love her, and the idea was a good one: she felt sure of it now.

Then the girl portrayed the wild desire which compels gratification. She danced as the priestesses of the Indies, as the Nubians of the cataracts of the Nile, as the bacchantes of Lydia. She turned and twisted from side to side like a flower shaken by the wind. The jewels in her ears leaped, the shred of silk which covered her back changed colour in the lights, and from her arms, from her feet, from her vesture, there shot forth invisible sparks which set the company aflame. A harp sang, and the crowd answered it with their acclamations. Opening her legs, but without bending her knees, she bent so low that her chin touched the floor. And the nomads inured to abstinence, Roman soldiers expert in debauchery, greedy publicans, old priests soured by disputes, all, with distended nostrils, quivered with lust.

Then she pirouetted round Herod's table frenziedly, swaying to and fro as sways a sorceress, and in a voice broken by sobs of passion, he said to her, "Come! Come!" She went on turning, the dulcimers crashed out as if they would burst, and the crowd shouted with all their strength. But the Tetrarch's voice was heard above the din: "Come! Come! Thou shalt have Capernaum! The plain of Tiberias! My strongholds! The half of my kingdom!"

She threw herself on her hands, with her heels in the air, and ran round the dais thus like a great beetle. Then, abruptly, she stopped.

Her neck and spine were at right angles; the sheaths of colour about her legs went up over her shoulders like rainbows, and encircled her face which was at a cubit from the ground. Her lips were painted, her eyebrows were deep black, her eyes were almost awful, and the beads of moisture on her brow were as vapour on white marble. She did not speak. They looked at each other.

There was a snapping of fingers in the balcony.

She went up into it, came down again, and, lisping a little, said with a childish air, " I wish that thou givest me in a dish the head . . ." She had forgotten the name, but went on again, smiling: " The head of Iaokanan! "

The Tetrarch sank back on his couch, crushed. He was bound by his word, and the people were waiting. Perhaps, thought he, if that death which had been predicted to him were awarded to another, his own might be averted. If Iaokanan were in truth Elias, he would be able to flee from it. If he were not, the murder was a matter of no importance.

Mannaëi was at his side and grasped his intention. Vitellius called him back and gave him the password for the sentinels guarding the pit.

That was a relief! In a minute all would be over.

Nevertheless, Mannaëi was not very quick at his work. He came back, but he was quite broken down.

For forty years he had been carrying out the duties of an executioner. It was he who had drowned Aristobulus, strangled Alexander, burnt Mattathias alive, beheaded Zosimus, Pappus, Joseph, Antipater, and yet he did not dare to kill Iaokanan. His teeth were chattering, and his whole body was trembling.

Before the pit he had seen the Great Angel of the Samaritans, covered all over with eyes, brandishing a huge sword, red and jagged like a flame. Two soldiers whom he brought as witnesses would say as much.

They had seen nothing, save a Jewish captain, who had rushed on them and was now no more.

Herodias's fury poured forth in a torrent of vulgar and cruel abuse. She broke her finger-nails on the

HERODIAS 153

lattice-work of the balcony, and the two carved lions seemed to be biting her shoulders and to be roaring with her.

Antipas followed her lead, as did the priests, soldiers, and Pharisees, all shouting for vengeance, while the rest were indignant that their pleasure should be delayed.

Mannaëi went out, hiding his face.

The guests found time passing even more slowly than it did earlier in the evening, and they began to feel bored.

Suddenly a noise of footsteps reverberated in the corridors. The feeling of uneasiness was becoming unbearable.

The head came in—Mannaëi holding it by the hair with outstretched arm, proud of the applause that met him.

Putting it on a dish, he offered it to Salome. She went quickly up into the balcony, and some minutes afterwards the head was brought back by that old woman whom the Tetrarch had noticed in the morning on the roof of a house, and, a little while before, in Herodias's chamber.

He drew back, so as not to see it. Vitellius glanced at it unconcernedly. Mannaëi came down from the dais and showed it to the Roman captains and then to all those who were dining on that side. They examined it. The sharp blade of his sword had glanced downwards and cut into the jaw. The corners of the mouth were drawn in a convulsion. Blood, already clotted, was sprinkled in the beard. The closed eyelids were pale as shells, and rays from the candelabra on the tables caught them.

It reached the table of the priests. A Pharisee turned it over curiously. Then Mannaëi setting it upright again, placed it before Aulus, whom it awakened. Through their half-opened lashes, the dead eyes of the one and the dulled eyes of the other seemed to say something to each other.

Then Mannaëi presented it to Antipas. Tears rolled down the Tetrarch's cheeks. The torches went out; the guests departed; and in the banqueting-hall there only remained Antipas, his hands pressed against his temples, ever gazing at the severed head, while Phanuel, erect in the middle of the great nave, with outstretched arms, was murmuring prayers.

. . . .

At the very moment when the sun rose, two men who had been sent out by Iaokanan a little while before, returned with their long-expected answer.

They confided it to Phanuel, who was enraptured with it.

Then he showed them the melancholy object on the dish in the midst of the remnants of the banquet.

One of the men said to him: " Be of good cheer! He has gone down to the dead to proclaim the Christ! "

The Essene now understood the meaning of those words, " That He may increase, I must decrease! "

And all three of them took the head of Iaokanan and went away towards Galilee. As it was very heavy, they took turns to carry it.

THE TEMPTATION OF
ST. ANTHONY

THE TEMPTATION OF ST ANTHONY

I

(High on a mountain of the Thebaïd, on a level space, curved like the crescent moon, and shut in by great rocks, stands the hermit's hut.

It is built of mud and reeds, and has a flat roof, and a doorway, but no door. Within, a pitcher and a loaf of black bread can be seen; in the middle, upon a wooden pedestal, a large book; on the floor, scattered about, bundles of fibre, two or three mats, a basket, a knife.

Out of the ground, some ten paces from the hut, rises a tall cross; and on the opposite side a gnarled and ancient palm-tree hangs over the abyss: for the mountain drops away precipitously, with what looks like a lake, formed by the Nile, at its foot.

The rampart of the rocks, to right and left, cuts off the view; but desertwards, like a succession of sea-beaches, vast ashy undulations rise up and up, parallel one behind the other; and beyond these pale sands, far in the distance, tower the Libyan mountains, wall-like, chalky-white, flecked here and there by violet mists; and behind them the sun is setting.

The northern sky is pearly-grey; and overhead, scattered like tufts of some tremendous plume, purple clouds spread across the blue vault. The fiery rays grow dim, the blue turns pale; everything—thickets, pebbles, soil—becomes hard as bronze; and there floats in the air a golden dust so minute that it mingles with the quivering light.

SAINT ANTHONY with long hair and beard, and wearing a goat-skin tunic, is sitting crosslegged, making mats. When the sun has gone, he sighs deeply, and with his eyes on the horizon he says :)

Another day! Another day gone!

And still there was a time when I was not altogether wretched! While it was yet dark I would say my prayers; and then go down to the stream for water, and climb the rough path with the leathern bottle on my shoulders, singing hymns as I climbed. When I had tidied my hut, I would pick up my tools, and try to make mats exactly of a size, and baskets beautifully light: for in those days I looked on even the most trivial toil as a duty which could never be unpleasant.

At fixed hours I would leave my work, and as with outstretched arms I betook myself to prayer I used to feel as though a fount of mercy were pouring from highest heaven into my heart. That fountain has dried up now. . . . Why?

(He walks, slowly, within the rocky circle.)

Everybody disapproved when I left home. My mother fell down fainting; my sister long stood beckoning me back; and little Ammonaria was crying, the child that I met every evening when she watered cattle at the cistern. I remember how she ran after me. The rings on her ankles glittered in the dust, and her tunic, open at the hips, fluttered in the wind. The old hermit who was taking me away shouted insults at her. Our two camels went galloping, galloping; and I have never seen any of my people from that day to this.

First of all, I chose a dwelling-place in the tomb of a Pharaoh. But these underground palaces are bewitched; and their darkness is heavy with the bygone fumes of incense. From out the depths of stone coffins I heard melancholy voices calling me; or sometimes I would see, come suddenly to life again, the abominable things pictured on the walls; and then I got me away to the shores of the Red Sea, to a citadel in ruins. There, my companions were scorpions that crawled among the stones, and eagles that wheeled unceasingly over my head against the blue sky. In the night I was torn by their talons, bitten by their beaks, brushed by their soft wings; and dreadful demons, howling in my ears, hurled me to the ground. Once, I recollect, travellers on their way to Alexandria rescued me, and took me along with them.

Next, I sat at the feet of that good old man Didymus. Blind though he was, none equalled him in understanding of the Scriptures. After a lecture, he used to take my arm and let me lead him along the Paneum, looking towards the lighthouse and the open sea. Then we would come back by the harbour, jostled by people of all lands—there were even men from the Crimea, wearing bearskins; and naked philosophers from the Ganges, smeared with cow-dung. But there was constant fighting in the streets, over Jews who would not pay their taxes, or agitators who wanted to drive out the Romans; and the city was full of heretics, disciples of Manes and Valentius and Basilides and Arius—all of them desperately eager to argue and convince.

Now and then their arguments come back to my memory still; but it is no use thinking about them—they do but distract me.

I fled away to Kolzum; and my contrition was so complete that no longer did I feel any fear of God. Certain men gathered about me to live as anchorites, and for them I drew up a practical rule of life, containing none of the vapourings of the mystics, or the exaggerations of the philosophers. Letters were brought to me from all parts, and men came long distances to visit me.

But Christians were being tortured in the cities, and a longing for martyrdom drew me to Alexandria, where I found, however, that the persecution had ended three days before I got there.

As I was turning back, I was stopped by a stream of people in front of the Temple of Serapis, and they told me that the Governor was making one last example: and there in broad daylight, in the centre of the portico, was a naked woman, lashed to a column, being flogged by soldiers with leather thongs; and at each blow her whole body writhed. She turned round, her mouth wide open—and over the heads of the crowd, amidst the long hair which partly hid her face, I thought that I recognized Ammonaria. . . .

And yet . . . that woman was taller . . . and beautiful . . . so wondrous beautiful!

(He smites his forehead with his hands.)

No! No! I must not think of it!

Another time, Athanasius wanted my help in his struggle against the Arians: but it all ended in sarcasm and mockery. He has been slandered since then, deprived of his bishopric, put to flight. . . . Where is he now? I know not! No one troubles

THE TEMPTATION OF ST. ANTHONY

to bring me news. My disciples have all left me—even Hilarion!

He must have been about fifteen when he came; and he was so quick-witted and always asking questions. And he listened so thoughtfully—and when I wanted things he would bring them to me so readily, as nimble as a young goat, and funny enough to have set the patriarchs laughing. He was as a son to me!

(The sky is red, the earth as dark as pitch. Trails of sand, like huge winding-sheets, spring up beneath the gusts of wind, then sink again. Across a bright patch of sky, suddenly, there comes a flight of birds, in formation like an arrow-head, and shining like a piece of solid metal with quivering edges.

Anthony watches them.)

Ah me! How gladly could I follow them! And how often have I enviously watched the boats, with their wing-like sails, and most of all when they were carrying off those whom I had welcomed as my guests! What happy times we had! And what confidences did we exchange! The man who interested me most of all was Ammon, who told me of his journey to Rome, and of the Colosseum and the catacombs, and the piety of the noble women who lived there, and ten thousand other things! . . . and I did not want him to go away! Why have I gone on living such a life? Better have stayed with the monks in the Nitrian desert, when they asked me! They have separate cells, yet see something of each other. A trumpet calls them to church on Sundays, and there are three cat-o'-nine-tails hanging ready for the punishment of wrongdoers and thieves and intruders, for their discipline is hard.

But a life such as theirs has its compensations. The faithful bring them eggs and fruit, and needles with which to pull thorns out of their feet. Round about Pisperi there are vineyards, and at Pabena they use a raft when they go to get food.

And possibly I might have served my brethren better by remaining a simple priest—helping poor people, ministering the sacraments, directing family life.

And even laymen are not all damned, and if I had chosen I might have been . . . let me see! . . . a grammarian, or a philosopher. There would have been a globe of reeds in my chamber, with writing-tablets ready at hand: young folk about me, and a wreath of laurel hanging over my door as a sign.

And yet, such success as that would have brought too much pride along with it. Possibly I had better have been a soldier. I was vigorous and bold enough—I could have pulled the ropes of the engines of war, marched through gloomy forests, entered smouldering cities with my helmet on my head! . . . And there was no reason why I should not have purchased with my savings the post of tax-collector at the toll-bar of some bridge; and travellers would have told me their adventures, while they showed me the curious things they had in their bags. . . .

The merchants of Alexandria go sailing at the mouth of the Nile on holidays, and they drink wine from lotus-cups, to the sound of the tambourines with which all the riverside taverns are a-tremble! Farther off, peaceful farms are sheltered from the

THE TEMPTATION OF ST. ANTHONY 163

south wind by clipped and pointed trees. The high roofs of the houses rest on slender columns, close together like trellis-bars; and stretched at his ease on a long seat the farmer can see, through these openings, his spreading lands about him, with sportsmen in the standing corn, the press where wine is made, the oxen treading out the grain. His children are playing on the floor, and his wife leans over to kiss him.

(Here and there, indistinct in the grey twilight, pointed muzzles appear, with ears pricked and eyes sparkling. Anthony goes towards them; but his footsteps dislodge some pebbles, and the creatures take to flight. They were jackals.
Only one of them has stayed, his flanks curled round the upright forepaws, his head raised with a sharp look of challenge.)

How grand he looks! I should like to stroke his back, very gently.

(Anthony whistles to him; but the jackal makes off.)

Ah! He has gone after the others! How lonely it is! How tired of it I am!

(Laughing bitterly :)

What a life it is! In the heat of the fire straining palm-branches to the shape of shepherds' crooks, twisting baskets, stitching mats, and then trading them with wandering tribes for bread so hard that it breaks one's teeth! Ah! Woe is me! Will it be ever thus? Death itself were better! I can bear no more of it! No more! No more!

(He stamps with his foot, then goes up and down among the rocks with hasty steps until, out of breath, he stops, bursts into tears, and at last flings himself exhausted to the ground.

The night is calm; multitudinous stars are twinkling; only the sound of the tarantulas is heard.

The arms of the cross cast their shadow on the sand; and Anthony, from amidst his tears, sees this.)

My God! Was I as weak as all that? Courage! Up we get!

(He enters the hut, uncovers some smouldering charcoal, kindles a torch and fixes it on the wooden pedestal, so that light falls upon the great book.)

If I were to look—the Acts of the Apostles? Yes! —and at random!

"*He . . . saw heaven opened, and a certain vessel descending unto him, as it had been a great sheet knit at the four corners . . . wherein were all manner of four-footed beasts of the earth, and wild beasts, and creeping things, and fowls of the air. . . . And there came a voice to him, Rise, Peter, kill and eat.*"

And so the Lord told His Apostle that he might eat of everything. . . . While I . . . ?

(Anthony rests his chin upon his breast, until the rustle of the pages, blown by the wind, makes him look up again: and once more he reads :)

"*The Jews smote all their enemies with the stroke of the sword, and slaughter, and destruction, and did what they would unto them that hated them.*"

Then comes the numbering of those slain: seventy-five thousand! They themselves had suffered so horribly! And besides, their enemies were enemies of the true God. And what joy to slaughter idolaters, in the very act of avenging oneself! The city must have overflowed with dead! Across the garden thresholds, on the stairways, and so piled up in the

THE TEMPTATION OF ST. ANTHONY

chambers that doors could no longer open and shut! . . . But here am I revelling in thoughts of murder and of blood!

(He opens the book in another place.)

"*Nebuchadnezzar fell upon his face, and worshipped Daniel.*"

Ah! That was as it should be! The Most High exalteth his prophets above kings; yet this king had eaten sumptuously, and was drunk continually with luxury and pride. And God, for his punishment, changed him into a brute, and he went crawling on all fours!

(Anthony bursts out laughing; and as he stretches his arms the tips of his fingers turn the pages of the book, and his eye falls on this sentence :)

"*Hezekiah was glad of them, and showed them the house of his precious things, the silver, and the gold, and the spices, and the precious ointment . . . and all that was found in his treasures. . . .*"

I can picture it to myself . . . they saw precious stones, diamonds and gold coins heaped right up to the ceilings. The possessor of such treasures is not as other men. He knows, as he handles these things, that he controls the results of labour without limit, and, as it were, the lives of multitudes of men whom he has gathered together, as one pumps water, and can spill abroad again. It is a wise precaution on the part of kings. The wisest of them all did not neglect it. His navy brought him ivory and apes. . . . Where does it say that, now? . . .

(He hurriedly turns the pages.)

Ah! Here we are!

"When the Queen of Sheba heard of the fame of Solomon . . . she came to prove him with hard questions."

How could she have hoped to tempt him? The devil indeed tried to tempt Jesus! But Jesus overcame him because he was God, and it may be that Solomon prevailed because he understood magic. A splendid thing, such knowledge as that! For the world, as a philosopher once explained to me, forms one great whole, in which everybody has power over everybody else. We should try, he said, to understand the mutual attractions and repulsions of things and then set them off one against another. . . . Might one not hope to modify in this way what appears to be the unchangeable order of things?

(At this moment, the looming shadow behind him, thrown by the arms of the cross, thrusts itself forward like a great pair of horns; Anthony cries :)

Help me, O my God!

(The shadow returns to its place.)

Ah! It was an illusion! Nothing more! It is silly of me to torture myself thus! There is nothing that I can do . . . positively nothing!

(He sits down and folds his arms.)

And yet . . . I thought I felt the approach of . . . But why should he come to me? And besides, am I ignorant of his devices? I drove away that hideous anchorite who grinningly offered me the little hot rolls; and the centaur who would have carried me away on his back . . . and the little blackamoor on the sandhills, who was so beautiful,

THE TEMPTATION OF ST. ANTHONY

and who told me that his name was " the Spirit of Incontinence."

(Anthony walks briskly to right and left.)

It was under my direction that this cluster of cells was built, and inhabited by monks who wear hairshirts beneath their goat-skin garments, and of whom there are enough to make an army! I have healed the sick while they still were far away; I have put evil spirits to flight; I have crossed a river swarming with crocodiles; the Emperor Constantine himself wrote to me thrice; Balacius, who spat at me, was torn asunder by his horses; the people of Alexandria, when I appeared once more among them, struggled to get a glance at me; and it was Athanasius himself who put me again upon my way. But what a life of labour it has been! For more than thirty years I have groaned here in the desert! Like Eusebius, I have carried four-score pounds of bronze upon my loins; I have exposed my body, like Macarius, to the stings of insects; I have kept awake for three and fifty nights in succession, like Pacomius, without ever closing an eyelid; and it may well be that those who were beheaded or tortured or even burnt alive won less merit than I, since my entire life has been one long martyrdom!

(He walks more slowly.)

I am sure there is no living man more utterly poverty-stricken than I! People are not nearly as charitable as they used to be; and nobody ever gives me anything in these days. My clothes are threadbare. I've no sandals, not even a bowl! I gave away all my own possessions to the poor and to my family, not keeping a single farthing for myself. If only to buy a few tools that are necessary for my work, I ought to have a little money. Not a great deal, of course! Just a few pence! . . . I would make them go such a long way! . . .

The Fathers of Nicæa in their purple robes looked like magi on their thrones, all along the wall; they were feasted sumptuously, and were highly esteemed, especially Paphnutius, who has been blind in one eye and crippled since the persecution of Diocletian! The Emperor himself kissed his empty eye-socket . . . more than once . . . and what a silly thing that was to do! After all, some of the members of that Council were unworthy! There was Theophilus, that bishop from Scythia; and another, John, of Persia; Spiridion—a keeper of beasts! . . . Alexander was too old. . . . Athanasius ought to have shown more gentleness towards the Arians, and then they would not have been so obstinate!

But I'm not so sure! They did not listen to me! That fellow who made those speeches . . . that tall young man with the curly beard—how calmly he tossed his specious arguments at me! And while I was feeling about for the proper answer, there they were, with their wicked faces, watching me, yelping like hyenas. Ah! Why could I not persuade the Emperor to banish the whole lot of them? . . . Or else thrash them, smash them, watch them suffer! *I* have suffered enough, anyhow!

(He leans wearily against the hut.)

It is because I have fasted too much! My strength

THE TEMPTATION OF ST. ANTHONY

is failing me! If I were to eat . . . just once in a way, the tiniest morsel of meat!

(He half closes his eyes, as though exhausted.)

Ah! Some good red flesh . . . a bunch of grapes to crunch . . . curds and whey wobbling on a dish! . . .

But stop! . . . Stop! . . . My heart rises and swells like the sea before a storm. Unspeakable languor bears me down; and upon the warm wind comes the sweet perfume of a woman's hair. And yet surely no woman is anywhere near? . . .

(He glances towards the pathway between the rocks.)

That is the way they come, balanced in their litters beneath the black arms of the eunuchs. They climb out, and clasping jewel-laden hands they kneel down before me and tell me all their troubles. A longing for joy that passes all human understanding so tortures them that they would welcome death itself, for in their dreams they say that they have seen God . . . heard him calling to them . . . and the edges of their garments trail about my feet. I thrust them from me, but "No!" they say, "Not yet! Tell us first what we must do!" And they are ready for every sort of penance, even for the roughest—to throw in their lots with me, to live here with me!

But it is long, now, since any of them have come! Perhaps one is on the road even now! Why not? If only suddenly . . . Surely I heard the tinkling of mule-bells on the mountain! Perhaps . . . ?

(Anthony climbs a rock near the pathway, and leans forward, peering into the shadows.)

Yes! Down there! Right at the bottom something moves, as though people were trying to find their way! She is there! . . . But they have missed the path. . . .

(He calls:)

Here you are! This way! This way!

(And the echoes repeat: " Way! Way! " while Anthony, half-dazed, slowly drops his arms.)

For shame! For shame! Alas! Poor Anthony!

(And a soft voice seems to whisper: " Poor Anthony.")

Somebody there? Answer me!

(The wind rises and falls among the rocks; and in its mingled tones he hears VOICES, as though the air itself were speaking. These voices are low, insinuating, shrill.)

FIRST VOICE: Do you desire women?
SECOND VOICE: Or great heaps of money?
THIRD VOICE: A shining sword?
OTHER VOICES: You are admired by everybody! Lie down and sleep! Slay them all! Yes! Slay them all!

(Meantime, a change takes place, and on the edge of the cliff the ancient palm-tree, with its clump of yellow branches, becomes the upper part of a woman's body, leaning over the abyss, with her long tresses flying.

Anthony turns towards his hut; and the pedestal supporting the book, its pages dotted with black letters, appears to him like a bush covered with swallows.)

It must be the flickering light of this torch—I will quench it!

(He extinguishes the torch, and the darkness becomes intense. And then, suddenly, across the sky there drift, first of all a splashing of water, then a painted harlot, the

THE TEMPTATION OF ST. ANTHONY

pinnacle of a temple, a warrior, a chariot with two rearing white horses.

These visions come abruptly, in a succession of jerks, and they stand out against the night as though outlined in scarlet upon ebony.

Their succession becomes more rapid, until at last they follow each other with dizzying speed. And then again they slacken, and grow faint by degrees, until they altogether die away, or else pass out of sight suddenly, and are instantly replaced by others.

Anthony closes his eyes.

The visions become more numerous than ever; they besiege him, throng him about. Unspeakable terror overwhelms him; and he is no longer conscious of anything but a fiery shrinking at the pit of his stomach. Spite of the tumult in his brain, he is conscious of a tremendous silence which separates him from the rest of the world. He tries to speak, but it is impossible! It is as though the chain of his existence had snapped; and, struggling no longer, Anthony falls upon the rush mat.)

II

(Then a shadow, more delicately fine than ordinary terrestrial shadows, and festooned along its edges by yet other shadows, falls upon the earth.

It is the Devil, leaning on the roof of the hut, and sheltering under his two wings—like a gigantic bat giving suck to its little ones—the Seven Deadly Sins, whose distorted heads can now and then be dimly seen.

With his eyes shut, Anthony lies motionless, his limbs stretched upon the mat.

It seems soft to him—softer and softer—and at last it even feels as though it were stuffed—and then it is lifted up so that it becomes a bed; and the bed becomes a boat, with water lapping against it.

To right and left rise two tongues of black soil, overlooked by cultivated fields, with a sycamore here and there. The sound of bells, of drums and of singing, comes from a distance, where there are people on their way to Canopus, to sleep in the temple of Serapis in hope that there they may dream dreams. Anthony knows this—and he glides propelled by the wind, between the two banks of the canal. Papyrus leaves, and red lotus-blossoms, taller than a man, hang over him. He lies stretched at the bottom of the boat; and at the stern an oar drags in the water. From time to time a warm breeze comes, and the slender reeds blow one against another. The murmuring of the little waves subsides. Drowsiness overtakes him. He dreams that he is a recluse in Egypt.

Then, with a start, he wakes up.)

Was I dreaming? . . . It was all so clear that I cannot be sure! . . . My tongue is burning! How thirsty I am!

(He goes into the hut, and feels about everywhere, at random.)

The ground is wet! . . . Has it been raining? See! something broken! My pitcher smashed! . . . Where is the leather bottle?

(He finds it.)

Empty! Not a drop left!

It will take a good three hours to go down to the stream; and the night is so dark that I should not see where I was going. I am pinched with hunger! Where is the bread?

(After searching for some time he finds a crust no bigger than an egg.)

What! Have the jackals stolen it? O curse!

(And in his rage he throws the morsel of bread on the ground.

He has scarcely done this when a table appears, laden with all manner of good things to eat.

The fine linen cloth, ribbed like the bands on the head of a sphinx, itself emits luminous vibrations. Upon it are great

THE TEMPTATION OF ST. ANTHONY

joints of meat; big fish; roasted birds in their feathers; four-footed creatures in their skins; fruit of a complexion almost as fair as a woman's; while blocks of clear ice, and goblets of bluish crystal, flash and sparkle one against the other. Anthony sees in the midst of the table a wild boar, steaming from every pore, his trotters tucked beneath his belly, his eyes half-closed—and the prospect of eating this formidable monster gives him intense joy.

Other things there are, too, which he has never seen before: rich dark dishes of mingled meat and vegetables; jellies the colour of gold; spiced stews in which mushrooms float, like water-lilies on a pond; creamy sweetmeats as light as clouds.

And the perfume of it all is like the salt smell of the sea, the freshness of fountains, the scattered scents of the woods. His nostrils open widely; he begins to dribble; he mutters to himself that there is enough for a year!—for ten years! —for a whole lifetime!

While his wide-open eyes gloat upon the food, other dishes constantly appear, and their number so increases that they form a pyramid slipping and crumbling at the corners. The various wines begin to flow; the fish quiver; the red gravy bubbles on the hot dishes; the ripe fruits proffer their pulp as lovers offer their lips—the table lifts itself to the level of his breast: then up to his chin . . . and now there is upon it but a single plate, and a small loaf of bread, just in front of him.

He is about to snatch the loaf, when other loaves appear.)

For me! . . . I want them all! But . . .

(He starts back.)

There was only one to begin with, and now look at them! . . . It is surely a miracle, such as that which the Lord worked!

What does it all mean? The thing is incredible! Ah-h-h! Satan! Get thee behind me! Get thee behind me!

(He kicks out at the table, and it disappears.)

What next? Anything else? . . . No!

(He takes a deep breath.)

What a temptation that was! But yet how valiantly did I resist!

(Anthony lifts his head while speaking, and stumbles over something that clatters.)

Whatever is that?

(He stoops down.)

Why! A drinking-cup! Some passer-by may have dropped it. Nothing unusual in that!

(He moistens a finger, and rubs the cup.)

It shines! It is of metal! Though I can hardly see whether . . . ?

(He lights his torch, and looks more closely.)

It is silver, with tiny ovals all along the edge; and there's a medallion at the bottom.

(He loosens the medallion with his finger-nail.)

It is a piece of money worth—a couple of shillings perhaps: not more! Never mind! It should be enough to buy me a sheep-skin.

(A gleam from the torch shows the cup more plainly.)

Impossible! . . . *Gold?* . . . It is, indeed! . . . Solid gold!

(Another coin, larger than the first, lies within the cup, and beneath that he finds several others.)

But that makes—enough for three oxen—and a little field!

(And then the cup is suddenly full to the brim with golden pieces.)

THE TEMPTATION OF ST. ANTHONY

Here we are! A hundred slaves, soldiers, attendants, money to spend!

(The ovals on the rim of the cup break away and shape themselves into a necklace of pearls.)

With such a bribe a man might purchase to himself even the Emperor's wife.

(Anthony jerks his arm, so that the necklace slips on to his wrist. In one hand he grasps the cup, and with the other lifts the torch to throw more light upon it. As water flows forth from a spring, so there trickles from the cup an endless stream of precious stones—diamonds, carbuncles, sapphires—so that soon there is a little heap upon the sand; and tangled among the jewels are great pieces of gold, stamped with the effigies of kings.)

Look! Look! Grecian coins and Persian; staters, darics! Alexander, Demetrius, the Ptolemies, Cæsar! But there was not one of them as rich as this! Everything is within my grasp now! No more hardship! ... How all this glitter dazzles me! Oh, my heart is overflowing! How good it all is! Yes! Yes! ... more and more! there's no end to it all! I might go on flinging money and jewels into the sea without a pause, and still have plenty. But why waste any of it? I will keep it all; without telling anybody; I will have scooped out in the rock a chamber, and it shall be lined inside with plates of bronze—and there will I sit and watch the piles of money slipping through my hands; I will thrust my arms into the gold as into sacks of corn. I want to bathe in it, lie down and sleep in it!

(He lets the torch fall, the better to embrace the mass; and casts himself outspread upon the earth. When he rises again, there is nothing there.)

What have I been doing?

If I had died in that moment, it would have meant hell for me! Inevitable hell!

(He trembles from head to foot.)

Am I then predestined to damnation? Ah, no! It is my fault, my own fault! I let myself be trapped in every snare! Never was there a bigger fool, a more infamous wretch than I! Would that I might break myself in pieces, or rather tear myself out of my body! I have restrained myself too long! I must be avenged, give blows, and kill! It is as though within my soul there were a drove of savage beasts. Would that I might, in the midst of a crowd, with strokes of an axe. . . . Ah! A dagger!

(He catches sight of his knife, and snatches at it. The knife slips from his hand, and Anthony stands crouched against the wall of the hut, open-mouthed, motionless, and with no longer any power to move.

He is unconscious of his surroundings, and fancies himself at Alexandria on the Paneum, an artificial hillock surrounded by a spiral staircase, standing up in the centre of the city.

In the foreground stretches Lake Mareotis, on the right is the sea, on the left the open country—and below him a tangle of flat roofs, cut across from north to south and from east to west by two streets which intersect and form two long lines of porticoes with Corinthian columns. The windows in the houses which overhang this double colonnade are filled with coloured glass, and some of them are fitted with wooden lattices, through which the fresh air pours.

Monuments in various architectural styles are crowded one against another. Egyptian gateways tower above Greek temples. Obelisks stand up like spears behind red brick battlements. In the middle of the squares are statues of Hermes with the pointed ears and Anubis with the dog's head. Anthony can see mosaics in the courtyards and curtains hung upon the beams of the ceilings.

THE TEMPTATION OF ST. ANTHONY

He takes in, with a single glance, the two harbours—the Great Harbour and the Eunostus—which are both of them round like amphitheatres, and separated from each other by a breakwater which joins Alexandria to the steep islet on which, to a height of five hundred cubits, and with nine storeys, rises the square tower of the Pharos, with a heap of black coals smoking on its summit.

Small inner basins open into the two larger ones. The breakwater, at either end, finishes in a bridge that is carried upon marble columns rising from the sea. Sails are moving beneath them; and heavy lighters crammed full of merchandise, state-barges incrusted with ivory, gondolas covered by awnings, triremes and biremes, every imaginable sort of vessel, either passes to and fro or is berthed beside the quays.

Round about the Great Harbour is an uninterrupted succession of royal buildings: the palace of the Ptolemies, the Museum, the Posidium, the Cæsareum, the Timonium where Mark Antony took refuge, the Soma where Alexander lies buried—whilst at the other end of the town, past the Eunostus, lies a suburb where are factories of glass and perfumes and papyrus.

Wandering pedlars, lumpers, donkeymen, hustle and jostle each other. Here and there a priest of Osiris with a panther's skin thrown across his shoulder, a Roman soldier in a helmet of bronze, and everywhere negroes. In the open shops women linger, and mechanics ply their trades; and the scrunching of the chariot-wheels scares the birds from the ground where they are picking up butchers' scraps and pieces of fish.

Over the flat unvarying whiteness of the houses the crisscross of the streets flings as it were a black net, beneath which the vegetable-markets look like green nosegays, the drying-grounds of the dyers like brightly coloured ornaments, and the gold on the temple pediments like sparks of fire—and all of it within the oval embrace of the greyish walls, beneath the blue vault of heaven, beside the still sea.

Suddenly the crowd stands still, and everybody gazes towards the west, where tremendous clouds of dust are whirling.

The monks of the Thebaïd are drawing near, clad in

goat-skins, armed with cudgels, and yelling a sort of religious battle-cry with the refrain: " Where are they? Where are they?"

Anthony knows that they have come to kill the Arians.

Quickly the streets are emptied—and nothing can be seen but flying feet.

And now the monks are in the city, twirling their terrible clubs, studded with nails which glitter like little steel suns. Crashing sounds are heard of things being broken in the houses. Then intervals of silence. And then once more loud shouts arise.

From end to end the streets are a seething confusion of terrified people.

Many have pikes in their hands. Now and then two groups will meet and intermingle; and the mass slips on the flagstones, is separated, then swoops together again. But always the men with the long hair are to be seen.

Spirals of smoke creep up from the corners of the buildings. Folding doors burst open. Side walls crumble. Architraves fall.

Anthony meets all his foes again, one after another. He even recognizes some that he had forgotten; and before he slays he insults them, disembowels them, throttles them, bludgeons them; drags old men about by their beards, crushes children, tramples on the wounded. And spiteful vengeance is wreaked upon culture and refinement; men who cannot read are destroying books; others smash, by hurling them to the ground, statues, pictures, furniture, coffers, a thousand and one dainty things of whose very uses they are ignorant, but with which, for just that reason, they are exasperated. Now and again they pause, for sheer lack of breath, and then begin again.

From the populace, who have rushed for safety into the courtyards, groans arise. Women lift naked arms towards heaven, and their eyes are full of tears. To turn the monks from their purpose, they hold them by the knees; but they are thrust away; and blood spurts as high as the ceilings, to be splashed back in sheets upon the walls; it streams from the trunks of headless bodies, fills the aqueducts, forms great red pools upon the ground.

Anthony is smeared with it up to his thighs. He wades in it; he tastes the spray of it upon his lips, and thrills

THE TEMPTATION OF ST. ANTHONY

with joy as he feels it upon his limbs, beneath his hair tunic which is soaked with it.

The night falls, and the dreadful noise dies down.

The monks have disappeared.

Suddenly, upon the outside galleries running round the nine storeys of the Pharos, Anthony notices thick dark lines, as though black crows were perching there. He runs thither and reaches the summit.

A great copper mirror, turned towards the open sea, reflects images of the ships thereon.

Anthony idly watches them, and as he watches their numbers increase.

They are gathered in a crescent-shaped bay. Behind them, on a promontory, stretches a new city of Roman architecture, with stone cupolas, conical roofs, pink and blue marbles, and a wealth of ornamental brass-work in the spirals of the Corinthian capitals, the ridges of the houses, and the cornice-angles. A cypress forest overhangs the city. The colour of the sea grows greener, and the air becomes more sharp. On the horizon there are snow-capped mountains.

While Anthony hesitates as to which way he shall go, a man approaches him and says: "Come! They are waiting for you!"

He crosses a market-place, enters a courtyard, and stoops beneath a doorway; and so reaches the front of the palace, which is decorated by a waxen group representing the Emperor Constantine striking down a dragon.

In the middle of a porphyry basin is a golden conch-shell filled with pistachio nuts. His guide bids him help himself, and he takes a handful.

And then it seems to him that he passes through one room after another.

There are depicted in mosaic all along the walls generals presenting conquered cities to the Emperor, holding them up in their hands. Basalt columns are everywhere, gratings of silver filigree, ivory benches, tapestries sewn with pearls. Light falls from the arched roofs, and Anthony goes on and on. Gentle vapours are spread about; he hears, now and then the wary pit-a-pat of sandals. Guards—stiff as mechanical figures—are stationed in the antechambers, with scarlet staves upon their shoulders.

He finds himself at last in a large hall, hung with

hyacinthine curtains at the far end. These are flung open, and the Emperor is revealed, seated on a throne, clad in purple tunic, and shod in red buskins laced with black.

A diadem of pearls surmounts his flowing locks, which are arranged symmetrically in ringlets. He has drooping eyelashes, a straight nose, and his countenance is dull and crafty-looking. At the corners of the canopy above his head are four golden doves; and two lions in enamel crouch at the foot of the throne. The doves utter melodious noises, the lions roar, the Emperor rolls his eyes, Anthony comes forward; and suddenly, without more ado, they are talking together of things that have happened. In the cities of Antioch, Ephesus and Alexandria, temples have been pillaged, and the images of the gods melted down into pots and pans; the Emperor laughs loudly at this. Anthony finds fault with his tolerance towards the Novatians. The Emperor grows angry : Novatians, Arians, Meletians—he is sick and tired of them all. But he approves of the Episcopate, since Christians are under the orders of their bishops, and the latter owe their positions to half-a-dozen eminent persons, so that one need only win over the bishops to secure the support of all the others. This was why he had not failed to supply them with large sums of money. But the Fathers of the Council of Nicæa he abominates. " Come and look at them ! " Anthony follows him.

And then they are on a terrace, on the same level.

It overlooks a hippodrome, full of people, and surrounded by porticoes where yet more people are walking. In the centre of the arena rises a narrow platform, on which are a little temple of Mercury, the statue of Constantine, three bronze serpents interlaced, and at one end some huge egg-shaped pieces of wood, and at the other seven dolphins with tails in the air.

Behind the imperial pavilion, the chamberlains, the major-domos and the nobles are arranged in ranks half-way up the walls of a church, all the windows of which are gay with women. On the right hand is the gallery of the blue faction, on the left that of the green; beneath them a picket of soldiers; and level with the arena a row of Corinthian archways, which give access to the stables.

The races are about to begin, and the horses draw up in line. Tall plumes, fastened between their ears, sway like branches in the wind; and the chariots quiver with the prancing of the steeds. These chariots are shaped like shells, and the drivers are clad in parti-coloured cuirasses, with sleeves that are tight at the wrists but loose about the arms; they have bare legs, full beards, and their foreheads are shaven after the fashion of the Huns.

Anthony is deafened for a while by the clatter of voices. From top to bottom he sees nothing but painted faces, many-coloured garments and jewelled ornaments; and the sand in the arena, glistening white, shines like a mirror.

The Emperor converses with him; confides to him many weighty and secret matters; makes confession to him concerning the assassination of his son; even asks advice about his health.

But Anthony catches sight of some prisoners at the back of the stables. They are the fathers of the Council of Nicæa, in rags, wretched. The martyr Paphnutius is combing the mane of one horse, while Theophilus washes the legs of another. John is blacking the feet of a third; Alexander scrapes manure into a basket.

Anthony goes amongst them. They draw themselves up in line; entreat him to intercede for them; kiss his hands. The multitudes hoot at them; and he rejoices unrestrainedly at their disgrace. He himself, on the other hand, is now become a great man about the Court, the confidant of the Emperor, his Prime Minister! And when on his brow the royal diadem is placed by Constantine, Anthony leaves it there, feeling that such honour is quite rightly paid to him.

And by and by amidst the shadows, there is revealed an immense hall, lit with golden candlesticks.

Columns, so lofty that they almost disappear in the darkness overhead, stretch in long lines beyond the tables which reach as far as eye can see—to where, in a luminous mist, staircases rise one above another, rows of arches, gigantic statues, turrets, and behind them all a vague background of palace-walls, topped by black masses of cedars, darker even than the black obscurity around.

The rows of guests, garlanded with violets, lean upon their elbows on low couches, and are constantly supplied with wine from tilted two-handled wine-jars—and at the very bottom, alone, decked out with tiara and covered with precious stones of fiery red, King Nebuchadnezzar eats and drinks.

To the right of him and to the left, assemblages of priests in pointed mitres are swinging censers. On the ground, at his feet, grovel the captive kings, with neither hands nor feet, and to them he tosses bones to gnaw; and lower still are his brethren, bandaged about the eyes—for they have all of them been blinded.

A never-ending lamentation rises from the depths of neighbouring penitentiaries. The sweet, slow sound of a water-driven organ alternates with the voices of choristers; and one realizes that all round the hall there is a city of boundless size, an ocean of humanity whose waves are beating against the walls.

Slaves bustle about, carrying dishes; women come and proffer wine; baskets creak under the weight of food; and a dromedary, laden with wine-skins pierced with holes, goes to and fro freshening the pavement by sprinkling it with verbena.

Some wild-beast keepers lead in their lions. Dancing-girls, with hair caught up in fillets, spin round and round upon their hands, and flames issue from their nostrils; negro mountebanks exhibit their tricks; naked children pelt each other with snowballs which fall into fragments as they strike the silver lattice-work. The uproar is so terrific that one would imagine a storm was raging; and a watery vapour hangs over the company, so much food is there about, and so many people breathing. Sparks now and then fall from the great torches, and are caught up by the wind and whirled through the night like shooting stars.

The King with the back of his hand wipes away the perfumes from his brow. He eats from hallowed vessels, then shatters them; he tells over to himself the numbers of his ships, his soldiers, his subjects. By and by, in sheer caprice, he will burn down his palace together with the guests who are gathered there. It is in his mind to rebuild the tower of Babel, and to dethrone God.

And Anthony can read, even from a distance, and as though written on his forehead, all his thoughts. They enter and fill his own mind—and he himself becomes Nebuchadnezzar.

Then, surfeited with lewdness and lust of destruction, he

THE TEMPTATION OF ST. ANTHONY

longs to drown himself in defilement. Since such degradation as shocks men is an assault upon their minds—one more of the means by which they are stupefied—and since there is nothing more vile than a brute beast, Anthony gets upon the table on all-fours, and bellows like a bull.

Something pricks his hand—perhaps it happened that he cut himself with a piece of flint—and he finds himself again outside his hut.

The rock-encircled space is deserted. The stars are shining. Everything is still.)

Once more have I been deceived! Whence come these imaginings? It is this body of mine that is in revolt. Ah! Wretch that I am!

(He rushes into the hut, snatches up a scourge whose cords have claws of metal tied in the ends, strips himself to the waist, and lifting his face towards heaven he cries :)

Accept this my penance, O God! Despise it not because it is so poor a thing. Let it be sharp; let it last a long time; let it be almost more than I can bear! . . . And now! . . . To begin! . . .

(He gives himself one stinging cut.)

Oh! Oh! . . . No! No mercy! . . .

(He begins again.)

Oh! Oh! Oh! . . . Each blow tears my skin, cuts my flesh, tortures me! But yet it is bearable! One gets used to it! It even almost seems . . .

(Anthony pauses.)

Go on, you coward! Go on! . . . There! There! . . . On my arms, and my back, and my chest, and my belly; all over me! Make the lash whistle; make it bite; make it tear me! I would have drops of my blood splashing up as high as the stars; I would break my bones, lay bare the very nerves!

Pinchers, the rack, melted lead! And more than that have the martyrs endured! Was it not so, Ammonaria?

(The shadow of the Devil's horns appears again.)

I might have been fastened to a column near to you, in front of you, under your very eyes, answering with my groans to your cries; and our sufferings would have mingled, our souls would have flowed together.

(He scourges himself furiously.)

There! There! Take that! Another! . . . But how it tingles now! What agony! And yet what rapture! Like—like a kiss! The marrow of my bones is melting! I am at the point of death!

(And he sees in front of him three riders in green robes, mounted on wild asses: lilies in their hands, and each exactly like the others.

Anthony turns round and sees yet three more riders, like the other three: and these also are on wild asses, and robed in green and holding lilies.

He starts back, and then the asses move towards him, pressing their muzzles against his body and biting at his clothes. He hears voices saying " This way, this way— here is the place "; and waving banners appear among the clefts of the mountains, with the heads of camels whose halters are of scarlet silk, and laden baggage-mules, and women wearing amber-coloured veils, astride on piebald horses.

The panting beasts kneel down; the slaves untie the bales of luggage; carpets of many hues are unrolled; shining things are spread about upon the ground.

A white elephant, covered with golden network, approaches, and the ostrich-plumes on his forehead shake from side to side.

Upon his back, cross-legged amongst piled-up cushions of blue wool, her eyelids half-closed and her head nodding backwards and forwards, is a woman so gorgeously clothed that her raiment scatters beams of light about her. The people fall upon their faces; the elephant bends his knees; and THE QUEEN OF SHEBA, descending from his shoulder, steps upon the carpet and moves towards Saint Anthony.

Her vesture of gold brocade, regularly divided by flounces worked in pearls and jet and sapphires, clings to her body like a sheath, and is coloured and enriched by twelve panels representing the signs of the Zodiac. She wears very high pattens, one of which is black, sprinkled with silver stars and a half moon, and the other white, covered with tiny golden drops with a sun in their midst.

Her long loose sleeves, trimmed with emeralds and feathers, reveal her delicately rounded bare arms, with ebony bracelets at the wrists, and jewel-laden hands with fingernails so finely pointed that their tips are nearly as sharp as needles.

A gold chain, under her chin and going upwards against each cheek, coils in spirals about her hair, which is sprinkled with blue powder; and then falls lightly about her shoulders, ending on her bosom in a scorpion set with diamonds, whose tongue shoots forth from between her breasts.

Two great golden pearls are set in her ears. Her eyelids are painted at their edges with black. On her left cheekbone is a brownish birth-mark; and she opens her mouth when she breathes, as though her corsage distressed her.

She plays, as she moves along, with an ivory-handled green parasol hung with scarlet bells—and twelve frizzly-haired negro-boys carry her long train, the end of which is held by an ape, who lifts it from time to time. She says :)

Ah! Sweet hermit! Sweet hermit! My heart fails me! ... In my impatience I have been tapping my heels together until they have grown hard, and one of my nails is broken. I have sent shepherds to watch upon the mountains, shading their eyes with their hands; and huntsmen to cry your name in the woods; and couriers to run along all the roads, asking everyone who passed: " Have you seen him?"

At night-time, I wept, with my face to the wall; and my tears at last cut two little channels in the mosaic, as sea-water cuts through the rocks; . . . for I love you! . . . Ah me! How I love you!

(She strokes his beard.)

Smile then, sweet hermit! Smile! For I can bring you such pleasure! You shall see! I play the lyre, I can dance like a bee, and tell story after story, each more amusing than the others!

You cannot dream how far we have come; but see how utterly worn out are the wild asses on which the green couriers rode—how dead they are with fatigue!

(The asses are stretched upon the ground, motionless.)

For three long moons they have galloped steadily, with pebbles between their teeth to help their breath, their tails streaming, their sinews taut, galloping, ever galloping! Never were such wild asses as these! They came to me from my mother's father, the Emperor Saharil, son of Iakhschab, son of Iaarab, son of Kastan. Ah! If they could still draw us we would yoke them to a litter and get quickly back to our home! But . . . what is it? . . . what are you thinking about?

(She looks closely at him.)

When you are my husband, I will have you beautifully dressed, and sweetly scented, and shaven and shorn.

(Anthony does not move: he is rigid as a column, colourless as a corpse.)

You are sad; is it because you are leaving your hut? But I—I have left everything for you—even

THE TEMPTATION OF ST. ANTHONY

King Solomon, though he has much wisdom, and twenty thousand chariots of war, and such a beautiful beard! I have brought you my wedding-gifts. Choose!

(She walks up and down between the rows of slaves and among the heaps of merchandise.)

Here is balm of Gennesaret, incense from Cape Guardafui, ladanum, cinnamon, and silphium for making sauces. In this bundle are Assyrian embroideries, ivory from the Ganges, purple from Elisa; and this cooling-box contains wine from Chalybon, such as is kept for the Kings of Assyria —it is quaffed unmixed from the horns of unicorns. There, too, are necklaces, and clasps, head-bands, parasols, gold dust from Baasa, silver alloy from Tartessus, blue wood from Pandio, white furs from Issidonia, carbuncles from the Island of Palaesimondus, and tooth-picks made of bristles from an extinct animal (*tachas*) that lived underground. Those cushions come from Macedonia, and these cloak-fringes from Palmyra. Here, on this Babylonian carpet there is . . . but come and look! Come! . . .

(She drags Saint Anthony by his sleeve. He resists. She goes on :)

This fine tissue, which crackles like fire between one's fingers, is the famous yellow cloth brought by merchants from Bactria, who must employ three-and-forty interpreters on the journey. I will have garments made from it, and you shall wear them when we are at home.

Undo the clasps of the sycamore case, and get

me my ivory casket that hangs on the elephant's saddle-bow!

(Something is taken out of a box, something round and wrapped in a veil; and they bring her a little carved chest.)

Would you have the shield of Dgian-ben-Dgian, the builder of the pyramids? It is there! It is made of seven dragon-skins, tanned in a parricide's bile, and fastened one upon the other with diamond screws. On one of its sides are pictured all the wars that have been fought since weapons first were made; and on the other all the wars that will be waged while the world lasts. Thunderbolts are repelled by it as though they were mere corks. When you go hunting, I will let you wear it on your arm.

And look at this little box! If you but knew what it holds! Turn it over and over, and try to open it! Nobody could ever do that; but kiss me, and I'll tell you how it's done.

(She takes Saint Anthony's face between her two hands; he holds her at arms' length.)

Once, in the night-time, King Solomon lost his head: and so we made a bargain. He got up, and going stealthily out . . .

(She pirouettes.)

Ah-ha! Sweet hermit! You shall not know! You shall not know!

(She shakes her parasol, so that all the tiny bells tinkle.)

And I have many other things besides, indeed I have! Treasures hid in galleries where you might lose yourself as in a forest. Trellis-work palaces of plaited rush for summertime, and palaces of black marble for the winter. In the middle of lakes that are as large as oceans I have islands, round as silver coins, all covered with mother-of-pearl; and as the warm waves roll and break they make sweet music on the sandy shores. My kitchen-slaves get birds from my aviaries and catch fish in my fish-ponds. Unceasingly do my engravers bend over their work of scooping out my portrait upon precious stones; breathless foundrymen are ever casting statues of me; and never do my perfumers finish their task of mingling fragrant extracts with vinegars, and of preparing my beauty-pastes. I have dressmakers cutting up my stuffs; goldsmiths fashioning my jewels; hairdressers to invent new styles for my hair; and careful workmen who paint the panelling with boiling resin and then cool it off with fans. I have maids enough to fill a harem, and my eunuchs would make up an army—but I have armies enough! I have whole nations! In the courtyard of my palace there is a guard of dwarfs with ivory trumpets on their shoulders.

(Anthony sighs.)

I have chariot-teams of gazelles, four-in-hands of elephants, pairs of camels by the hundred, and mares with manes so long that their feet become entangled as they gallop—and cattle whose horns are so wide that the trees in front of them must be cut down before they can go forth to feed. There are giraffes in my gardens, which stretch their heads over the edges of my roofs while I take the air after dinner.

Reclining in a shell, and drawn by dolphins, I go up and down in grottos listening to the water as it falls from stalactites. And then I reach the land of diamonds, where my friends the magicians let me choose the finest for myself, and then I come back to the open air again and go home.

(She utters a shrill whistle—and a great bird, swooping down from the sky, alights upon her head, scattering the blue powder with which her hair is sprinkled.

Its plumage, orange-coloured, looks as though it were composed of metal scales. Its tiny head, topped by a silver crest, is like a human face. It has four wings, the feet of a vulture, and a large tail like that of a peacock, which spreads out in a circle.

It takes the Queen's parasol in its beak, hovers for a moment to regain its balance, and fluffs its feathers—then remains motionless.)

Thanks, my beautiful Simorg-Anka! It was you who told me where to find my lover! Thanks! Thanks! My heart's forerunner!

He can fly as fast as thought and go right round the world in a day. At evening he comes back and perches at the foot of my couch; he tells me what he has seen—seas with their fishes and their ships over which he has flown, the great empty deserts upon which he has gazed from the heights of heaven, the waving harvests on cultivated land, the weeds that spring up on the walls of forsaken cities.

(She twists her hands together languidly.)

Oh! If you but would! If you but would! . . . I have a pavilion upon a promontory on an isthmus dividing two oceans. It is wainscoted with sheets of glass, and paved with tortoise-shell, and it lies open to the four winds of heaven. I can look down and see the approach of my fleets, and watch the people coming up the hill with the cargoes on their

THE TEMPTATION OF ST. ANTHONY

shoulders. . . . We should sleep on pillows softer than the clouds, drink cooling draughts out of the rinds of fruit, and gaze at the sun through emeralds! Come . . . !

(Anthony starts back. She comes nearer to him; and speaks with irritation :)

What? Not a wealthy woman, nor a stylish one, nor a fond and loving one? None of these for you, eh? . . . But a lustful one, smutty, with raucous voice, and hair as red as fire and quantities of flesh. Would you rather have in your arms a body cold like a serpent's skin, or do you choose big black eyes, darker than magic caverns? Look at them! Look at my eyes!

(Anthony, in spite of himself, gazes into her eyes.)

All the women you have ever met, from the strumpet at the cross-roads singing by lantern-light, to the haughty lady in her litter, dropping rose-bud petals round about her—all the faces you have glimpsed, all that you have imagined and desired— they can all be yours! I am not just one woman, I am an entire world! If I do but put aside my garments, you shall discover in my one body a whole universe of mysteries!

(Anthony's teeth chatter.)

If you were to touch my shoulders with the tip of your finger, it would be as though a trail of fire went darting through your veins. Possession of but the tiniest part of me will give you joys more intense than could the conquest of an Empire.

Put your lips on mine! My kisses have such savour that you feel as though rare fruit were melting within your very heart! Ah! How you will lose yourself in my hair; breathe the sweetness of my bosom; be amazed by the marvel of my body, and, scorched by the light of my eyes, clasped close in my arms, in the whirlwind . . .

(Anthony makes the sign of the cross.)

You scorn me! Then farewell!

(She withdraws, weeping; but turns towards him again :)

Are you quite, quite sure? . . . A woman so lovely?

(She laughs, and the ape that carries the end of her train lifts it up.)

You'll be sorry, sweet hermit! You will hate yourself, and you will groan aloud! But that will be nothing to me! La! la! la! Tra-la-la! Tra-la-la!

(She goes skipping off, her face hidden in her hands.
The slaves march past Saint Anthony, the horses, the dromedaries, the elephant, the maidens, the reladen mules, the negro-boys, the ape, the green couriers, each with a broken lily in his hand . . . and the Queen of Sheba withdraws, shaken by a convulsion that might be either a sob or a sneer.)

III

(When she has gone, Anthony sees a child on the threshold of his hut.)

It must be one of the Queen's servants (*he thinks*).

(This child is no bigger than a dwarf, and yet thick-set like the Cabiri, distorted, and of wretched appearance. He has an astonishingly large head, covered with white hair;

and he shivers in a poor little tunic, and holds a roll of papyrus tightly in his hand.

The light of the moon, as it passes through a cloud, falls upon him.)

ANTHONY (*observes him from a distance and is afraid of him*): Who are you?

THE CHILD (*replies*): I am Hilarion, your old disciple!

ANTHONY: It is a lie! Hilarion has been living in Palestine these many years.

HILARION: I have come back! It is truly I!

ANTHONY (*goes near and looks closely at him*): But his face was as bright as the dawn, open, joyful. Yours is the face of one grown gloomy and old.

HILARION: I am worn out with long labours!

ANTHONY: And the voice also is different. It chills one!

HILARION: That is because I have been fed with bitter food.

ANTHONY: And your white hair?

HILARION: I have had so many sorrows!

ANTHONY (*aside*): Can it be possible . . . ?

HILARION: I was not so far away as you suppose. Paul the hermit came to see you this year in the month of Schebar. It is exactly twenty days since the Nomads brought you bread. You told a sailor the day before yesterday to have three bodkins sent to you.

ANTHONY: He knows everything!

HILARION: Realize, then, that I have never left you: though there are long periods when you do not perceive me.

ANTHONY: How can that be? It is true that my head gives me much trouble. Especially to-night . . .

HILARION: All the Deadly Sins have been here. But their paltry snares are powerless against such a Saint as you.

ANTHONY: Oh! No . . . No! I fail at every moment! Why was I not one of those whose souls are ever brave, and their spirits strong—like the great Athanasius, for instance?

HILARION: He was irregularly ordained by seven bishops.

ANTHONY: What did that matter! If his virtue . . .

HILARION: Nonsense! A proud man, and a cruel; always intriguing, and at last exiled because he had cornered the market.

ANTHONY: A false accusation!

HILARION: You cannot deny that he tried to corrupt Eustates, the almoner?

ANTHONY: That was said of him, I admit.

HILARION: He burned the house of Arsenius, in revenge!

ANTHONY: Alas!

HILARION: At the Council of Nicæa, speaking of Jesus, he called Him " the man of God."

ANTHONY: Ah! That was blasphemy!

HILARION: And so unintelligent, besides, that he vows he can make nothing of " the Word."

ANTHONY (*smiling with satisfaction*): His intelligence, indeed, is not what you would call—high!

HILARION: Now if *you* had been put in his place, it would have been a blessing for your brethren as

THE TEMPTATION OF ST. ANTHONY

well as for yourself. In this solitary life a man deteriorates.

ANTHONY: On the contrary! Man, being spiritual, must withdraw himself from worldly concerns. Material things degrade him. I would have no more to do with this earth—not even would I plant my foot upon it!

HILARION: Hypocrite! Thus to bury yourself in solitude only the better to indulge your dissolute lusts! You deny yourself in food and drink and warmth and slaves and honours; but in imagination you accept offers of banquets, perfumes, naked women and applauding crowds! Your chastity is but a more cunning corruptness, and your contempt of the world merely weak hatred against it! That is what makes you and other men of your sort so dismal; or else it is because you no longer believe. Truth brings joy to its possessor. Was Jesus sad? He went about surrounded by friends, slept in the shade of olive trees, ate with publicans, was a wine-bibber, forgave the woman who was a sinner, healed all manner of sickness. You—you feel pity only for your own misfortunes. It is remorse which troubles you, and your savage madness makes you reject the fawning of a dog or the smile of a little child.

ANTHONY (*bursting into sobs*): Enough! Enough! You stir my heart too deeply!

HILARION: Shake the vermin out of your rags! Get up out of your filth! Your God is not a Moloch to demand human flesh as a sacrifice!

ANTHONY: And yet suffering is blessed. The cherubim stoop to catch the blood of the confessors.

HILARION: Then of course you will admire the Montanists, who outdo all others!

ANTHONY: But truth of doctrine it is which makes true martyrdom!

HILARION: How can martyrdom prove the worth of doctrine, since it witnesses quite as often for error?

ANTHONY: Be silent! Do! You venomous beast!

HILARION: Perchance martyrdom is not so very difficult after all! The encouragement of one's friends, the joy of being unusual, the oath which one has taken, the excitement—a thousand things all help!

(Anthony goes away from Hilarion; but Hilarion follows him.)

Besides, this manner of death brings serious disorder along with it. Dionysius, Cyprian and Gregory deliberately avoided it. Peter of Alexandria has declared it to be of doubtful merit, and the Council of Elvira . . .

ANTHONY (*stops his ears*): I will hear no more!

HILARION (*raising his voice*): There you are! Falling yet again into your besetting sin, which is sloth. Ignorance is the scum upon the top of pride. A man says: "I have made up my mind; there's nothing to argue about!" And so he despises doctors, philosophers, tradition, and even the text of that Law which he has neglected. Do you fancy that you hold all wisdom within your grasp?

ANTHONY: I can hear him still! My head is full of his noisy words.

HILARION: Better than the mortifications, by which you hope to persuade God, would be an endeavour to comprehend him. Our only true deserving comes with our thirst for truth. Religion by itself cannot explain everything; and a solution of the problems which you ignore would render it yet stronger and more lofty than it is. Therefore a man, for the sake of his own salvation, should go amongst his brethren —else is the Church, the congregation of the faithful, no more than a mere name—and he should hear all sides, despising nothing, neglecting nobody. Balaam the sorcerer, Æschylus the poet, and the Cumæan Sibyl, all foretold our Saviour. Dionysius of Alexandria received a command from heaven that he was to read all sorts of books. Saint Clement bids us study Greek literature. Hermas was converted by the apparition of a woman whom he had loved. . . .

ANTHONY: With what assumption of authority you speak! And it seems to me that you are growing taller. . . .

(Hilarion's height indeed increases gradually; and Anthony shuts his eyes so that he may no longer look upon him.)

HILARION: Be at ease, good hermit! Let us seat ourselves on this big stone—as in olden days we were wont to sit, when at break of day I would salute you, calling you " the bright morning-star ": and then straightway you would begin to teach me. Nor even yet is that teaching finished! The moon gives light enough. I listen.

(He has taken a reed-pen from his girdle; and cross-legged on the ground, with the roll of papyrus in his hand, he lifts his face towards Saint Anthony, who sits with dejected head.

After a moment of silence, Hilarion begins again :)

Is it not a fact that the word of God is confirmed by miracles? And yet Pharaoh's magicians also worked miracles; other impostors might do likewise, and so we should be deceived. For what, after all, is a miracle? Something or other which appears to us to be outside the ordinary operations of nature. But are we so sure that we really know what those operations are? Merely because we are so accustomed to anything that it does not astonish us, does it therefore follow that we really understand that thing?

ANTHONY: It doesn't matter much, so long as we believe the Scriptures.

HILARION: Saint Paul, Origen, and many others did not take the Scriptures literally; but once you begin to explain it allegorically it becomes the portion of just a few, and so the evidence for the truth vanishes. What is to be done?

ANTHONY: Trust the Church!

HILARION: You mean to say, then, that the Scriptures are worthless?

ANTHONY: By no means! Though I must admit that in the Old Testament there are some things . . . Well! some rather doubtful things. . . . But the New Testament shines with no uncertain light!

HILARION: And yet the Angel of the Annunciation, in Matthew, appears to Joseph, whilst in Luke it is to Mary that he comes. The anointing of the feet of Jesus by a woman happens, according to the first Gospel, at the very beginning of his public life, whereas according to the other three it was only a few days before his death. The cup offered as he hung on the cross was vinegar mingled with gall in

THE TEMPTATION OF ST. ANTHONY 199

Matthew, but Mark says that it was wine and myrrh. According to Luke and Matthew, the Apostles were to take with them neither money nor scrip—not even sandals or staff; in Mark, on the contrary, Jesus forbids them to take anything except their sandals and their staff. For my part I find this all very confusing! . . .

ANTHONY (*in perplexity*): Truly . . . truly. . . .

HILARION: When he was touched by the woman who had an issue of blood, Jesus turned himself and said, "Who touched me?" showing that he did not know who it was that had touched him. That rather seems to do away with the omniscience of Jesus, doesn't it? If the tomb was watched by guards, there was no reason why the women should have worried about getting help to roll the stone from the tomb. And so either there was no watch, or else the holy women never went there at all. After the resurrection, he eats with his disciples and tells them to handle his wounds. It was a human body, a material object, it had weight—and yet it could pass through walls. Is that possible?

ANTHONY: It would take a long time to answer you!

HILARION: Why did he receive the Holy Spirit, who was himself the Son? What need had he of baptism if he was himself the Word? How could the Devil have tempted him, who himself was God?

Have these problems never puzzled you?

ANTHONY: Yes! Often! Often! Sometimes benumbed, and sometimes raging, they are ever in my mind. I beat them down; but up they spring again and choke me; so that ofttimes I fear that I am accursed.

HILARION: Then what use is there in your serving God?

ANTHONY: I must ever adore him!

(After a long silence Hilarion goes on again:)

But, doctrine apart, wide liberty of research is permitted us. Would you understand the hierarchy of the angels, the meanings of numbers, the essential truth of germs and metamorphoses?

ANTHONY: Yes! Yes! My thoughts struggle to escape out of their prison, and it seems to me that if I put forth all my strength I shall succeed. Now and then, for as long as a flash of lightning lasts, I feel myself lifted up—then back again I fall!

HILARION: The secret thing that you would grasp is guarded by sages in a distant land, who sit beneath gigantic trees, white-robed and serene gods. Warm air sustains them, and they need no other food. Round about them leopards move upon the greensward. The sound of running water and the neighing of unicorns blend with their voices. You shall hear them: and the face of the unknown shall be unveiled!

ANTHONY (*sighing*): The way is long, and I myself grow old!

HILARION: Oh-ho! Wise men are not scarce! There are some of them quite close to you; here! Let us enter!

THE TEMPTATION OF ST. ANTHONY

IV

(And Anthony perceives a great basilica.

Light is flowing from the apse, brilliant as the rays of a multi-coloured sun. It plays upon the heads of the vast concourse of men and women which fills the nave and ebbs between the columns, towards the side-aisles—where behind the wooden screens are to be seen altars, couches, chains of little blue stones, and painted constellations on the walls.

In the midst of the crowd, here and there, are motionless groups. Men deliver harangues, standing on stools, with upraised hands; others pray, with arms outstretched in the form of a cross; some lie prostrate on the ground, sing hymns, or drink wine; round about a table, the faithful are holding a love-feast; martyrs unswathe their limbs and show their wounds; old men, leaning on their sticks, relate the story of their travels.

Some there are from the country of the Germans, from Thrace, and from Gaul, from Scythia and the Indies—with snow on their beards, feathers in their hair, thorns on the fringes of their garments, sandals black with mud, skin burned by the sun. All manner of costumes there are, too—purple mantles, and linen robes, embroidered dalmatics, hair-shirts, sailors' caps, bishops' mitres. It is extraordinary to see how their eyes flash like lightning. Some of them look like executioners, and some like eunuchs.

Hilarion goes forward into the crowd. Everybody salutes him; while Anthony, keeping close at his side, attentively watches the people round about him. He sees that there are many women; and that some of them are dressed like men, with short hair; and of these he is afraid.)

HILARION: Those are Christian women who have converted their husbands. It seems as though women are always for Jesus, even among the idolaters—Procula, for instance, Pilate's wife, and Nero's concubine, Poppæa. Do not be afraid! Come on!

(And all the time other people are arriving.

They multiply, they redouble their numbers; insubstantial as shadows, and yet producing an amazing uproar, in which are intermingled howls of rage, the songs of lovers, canticles and objurgations.)

ANTHONY (*in a low voice*) : What is it they want?

HILARION : The Lord once said : " I have yet many things to say unto you." These people have knowledge of those things.

(And he pushes Anthony towards a golden throne with five steps, upon which, surrounded by ninety-five disciples, their bodies shining with oil, and all very lean and pale, sits the prophet Manes—handsome as an archangel, motionless as a statue, wearing an Indian cloak, with carbuncles in his plaited hair : in his left hand a book with coloured pictures, and under his right a globe. The pictures represent the creatures which lay dormant in chaos. Anthony leans forward to look at them. Then MANES makes the globe revolve; and accompanying his words on a lyre which gives forth sounds of crystal clearness :)

The celestial land is in the topmost height : the terrestrial world is at the lowest depth. Two angels bear it up—Splenditenens, and Omophorus who has six faces.

In the highest point of utmost Heaven dwells God himself, God the impassible; and below him, face to face, are the Son of God and the Prince of Darkness.

When darkness reached the edges of his Kingdom, God sent forth from his own essence a principle from which was evolved the first man, and encircled him with the five elements. But the evil spirits of darkness robbed man of a part of his nature, and that part was his soul.

There is but one single soul—spread everywhere abroad, as the waters of one river divide into many

THE TEMPTATION OF ST. ANTHONY

streams. It is this single soul which sighs in the wind, rasps upon saws while they cut through marble, roars in the waves of the sea; and it is this same soul which sheds milk-white tears when a leaf is broken from a fig-tree.

When souls go out from this world, they travel towards the stars, which themselves are alive.

ANTHONY (*beginning to laugh*): Ah-ha! What foolish fancies!

A MAN (*beardless and of stern appearance*): In what are they either foolish or fanciful?

(Anthony would reply: but Hilarion whispers to him that this man is the mighty Origen; and MANES goes on again:)

At first they stay for a while in the moon, where they are purified. Then they mount upward to the sun.

ANTHONY (*slowly*): I do not know of anything—to hinder us—from believing that.

MANES: The proper end of every creature is the liberation of the heavenly gleam enclosed in matter. The gleam escapes most easily with help from such things as perfumes, aromatic spices, the bouquet of wines, things in themselves so unsubstantial that they almost resemble thoughts. Bodily acts, on the other hand, retain it in its prison. The murderer must be born again in the body of a victim; he who slays an animal will become that animal; when you plant a vine, your being becomes inevitably bound among its branches. The eating of food absorbs the gleam. Be therefore always abstemious! You must fast!

HILARION: They are temperate enough, you see!

MANES: There is much of it in flesh-meats; but less in herbs. Those who are called the "Pure Ones," by reason of their extraordinary merit, extract from vegetation this luminous quality, and so it re-ascends to its source; whereas mere animals, by the act of generation, re-imprison it in flesh. Therefore, no women!

HILARION: And continent too!

MANES: Or, rather, take care that women do not conceive—better for the soul of man to be spread abroad upon the earth than to languish in fleshly entanglement. . . .

ANTHONY: Oh! How abominable!

HILARION: But why trouble yourself with these successive degrees of depravity, when the Church has once for all made marriage a sacrament?

SATURNINUS (*in Syrian costume*): It is a depressing version of affairs that he sets forth! The Father, to punish the rebel angels, commanded them to create the world. Christ came, and so the Jewish God, who was one of these angels. . . .

ANTHONY: An angel! He! The Creator!

CERDO: Did he not try to kill Moses, and were not prophets deceived by him, and nations led astray—did he not scatter falsehood and idolatry everywhere?

MARCION: Of a surety, the Creator is not the one true God!

ST. CLEMENT OF ALEXANDRIA: Matter is eternal!

BARDESANES (*who appears as a Babylonian mage*): It was formed by the Seven Planetary Spirits.

THE HERMIANS: It was the angels who made souls!

THE PRICILLIANISTS: It was the Devil who made the world!

ANTHONY (*staggering backwards*): Horror!

HILARION (*holding him up*): You despair too quickly! You do not really understand what it is they teach! Here is one who learnt from Theodas, the friend of St. Paul. Listen to him!

(And at a sign from Hilarion VALENTINE comes forward, clad in tunic of cloth of silver; his cranium is high and pointed; his voice wheezing:)

The world is the work of a God in delirium.

ANTHONY (*with bowed head*): The work of a God in delirium! (*After a long silence*): How can that be?

VALENTINE: The most perfect of beings, of the Æons, called the Abyss, reposed in the womb of the Deep, together with Thought. From their union sprang Intelligence, with Truth as a companion.

Intelligence and Truth begat the Word and Life, who in their turn begat Man and the Church—and so there were eight Æons.

(He reckons them up on his fingers.)

The Word and Truth produced ten other Æons—five couples, that is. Man and the Church produced yet other twelve, among them the Paraclete and Faith, Hope and Charity, Perfection and Wisdom—Sophia.

The harmony of these thirty Æons constitutes the Pleroma, or Universality of God: and thus, like the echo of a voice withdrawn, like the fading scent of a scattered perfume, like the rays of the setting sun, the Powers that emanated from the Principle grow ever fainter and yet more faint.

But Sophia, filled with desire for the Father, broke away from Pleroma—and then the Word made another couple, Christ and the Holy Spirit; and in them are reunited all the Æons; and between them all they constituted Jesus, the flower of the Pleroma.

However, Sophia, as she struggled to escape, had left in the void a reproduction of herself, an evil substance, Acharamoth by name. The Saviour had compassion on her and released her from all passions, and from the smile of Acharamoth thus released Light was born; her tears formed the waters, and from her sorrows dark matter sprang.

From Acharamoth came forth the Demiurge, maker of the worlds, of the heavens and of the Devil. He dwells far below the Pleroma, so far below that he knows nothing about it, and so conceives of himself as the true God, repeating by the mouths of his prophets the constant formula: "There is no other God than I!" Then he made man, and put into his soul that immaterial principle which was the Church, a reflection of that other Church within the Pleroma.

The time will come when Acharamoth, attaining to the highest region of all, shall be one with the Saviour; when the fire concealed within the world shall annihilate all matter, shall consume even itself; and when men, become pure spirit, shall espouse the angels!

ORIGEN: Then shall the Demon be overcome, and the reign of God begin!

(Anthony is about to cry out but checks himself; and then BASILIDES, taking him by the arm :)

The Supreme Being, with all his emanations, is called Abraxas; and the Saviour, with all his virtues, is Kaulakau—that is to say, " Line-upon-line, Uprightness-upon-uprightness."

We can exert the power of Kaulakau by using certain words, inscribed, in order that they may not be forgotten, upon this chalcedony.

(And he shows a little stone hanging at his neck, on which strange symbols are engraved.)

And so you will be transported into the Invisible; and being above the Law you will treat everything, even virtue itself, with disdain.

We others, the Pure Ones, must shun sorrow, after the example of Kaulakau.

ANTHONY: Why, what about the cross?

THE ELKESAITES (*in hyacinthine robes, reply to him*): The sadness, the degradation, the condemnation and the oppression of our fathers are blotted out, thanks to the evangel which came!

We may deny the inferior Christ, Jesus the man; but we must adore the other Christ, produced in his person under the wing of the Dove.

Marriage is honourable! The Holy Spirit is of female sex.

(Hilarion has vanished; and Anthony, carried forward by the crowd, comes to where THE CARPOCRATIANS are stretched upon scarlet cushions, in company with women.)

Before regaining the Alone, you will pass through a series of states and actions. If you would break your way out of the darkness, do the deeds of darkness here and now. Let the husband say to the wife: " Show benevolence to your brother," and then she'll kiss you.

THE NICOLAITANES (*gathered round a smoking dish*): This is meat offered to idols; partake of it! Apostasy is allowable if only the heart be pure. Gorge thy flesh with that for which it craves. Put an end to desire by dint of debauchery! Prounikos, the Mother of Heaven, wallowed in infamy.

THE MARKOSIANS (*wearing gold rings, and streaming with balsam*): Throw in your lot with us, if you would be one with the Spirit! Come with us if you would fain taste of immortality!

(And one of them exhibits to him, behind a hanging, the body of a man, surmounted by the head of an ass, representing Sabaoth, father of the Devil. He spits upon it, to show his hatred.

Another shows him a very low couch, strewn with flowers, and says :)

The spiritual marriage is now to be consummated.

(A third utters an invocation; and blood appears in the goblet of glass which he holds :)

See! See! The blood of Christ!

(Anthony is moving off, when water, splashed from a vat, besprinkles him. THE HELVIDIANS are plunging into it head-foremost and mumbling :)

A man who has been born again by baptism can sin no more!

(Then he passes a large fire, round which are gathered the Adamites, who go naked in emulation of the purity of Paradise; and he stumbles over THE MESSALIANS lying on the pavement, half-asleep, inanimate :)

Trample upon us if you will! We shall not stir.

Activity is always evil; every sort of occupation wicked!

(Behind these, the wretched PATERNIANS, men, women and children, lying promiscuously upon heaps of filth, lift their hideous faces, besmeared with wine :)

The baser parts of the body were made by the Devil, and they belong to him. Eat, therefore, drink, and fornicate!

ÆTIUS: Wickedness is inevitable and unworthy of the notice of God!

(But suddenly A MAN clothed in a Carthaginian mantle, leaps into the middle of them, a bundle of thongs in his hand; and hitting out vigorously to right and left of him indiscriminately :)

Ah! Cheats, robbers, simonists, heretics, devils! Scholastic vermin and dregs of hell! Marcion, there, is a sailor from Sinope, excommunicated for incest; Carpocrates was banished as a magician; Ætius stole his concubine, and Nicolas prostituted his wife; and Manes, who calls himself the Buddha, but whose real name is Cubricus, was skinned alive with a pointed reed, and his dried skin still hangs on the gates of Ctesiphon!

ANTHONY (*recognizing Tertullian, rushes towards him*): Master! Help! Help!

TERTULLIAN (*continues*): Break the images! Veil the virgins! Pray, fast, weep, subdue yourselves! No more vain philosophy! No more studying of books! Beside Jesus, all learning is worthless!

(The people have fled; and, instead of Tertullian, Anthony beholds a woman sitting upon a stone bench.

She is sobbing, with her head resting on a column; her hair hangs down, and her tired body is covered by a long, thin, brown dress.

And then they are face to face, far away from the crowd—and silence falls, an extraordinary calm, as when in the woods the wind is suddenly hushed, and all the leaves are still.

The woman is very beautiful, if somewhat faded, and of sepulchral pallor. They gaze at each other: and their eyes exchange as it were a stream of thoughts, a thousand things of long ago, confused, intense. At last PRISCILLA begins to speak :)

I was in the cooling chamber after my bath, and the rumbling of the streets lulled me to sleep.

Of a sudden I heard a clamour. They were crying out: "He's a magician! It is the Devil!" And the people stopped at our house, in front of the temple of Æsculapius. I drew myself up by my hands to the level of the window.

On the peristyle of the temple was a man with an iron collar about his neck. He took red coals from a chafing-dish, and with them traced long lines across his breast, calling out: "Jesus, Jesus!" The people shouted: "This is abominable! Let him be stoned!" But he heeded them not. The thing was unheard of, crazy! Flowers as large as the sun were turning round and round before my eyes, and I heard in space the vibrations of a golden harp. The daylight died. My arms loosed their hold of the window-bars, my strength failed me; and when he had led me to his house . . .

ANTHONY: But of whom are you speaking?
PRISCILLA: Why, of Montanus!
ANTHONY: But Montanus is dead!
PRISCILLA: That is not true.
A VOICE: No, Montanus is not dead!

(Anthony turns round; and near him, on the other side,

THE TEMPTATION OF ST. ANTHONY

on the bench, a second woman is sitting—fair, this latter, and even paler than the other, with swellings under her eyes, as though she had been long weeping. Without his questioning her, she says :)

MAXIMILLA: We were coming back over the mountains from Tarsus, when we saw a man under a fig-tree at a turn in the road.

He cried to us from afar: "Stop!" and he rushed towards us, abusing us. The slaves hurried up. The man burst out laughing. The horses became restive. The watch-dogs were all howling.

There he stood. Sweat was streaming down his face. His cloak flapped in the wind.

Calling us by our names, he upbraided us with the emptiness of our lives, the vileness of our bodies; and he shook his fist at the silver bells which were fastened under the cheeks of the dromedaries.

His anger brought my heart into my mouth; and yet from it also I derived pleasure which soothed and even intoxicated me.

First came the slaves. "Master," said they, "our beasts are weary"; next it was the women: "We are afraid"; and the slaves went away. Then the children began to cry: "We are hungry!" And since no reply was given to the women, they also disappeared.

He was still speaking. I felt that someone was near me. It was my own husband; but I had ears only for the other. Dragging himself along amidst the stones, my husband cried: "Are you leaving me?" And I answered: "Yes, go away"—so that I might follow Montanus.

ANTHONY: A eunuch!

PRISCILLA: And need that surprise you, foul-minded fellow that you are? The love of Martha and Joanna and Susanna and of Mary Magdalene for the Saviour was all spiritual. Souls, no less than bodies, can join in the excitement of an embrace. Leonteus, the bishop, by self-mutilation, made it possible for Eustolia to remain in his house—loving his love more than he loved his manhood. And besides, it was no doing of mine; I was driven to it by some force outside myself; Sotades could not cure me. But it was cruel, none the less! I do not mind! I am the last of the prophetesses; and after me the end of the world will come.

MAXIMILLA: It was upon me that he heaped his favours. And, what is more, there is none who loves him more than I, none who is more loved by him!

PRISCILLA: You lie! It is I who am first!

MAXIMILLA: Nay, indeed, it is I!

(They fight. A negro's head appears between their shoulders.)

MONTANUS (*in a black mantle, fastened by cross-bones*): Be still, my doves! Earthly bliss is not for us, but by our union we enjoy a spiritual plenitude. After the period of the Father, the period of the Son; and it is I who inaugurate the third, which is that of the Paraclete. His light came down upon me when for forty nights, over my home at Pepuza, the heavenly Jerusalem blazed in the firmament.

Ah! How you cry out in agony under the scourge! How your afflicted members offer themselves to my spiritual ardours! How you faint upon

THE TEMPTATION OF ST. ANTHONY

my breast with longing that can never be satisfied! Your love is so strong that it has revealed whole worlds to you, and with your bodily eyes you can even behold the souls of men.

(Anthony gives a start of astonishment. TERTULLIAN, appearing again beside Montanus:)

No doubt: since the soul has a body, and things which have no bodies simply do not exist.

MONTANUS: To render it more subtle still, I have ordained many mortifications, three Lents in each year, and nightly prayers where no word is spoken—lest the breath which issues from an open mouth should tarnish thought. No second marriages, or, better still, no marriage at all! It was with women that the angels sinned.

THE ARCONTICS (*in hair-shirts*): The Saviour said: "I am come to destroy the works of the woman."

THE TATIANIANS (*in shirts of woven reed*): She is the tree of evil! Our bodies are garments of skin.

(And going farther along the same side, Anthony meets THE VALESIANS stretched upon the ground, with red clots under their bellies, beneath their tunics. They offer him a knife:)

Do as Origen did, and what we have done! Is it the pain you are afraid of, you coward? Is it love of the flesh which withholds you, you hypocrite?

(And as he watches them struggling, stretched upon their backs in pools of their own blood, THE CAINITES, their hair knitted together by vipers, pass near him, clamouring in his ear:)

Glory be to Cain! Glory be to Sodom! Glory be to Judas!

Cain was the father of all strong men. Sodom, by the chastisement which she endured, terrified the world, and Judas was the instrument by which God saved the world! . . . Yea, Judas! But for him no atoning death, and therefore no redemption!

(They vanish amid the hordes of CIRCONCELLIONS, clad in wolfskins, crowned with thorns, and carrying iron clubs :)

Trample on the fruit! Trouble the spring! Drown the child! Plunder the rich man who is happy, with plenty to eat! Beat the poor man who envies the ass his covering, the dog his food, and the bird her nest, and who grieves because others are not all as miserable as he.

It is for us, the saints, to poison, burn, massacre, so that the end of the world may be hastened!

There is salvation only in martyrdom. We give ourselves to martyrdom. We drag the skin from our heads with pincers; we spread our bodies under the plough; we cast ourselves into the mouths of ovens!

Shame upon baptism! Shame on the eucharist! Shame upon marriage! Damnation upon all!

(Then, all through the basilica, the raging is redoubled. The Audæans shoot arrows at the Devil; the Collyridians cast blue veils towards the roof; the Ascites prostrate themselves before a wine-skin; the Marcionites baptize a corpse with oil. Near Appelles, a woman tries to explain her meaning by showing a wafer inside a bottle; another, among the Sampseans, distributes dust from her sandals as though it were a sacrament. Upon the rose-strewn couch of the Marcosians, two lovers embrace. The Circoncellions are cutting one another's throats; the death-rattle is heard among the Valesians; Bardesanes sings; Carpocras dances; Maximilla and Priscilla utter loud groans—and the false prophetess of Cappadocia, naked, leaning on a lion and shaking three torches, yells the Terrible Invocation aloud.

THE TEMPTATION OF ST. ANTHONY 215

The columns rock like tree-trunks; fiery gleams cross one another from the amulets on the heresiarchs' necks; the constellations in the chapels quiver; and the walls seem to recoil from the moving to and fro of the crowd, each head in which is a wave which leaps and roars.

And out of the depth of the clamour a song arises, in bursts of laughter, amidst which the name of Jesus recurs again and again.

These are some of the rabble, and they are clapping their hands in time with the song. In their midst is ARIUS in the vesture of a deacon :)

The fools who rant against me profess to explain the unreasonable; and for their utter confusion I have composed some little poems so comical that they are known by heart in the mills, in the taverns, and on the wharves.

A thousand times no! The Son is not co-eternal with the Father, nor of the same substance! Or he would never have said: "Father, take away this cup from me!"—"Why callest thou me good? None is good save one, that is God"—"I go to My God and to your God!"—and other words bearing witness to his created nature. This is proved to us, further, by all his names: Lamb, Shepherd, Fountain, Wisdom, Son of Man, Prophet, the Way, the Corner-Stone!

SABELLIUS: For my part I maintain that the two of them are identical!

ARIUS: The Council of Antioch decided the contrary.

ANTHONY: Then what is the Word? What was Jesus?

THE VALENTINIANS: He was the husband of Acharamoth repentant.

THE SETHIANIANS: He was Shem, the son of Noah.

THE THEODOTIANS: He was Melchizedeck.

THE MERINTHIANS: He was nothing but a man.

THE APPOLINARIANS: He took the appearance of one! His passion was a pretence.

MARCEL OF ANCYRA: He was an unfolding of the Father!

POPE CALIXTUS: Father and Son are two manifestations of one only God!

METHODIUS: First he was in Adam, then in man.

CERINTHUS: And he will rise again.

VALENTINE: Impossible—His body being celestial.

PAUL OF SAMOSATA: He was God only from the moment of his baptism!

HERMOGENES: He dwells in the sun!

(And all the heresiarchs form a circle about Anthony, who covers his face with his hands, and weeps.

A JEW, red-bearded, and spotted with leprosy, comes close to him, and with a horrible titter :)

His soul was the soul of Esau! He suffered from the mania of Bellerophon, who tried to ascend to heaven, and his mother, a seller of perfumes, surrendered herself to Pantheus, a Roman soldier, among the sheafs of maize, one evening in harvest-time.

(ANTHONY suddenly lifts his head, looks at them without speaking; then goes straight towards them :)

Doctors, magicians, bishops and deacons, men and phantoms! Begone! Begone! You are all of you lies!

THE HERESIARCHS: We have our martyrs, who were more truly martyrs than yours; our prayers are more laborious, our outbursts of love more sublime, our ecstasies more intense.

ANTHONY: But no revelation! No proofs!

(Then they all wave in the air rolls of papyrus, tablets of wood, pieces of leather, bundles of stuff—and pushing one against another:)

THE CERINTHIANS: Behold the Gospel of the Hebrews!
THE MARCIONITES: The Gospel of the Lord!
THE MARCOSIANS: The Gospel of Eve!
THE ENCRATITES: The Gospel of Thomas!
THE CAINITES: The Gospel of Judas!
BASILIDES: The treatise on the Destiny of the Soul!
MANES: The Prophecy of Barcouf!

(Anthony struggles to escape from them—and he perceives amongst the shadows in a dark corner THE OLD EBIONITES, dried up like mummies, dull of vision, and white-bearded. With quivering voices they exclaim:)

We, for our part, have known him, the carpenter's son. We were contemporary with him, we lived in his street. He used when at play to make little birds of clay; he was not afraid of the sharp edge of the abacus; he used to help his father in the workshop, or put together for his mother the balls of coloured wool. Then he travelled to Egypt, and thence returned with wonderful secrets. We were at Jericho when he came to seek the locust-eater. They talked with low voices, so that no one could hear what they said. But it was from that time onward that men spoke of him in Galilee, and that many legends were set to his account.

(*They repeat tremulously*): We knew him! Yes! We knew him!

ANTHONY: Ah! Speak! Tell us more! What did he look like?

TERTULLIAN: Of savage and repellent aspect—for he bore all the crimes, all the sorrows, and all the ugliness of the world.

ANTHONY: Oh! No! no! It seems to me, on the contrary, that his presence must always have had a beauty more than human.

EUSEBIUS OF CÆSAREA: There is indeed at Paneades, near an ancient ruin, in a tangled mass of vegetation, a stone statue which was set up, so they say, by the woman with an issue of blood. But time has eaten into the face of the statue, and the inscription has been worn away by the weather.

(A woman comes out from among the Carpocratians.)

MARCELLINA: Once was I deaconess at a little church in Rome, where it was my task to show to the faithful the silver images of Paul, Homer, Pythagoras and Jesus Christ. But only his have I kept.

(She opens her mantle a little way :)

Would you like it?

A VOICE: He himself appears again when we call on him! This is the time! Come!

(And Anthony feels a rough hand fall upon his arm, which drags him away. He ascends a staircase in complete darkness, and after mounting many steps he stops in front of a door.

Then his guide (is it Hilarion? He knows not) whispers in someone's ear: "The Lord is just coming"—and they are taken into an unfurnished room, with a low ceiling.

The first thing he notices is, right in front of him, a large chrysalis, the colour of blood, with a human head from which

THE TEMPTATION OF ST. ANTHONY

rays are darting out; and round about it, in Greek letters, the name KNOUPHIS. This head looks down from the shaft of a column set in a base. On the other side of the room there are bright iron medallions, representing the heads of various creatures, such as an ox, a lion, an eagle, a dog, and yet once again the head of an ass!

Earthenware lamps, burning before these images, give an uncertain light. Through a hole in the wall, Anthony sees the moon shining far off across the waves, and he can even distinguish their little splashings, and hear the occasional heavy thud of a boat's keel against the stones of a breakwater.

Men, squatting on the ground, their faces hidden in their mantles, now and then make noises like the smothered barking of dogs. Women sleep, with their foreheads on their two arms supported by their knees, so covered up in their clothing that they look like bundles of stuff all along the wall. Near them, half-naked children, crawling with vermin, stare foolishly at the burning lamps—and nobody does anything, because everybody is waiting for something to happen.

They talk in low voices of domestic affairs, or of the treatment of disease. For some of them the persecution has become more than they can bear, and they are to embark at daybreak. And yet it is easy enough to deceive the heathen : " The fools believe that we adore Knouphis! "

But one of the brethren, moved by sudden inspiration, goes and stands by the column, on which a basket has been placed, containing a loaf of bread which lies on yellow leaves and creepers.

The others stand up in their places, forming three parallel lines.

THE INSPIRED BROTHER unrolls a bill covered with intermingling cylinders, and speaks as follows :)

Among the shadows descended the ray of the Word, and from it issued a vehement cry, as it had been the voice of Light itself.

ALL TOGETHER (*respond, swaying their bodies*) : Have mercy, Lord!

THE BROTHER : Next was man created by the

notorious God of Israel, with those as his helpers. (*He points to the medallions*.) Astophaios, Oraios, Sabaoth, Adonai, Eloi, Iao!

And there was man, lying in the mud, hideous, feeble, formless, unconscious.

ALL (*in sorrowful accents*): Have mercy, Lord!

THE BROTHER: But Sophia, in pity, bestowed life upon him by the gift of a particle of her own soul.

Then, seeing man so beautiful, God was jealous, and confined him within his own territory, forbidding him to touch the Tree of Knowledge.

But once more the other helped him. She sent the serpent who found cunning means of moving him to disobedience against this spiteful law.

And man, when once he had tasted knowledge, understood celestial things.

ALL (*loudly*): Have mercy, Lord!

THE BROTHER: But Iabdalaoth, for vengeance' sake, hurled man down amongst material things, and the serpent with him!

ALL (*very quietly*): Have mercy, Lord!

(They cease, and then there is silence. Smells from off the wharves mingle in the warm air with the smoke of the lamps. The wicks flicker, on the point of extinction; large mosquitoes circle about them; and Anthony groans in anguish, for he feels that some horrible thing is drifting round him, some dreadful deed that is near accomplishment. But THE BROTHER, stamping with his heel, cracking his fingers, jerking his head, chants in furious rhythm, to the accompaniment of cymbals and the piercing sound of a flute :)

Come! Come! Come forth from thy cavern! Swift runner that has no feet, captor without hands!

THE TEMPTATION OF ST. ANTHONY

Winding like the rivers; spherical as the sun; black, and flecked with gold, as the firmament is sown with stars! Like the curlings of a vine, or the circumvolution of entrails!

Unbegotten! Eater of earth! Ever young! Quick of understanding! Honoured at Epidaurus! Benevolent towards men! Who didst heal King Ptolemy, and the soldiers of Moses, and Glaucus, the son of Minos!

Come! Come! Come forth from thy cavern!

ALL (*repeat*): Come! Come! Come forth from thy cavern!

(But nothing appears.)

Why! What is the matter?

(And they consult together, proposing various things. An old man offers a clod of turf. Then there is a movement in the basket. The leaves shake, some flowers fall—and the head of a python appears.

It goes slowly round the loaf of bread, like a wheel turning about a rigid disc, then unfolds and stretches itself out. It is of enormous size and of great weight. To keep it from touching the ground, men support it against their breasts, women hold it on their heads, children lift it up in their arms—and its tail, passing through the hole in the wall, reaches away indefinitely even to the bottom of the sea. Its coils multiply, filling the chamber, hemming Anthony in.

THE FAITHFUL, glueing their lips upon its skin, snatching from each other pieces of bread which the python has bitten off :)

It is thou! It is thou!
Lifted up by Moses in the wilderness, broken in pieces by Hezekiah, restored by the Messiah! He drank of thee in the waters of baptism; but in the

Garden of Olives thou didst leave him, and there he realized all his weakness.

Twisted along the arms of the cross, and above his head, dribbling on the crown of thorns, thou didst see him die. For thou art not Jesus; but thou art the Word! Thou art the Christ!

(Anthony faints with horror, falling back upon some pieces of wood, where in front of his hut, the torch that has slipped from his hand is slowly burning.

The shock awakens him; and he sees the Nile, clear under the whiteness of the moon, like a great serpent undulating among the sands; and illusion overtakes him again—he is still among the Ophites; they surround him, they call out to him; they are carrying baggage down to the wharf. He accompanies them, and goes on board ship.

A period of time, of which he has no clear consciousness, elapses.

Then he is within a vaulted prison. The bars in front of him make black lines against the background of blue sky, and on either side, in dim light, there are men and women weeping and praying, surrounded by others who are trying to comfort them.

Without, the buzzing as of a crowd of people, and the splendour of a summer's day.

Shrill voices are offering water-melons for sale, and water, and iced drinks, and seat-cushions of woven grass. Now and then applause breaks out. He can hear footsteps overhead.

Suddenly there comes a bellowing roar, deep and long drawn-out—hollow as the sound of water in an aqueduct.

And he sees, right in front of him, behind the barriers of another cell, a lion walking about—then a line of sandals, bare legs and purple fringes. Beyond that, ever-rising tiers of spectators in circles that are smaller at the bottom, on the edge of the arena, and widest at the top, where wooden masts uphold an awning of hyacinth, stretched on cords across the entire space. These great circles of stone are intersected by stairways which at regular intervals from each other converge towards the arena.

THE TEMPTATION OF ST. ANTHONY 223

The seats are full of people, knights, senators, soldiers, plebeians, vestal virgins and courtesans—in woollen hoods, silken maniples, grey tunics, with jewelled aigrettes, feathered tufts, and lictors' rods; and all this seething, shouting, excited, furious multitude, like a huge boiling vat, stupefies him. In the middle of the arena smoke of incense rises from an altar.

And he understands that the men and women round about him are Christians, condemned to the lions. The men wear the crimson mantles of priests of Saturn, the women the fillets of Ceres. Their friends are selecting and appropriating for themselves odds and ends of their garments and their rings. They had, say these friends, to spend a good deal of money to get into the prison. But what matter! They will stay till the end.

Among these sympathizers, Anthony notices a man with a bald head, and in a black mantle, whose face he remembers to have seen somewhere. He is speaking to them of the nothingness of this world, and the felicity of the chosen; and, as he listens, Anthony is transported by heavenly love, and longs to lay down his life for the Saviour, not clearly knowing whether or not he himself is one of the martyrs.

Yet all of them, save a long-haired Phrygian, who stands with arms uplifted, have a dejected air. An old man, on a bench, is sobbing; and a youth stands, with drooping head, and dreams.

THE OLD MAN, who has refused to pay honour to a statue of Minerva at the cross-roads, gazes at his companions as though he were thinking :)

Something should have been done to help me! Associations can so easily arrange for their members to be left in peace. Many Christians have got forged letters certifying that they have sacrificed to idols.

(*Aloud, he asks*): Was it not Petrus of Alexandria who decided what should be done about those who give way under torture?

(*Then, to himself*): Ah! It is hard at my time of life! My infirmities make me so weak. Yet I might have gone on living until next winter, or even longer!

(He thinks of his little garden—and his eyes turn towards the altar.
THE YOUNG MAN, who violently interrupted a festival of Apollo, murmurs:)

And it would have been so simple for me to have fled to the mountains!

The soldiers would have caught you (*says one of the brethren*).

Oh! I would have done what Cyprian did; I would have come back; and the second time, surely, I should have been stronger!

(Then he thinks of the countless days he might have lived; of all the unknown delights which now he can never know—and he, too, looks towards the altar: but THE MAN IN THE BLACK TUNIC hastens to his side:)

For shame! What! You! A victim chosen by God! Look at all those women who are watching you! And sometimes it even happens that God works miracles. Pionius made powerless the hand of his executioner; the blood of Polycarp quenched the flames around his stake! (*He turns to the old man.*) Father! Father! You must edify us by your death. If you cling to life, you will only be guilty, sooner or later, of some sin that will destroy the fruit of all your good deeds. God's power is infinite; and it may happen that the whole populace will be converted by your example.

(And in the den near by, the lions go up and down unceasingly, swift, monotonous. The largest lion of them all suddenly looks straight at Anthony, and roars—and breath issues from his jaws like steam.

The women are huddled against the men.)

THE CONSOLER (*going from one to another*): What would you say, what would any of you say, if you were about to be burned with red-hot irons, torn to pieces by horses, or if your bodies were to be plastered with honey and then devoured by flies! As it is, you will but die the death of a hunter who is taken by surprise in a wood.

(Anthony thinks that he would choose any one of those deaths rather than face these awful wild beasts; he can almost feel their teeth, their claws—hear his bones cracking in their jaws.

A keeper enters the dungeon; the martyrs tremble.

There is only one who appears unmoved: the Phrygian, who is praying by himself. He has burned three temples; and he comes forward with his arms raised, his mouth open, his face turned upward, seeing nothing, like a sleep-walker.)

THE CONSOLER (*cries*): Back! Back! The spirit of Montanus might lay hold of you.

ALL (*recoil, with loud outcries of*): Damnation to the Montanists!

(They insult him, spit at him, make to strike at him. The restless lions bite each others' manes.)

THE PEOPLE (*howl*): To the wild beasts! To the wild beasts!

(The martyrs cling to each other, and burst into sobs. A cup of stupefying wine is offered to them, and it passes quickly from hand to hand.

Against the door of the cell, another keeper awaits the signal. It is given; the door opens; a lion goes out.

With long, slanting steps he crosses the arena. Behind him, one by one, appear other lions, then a bear, three panthers and some leopards. They scatter—like a herd in a meadow.

The crack of a whip is heard. The Christians waver—but, the sooner to make an end, their brethren push them forward. Anthony closes his eyes.

He opens them again. But he is surrounded by shadows.

After a while, the shadows clear away; and he can discern an arid plain on which are little mounds, such as one sees near worked-out quarries.

Here and there, level with the ground, are slabs of stone, with clusters of shrubs growing between them; and over the slabs white forms, insubstantial as clouds, are bending.

Others come quietly up, their eyes shining through openings in their long veils. By the calm ease of their walk, and by the perfume which surrounds them, Anthony knows that these women are patricians. There are men, too, but of inferior station, since their faces are both simple and coarse.)

A WOMAN (*taking a deep breath*): Ah! How sweet the air of this cool night, amongst the sepulchres! I am so weary of soft beds, of the turmoil of daily life, of the oppressive heat of the sun!

(Her maid takes a torch from a canvas bag and lights it. From this, other torches are kindled by the faithful, who then place them on the tombs.)

A WOMAN (*panting*): Ah-h-h! Here I am, at last! What a thing it is to have an idolater for one's husband!

ANOTHER: Our visits to the prisons, the meetings with our brethren, all seem suspicious to our husbands, and even if we make the sign of the cross, we must do it unobserved: they would take it for some magical enchantment.

ANOTHER: In my case, it meant constant quarrelling; I would not submit my body to his perverted lusts, and in revenge he has had me prosecuted as a Christian.

ANOTHER: You remember Lucius, that handsome young man, who was dragged by the heels behind a chariot, like Hector, from the Esquiline Gate to the mountains of Tiber—and on both sides of the way his blood spattered the thickets! See! I gathered some of the drops.

(She draws from her bosom a blackened sponge, covers it with kisses, then flings herself upon the slabs, crying :)

O my friend! My friend!

A MAN: It is three years to this very day since Domitilla died. She was stoned in the forest of Proserpine. I gathered up her bones, which shone like fire-flies on the grass. The earth has now reclaimed them!

(He throws himself upon a tomb.)

O my beloved! My betrothed!

ALL THE OTHERS (*scattered about the plain*): O my sister! O my brother! O my child! O my mother!

(They are kneeling, faces covered by their hands; or else they are flat on the ground, with arms extended—and their smothered sobs seem to tear them asunder. Now and then they look heavenward, and say :)

Have pity on her soul, O God! She languishes in Hades: let her of thy mercy attain unto thy resurrection, that she may enjoy light in thee!

(Or, with eyes downcast, they murmur :)

Your sufferings are ended: be at rest! Here is wine for you, and food.

A WIDOW: I have made pottage, such as he loved, with eggs and a double measure of flour! We are going to eat together now, are we not? as in days of old!

(She lifts a morsel to her lips, and then suddenly begins to laugh, unrestrainedly, frantically. And others imitate her, nibbling little bits, drinking mouthfuls.

They tell the stories of their martyrs; grief gives way to excitement; more and more wine is drunk. They fix their eyes, flooded with tears, upon each other. They stammer with mingled intoxication and grief; little by little their hands touch, their lips meet, their veils are pushed aside, and they lie entangled on the tombs, among the torches and the cups.

The sky begins to brighten. The fog soaks their garments—without looking at each other they go off separately, each on her several way, into the surrounding country.

The sun shines; the vegetation has shot up, the whole appearance of the plain is altered.

And Anthony, looking between some bamboos, sees clearly a forest of bluish-grey columns. They are tree-trunks all growing from one single root. From every branch of the latter other branches fall and bury themselves in the ground; and the appearance of all these horizontal and perpendicular lines, so many times repeated, would have been that of an enormous frame-work, if there had not been growing upon them, here and there, a number of small figs, and dark-coloured foliage, like that of the sycamore.

In the forks of this tree he sees clusters of yellow flowers, together with purple blossoms and ferns, like birds' plumage.

Beneath the lowest branches the horns of buffalo appear, and the bright eyes of antelopes; there are twittering paroquets, hovering butterflies, crawling lizards, buzzing flies; and in the midst of the silence one feels that under the surface there is throbbing life.

At the entrance to the wood, on a sort of pyre, a strange

THE TEMPTATION OF ST. ANTHONY

sight is to be seen—a man—covered with cow-dung, completely naked, more shrivelled than a mummy; his joints form knots at the ends of bones that look like sticks. Bunches of shells hang at his ears; his face is unusually long; and his nose like a vulture's beak.

His left arm has been held out for so long that the joint has stiffened, and it is now as straight as a post—and he has been sitting there for so many years that birds have come and nested in his hair. On the four sides of his pyre fires are burning. The sun shines full in his face, and he gazes at it with wide-open eyes.

He addresses Anthony, without looking at him :)

Brahman from the banks of the Nile, what do you think of it all?

(Flames burst forth on all sides of him, between the beams of the pyre; and THE GYMNOSOPHIST continues :)

Like the rhinoceros, I have buried myself in solitude. My home is in the tree behind me.

(Looking more closely at the great fig-tree, one does indeed discover, amongst its flutings, a natural hollow large enough to hold a man.)

My food has been flowers and fruit, and so carefully have I kept my rule that never even a dog has watched me eat.

Since life comes forth from corruption, corruption from desire, desire from excitement, excitement from contact, I have shunned all action, every contact, and —as still as the stone of a tomb, breathing through my nostrils, my look fixed steadily upon my nose, contemplating space in my mind, the world in my own members, the moon in my heart—I have dreamed of the essence of that great Soul whence issue continually, like sparks from a fire, the principles of existence.

I found at last the supreme Soul in all beings, all beings in the supreme Soul—and into that Soul my own being has now entered, even as into it I had gathered all my bodily senses.

Knowledge comes to me direct from heaven, as the bird Tchataka quenches his thirst only with the falling rain-drops.

In just so far as I know things, things for me no longer exist.

For me, now, there can be no more hope and no more anguish, no happiness, no virtue, neither day nor night, neither thou nor I—unalterable nothingness!

My frightful austerities have made me superior to the Powers. A drawing together of my thought could kill the sons of a hundred kings, dethrone the gods, overthrow the world.

(He has been speaking in a monotonous voice. The leaves round about shrivel up. Rats flee away along the ground. He slowly turns his eyes downward to the rising flames, and proceeds :)

I have learned to hate form and perception, and even knowledge itself—for thought does not survive the transitory fact which caused it; and mind, like everything else, is but illusion.

All that is begotten will perish, all that dies must live again; beings now invisible will tarry within wombs that are yet unformed, to issue thence once more upon the earth for painful service of other creatures.

But whereas hitherto I have revolved in countless existences, under the guise of gods, and animals, and men, I here renounce further journeyings: I will have no more of this weary business! I forsake the filthy tavern of my body, built of flesh, reddened with blood, covered with horrible skin, full of uncleanness—and, instead, I go at last to slumber in the very depth of the Absolute, in Annihilation.

(The flames have mounted level with his breast—and then they wrap him round, his head thrust up out of them, as though through a hole in a wall, and his staring eyes at gaze.

Anthony rises. The torch, on the ground, has kindled the splinters of wood; and flames have singed his beard.

Crying aloud, Anthony stamps out the fire—and when nothing remains but a heap of ashes, he says :)

But where is Hilarion? He was there just now. I saw him! What! No, that is impossible! I was mistaken! But why? . . . Perchance my hut, these stones, the sand, are no longer real. I am going mad. I must be calm! Where was I? What happened?

Ah! The gymnosophist! . . . Such deaths are common among the Hindu philosophers. Kalanos burned himself in the presence of Alexander; there was another who did likewise in the time of Augustus. How they must have hated life! Unless it was pride that urged them? . . . No matter, theirs was the unshaken courage of martyrs! . . . And as for the martyrs themselves, I believe now all that I have heard of the debauchery they cause.

And before that? Yes, I remember! The crowd of heresiarchs—how noisy they were! How their eyes shone! . . . But why with their bodies must they go such outrageous lengths? And wherefore such wanderings of the spirit?

But since along their various roads they claim to be seeking God, how shall I blame them, I, who so often stumble in mine? When they disappeared, I may have been just on the point of learning more. Everything whirled too quickly about me; I had no time for an answer. Now there seems to be in my mind more room, more light. I am calm. I feel that I could—but what is this? I put out the fire, I thought!

(A light is fluttering among the rocks, and soon by fits and starts a voice is heard, far off, in the mountain.)

Is it the howling of a hyena—or perhaps the sobbing of a traveller who has lost his way?

(Anthony listens. The light comes nearer.
And he sees a weeping woman, leaning on the shoulder of a white-bearded man.
Her purple robe is in rags. He has a tunic of the same colour, and carries a bronze vessel, from which a little blue flame rises. They are both bare-headed.
Anthony is uneasy—wondering who the woman may be.)

THE STRANGER (*Simon*): Wherever I go, I take with me this young girl, this poor child.

(He lifts up the bronze lamp, and by its flickering light Anthony looks closely at the girl.
Her face bears the marks of teeth, and there are bruises on her arms; her disordered hair is caught in her tattered rags; her eyes seem to be insensible to light.)

SIMON: She is like this, sometimes, for very long periods, neither speaking nor eating; and then she will rouse herself, and utter wonderful things.

ANTHONY: Yes?

SIMON: Ennoia! Ennoia! Ennoia! Tell us what you have to say!

(She turns her eyeballs as though awakening from a dream; passes her fingers slowly across her brows; and in a doleful voice :)

HELENA (*Ennoia*): I remember a distant country, green as an emerald. A single tree is there. . . .

(Anthony starts.)

In each storey of its large branches, a pair of spirits have their airy home. The branches round about them lace together, like the veins in a body: and they can see the life eternal circulating from the roots hidden in darkness to the sun-lit summit. I, on the second branch, lit up the summer nights with my loveliness.

ANTHONY (*tapping his forehead*): Ah-ha! I understand! Her head . . .

SIMON (*finger on lips*): Hush!

HELENA: The sail bulged, the keel broke through the foam. He said to me: " What matter if my country suffers, if I lose my kingdom! I shall possess you, in my own house! "

And how sweet was that lofty chamber in his palace! He lay upon the ivory bed, fondling my tresses, and singing songs of love.

At close of day I saw the two camps, and the blazing beacons, Ulysses at the door of his tent, Achilles in full armour driving his chariot on the sea-beach.

ANTHONY: But she is quite mad! Why . . . ?

SIMON: Hush! Hush!

HELENA: They anointed me with fragrant oils, and sold me to the people for their entertainment.

One evening, I stood with the sistrum in my hand, and made dance-music for some Greek sailors. Rain fell in torrents upon the tavern, and the cups of hot wine were steaming. A man came in, though the door was not opened . . .

SIMON: It was I! I had found you again!

Look at her, Anthony, her whom men call Sigeh, Ennoia, Barbelo, Prounikos! The spirits that rule the world were jealous of her, and imprisoned her within this body of a woman.

She has been Helen of Troy, whose memory the poet Stesichorus cursed. She has been Lucretia, the patrician woman who was ravished by kings. She has been Delilah, who shore away the lock of Samson. She was that maiden who shamed the people of Israel. She has been enamoured of idolatry and lying and adultery and all kinds of foolishness. She has been a prostitute among all the nations. She has sung at all the cross-roads, and kissed the mouths of all men.

As the Syrian woman, she was mistress of the robbers at Tyre. She drank with them all through the night, and hid assassins among the riff-raff of her careless bed.

ANTHONY: But what is all this to me?

SIMON (*angrily*): I have redeemed her, I tell you, and restored her to her splendour; so that it was with her that Caius Cæsar Caligula fell in love when he longed to embrace the Moon!

ANTHONY: But surely . . . ?

SIMON: She herself is the Moon! Did not Pope Clement write of how she was imprisoned in a tower? Three hundred people surrounded the tower; and from every loophole, at one and the same moment, they saw the moon look out—though there are not in existence many moons, nor several Ennoias.

THE TEMPTATION OF ST. ANTHONY

ANTHONY: Yes—I think I remember . . .

(And he falls into a reverie.)

SIMON: Innocent as the Christ, who died for men, so did she give herself up for women. For the powerlessness of Jehovah is shown by the transgression of Adam, and we must free ourselves from the old law, which is contrary to the order of things.

I have proclaimed this revival in Ephraim and in Issachar, by the torrent of Bizor, beyond the lake of Houleh, in the valley of Megiddo, farther off than the mountains, at Bostra and at Damascus. Let such come to me as are drowned in wine, or covered with mud, or stained with blood, and I will take away their defilement with the Holy Spirit, whom the Greeks call Minerva! She is the Holy Spirit! And I am Jupiter, Apollo, the Christ, the Paraclete, the almighty power of God, incarnate in the person of Simon!

ANTHONY: Ah! It is you, then! . . . You are he!

But I know about your wickedness!

You were born at Gittoi, near Samaria. Your first master, Dositheus, dismissed you. You cursed St. Paul for converting one of your women; and then, when you were overcome by St. Peter—in your rage and terror you cast into the water your bagful of tricks!

SIMON: Would you like them?

(Anthony looks at him, and an inner voice whispers within his breast: "Why not?")

SIMON (*continues*): He who understands the forces of nature and the inner quality of spirits can work miracles. That has been the dream of all the sages; and that—confess it now!—is the desire by which you are tormented.

In the amphitheatre, with the Romans all round me, I flew so high up in the air that I was seen no more. Nero ordered me to be beheaded; but it was a sheep's head which fell to the ground instead of mine. And at last, when they burned me alive, I rose again the third day. And the proof of this is, that here I am!

(He holds out his hands; and Anthony recoils, for their smell is as the smell of a corpse.)

I can make bronze serpents move, and marble statues laugh, and dogs speak. I will show you mountains of gold; I will make and unmake kings; you shall see the nations adore me! I can walk on the clouds and upon the waves, pass over mountains, make myself appear as a youth, as an old man, a tiger or an ant; assume your countenance, or give you mine. I can direct the thunderbolt! Do you hear it?

(The thunder rumbles, and there are flashes of lightning.)

It is the voice of the Most High! "For the Lord thy God is a consuming fire"; and all creation is controlled by flashings-forth from this furnace.

You shall be baptized therein, even now—with that second baptism proclaimed by Jesus, which fell upon the Apostles one stormy day when the window was open!

(And moving the flame, which he holds in his hand, backwards and forwards, slowly, as though about to sprinkle Anthony therewith :)

Mother of mercies, who dost reveal all secret things, and by whom we attain peace in the eighth dwelling-place. . . .

ANTHONY (*cries out*): Alas! If only I had here some holy water!

(The flame is extinguished, amidst whirls of smoke.
Ennoia and Simon have disappeared.
Fog fills the scene, extremely cold, opaque, and fetid.)

ANTHONY (*stretching out his arms like a blind man*): Where am I? . . . I may fall into the abyss. And the cross, I know, is too far away. . . . Ah! What a night it is! What an awful night!

(A gust of wind makes an opening in the fog—and he sees two men, clothed in long white tunics.
One of them is tall, with a gentle face, and of grave deportment. His brown hair, parted as in pictures of the Christ, falls uniformly upon his shoulders.
He has laid aside a wand which he was carrying in his hand, but which his companion now holds, having made as he received it an oriental obeisance.
This other man is short, fat, snub-nosed, bull-necked, curly-haired, simple-looking.
They are both barefoot, bareheaded, and covered with dust like men newly come from a journey.)

ANTHONY (*leaping up*): What do you want? Speak! . . . Begone!

DAMIS (*who is the little man*): There, there! . . . Good hermit! What do I want? I do not know; but here is the master!

(He sits down: the other remains standing. Silence.)

ANTHONY (*begins again*): And so you have come . . . ?

DAMIS: Oh! From far away—from very far away!

ANTHONY: And you are going . . . ?

DAMIS (*pointing to the other*): Where he chooses!

ANTHONY: But who is he?

DAMIS: Have you looked upon him?

ANTHONY (*aside*): He looks like a saint! If I only dared . . .

(The smoke and the fog have gone. The night is very clear. The moon shines.)

DAMIS: Why don't you speak? What are you thinking?

ANTHONY: I fancied—Oh! Nothing!

(Damis, bending low, with his eyes on the ground, approaches Apollonius, and goes round about him several times:)

Master! It is a Galilæan hermit who asks to know the beginnings of wisdom.

APOLLONIUS: Let him come near!

(Anthony hesitates.)

DAMIS: Approach.

APOLLONIUS (*in a voice of thunder*): Approach! You would know who I am, what I have done, what I think? Is it not so, my son?

ANTHONY: But only if such things can help to my salvation.

APOLLONIUS: Be glad, then, for I will speak!

DAMIS (*aside to Anthony*): Incredible! He must have seen in you at the very first glance some unusual talent for philosophy! I also will try to profit!

APOLLONIUS: I will tell you, to begin with, by how long a road I travelled to win this knowledge, and if in all my life you find one evil action you must

THE TEMPTATION OF ST. ANTHONY

tell me—for he who has done wrong by his actions may cause others to stumble by his words.

DAMIS (*to Anthony*): What a righteous man! Eh?

ANTHONY: There's no doubt of his sincerity.

APOLLONIUS: The night that I was born, my mother dreamed that she was gathering flowers on the edge of a lake. There came a flash of lightning, and she gave me birth, amid the music of swans that sang to her in her dream.

Until my fifteenth year, thrice was I plunged, each day, in the fountain of Asbadeus, whose waters affect perjurers with dropsy; and my body was rubbed with nettle-leaves, to keep me chaste.

A princess from Palmyra came to me one evening, offering to show me the whereabouts of treasures that she had found in some tombs. A temple-servant of Diana, in despair, slew herself with the sacrificial knife; and the Governor of Cilicia, when all his blandishments had proved of no avail, cried out, before all my family, that he would have me put to death; but it was he who died, three days later, assassinated by the Romans.

DAMIS (*to Anthony, nudging him with his elbow*): Eh! What did I tell you? What a man!

APOLLONIUS: Four successive years did I preserve the Pythagorean silence. Not even the most sudden pain could draw a sigh from me; and when I entered the theatre, folk withdrew from me as from a phantom.

DAMIS (*to Anthony*): And you—could you have done that?

APOLLONIUS: When my novitiate was ended, I

undertook the instruction of priests who had lost the tradition.

ANTHONY: What tradition?

DAMIS: Be quiet! Let him go on!

APOLLONIUS: I have shared familiar talk with the Samaneans of the Ganges, the astrologers of Chaldæa, the mages of Babylon, with the Druids in Gaul, and with negro medicine-men! I have climbed the fourteen Olympian peaks, sounded the Scythian lakes, measured the width and the breadth of the Great Desert!

DAMIS: Every word is true; for I myself was with him!

APOLLONIUS: But before that I had been as far as the Caspian Sea. I made the tour of it, and then came down, through the country of the Baraomutæ where Bucephalus is buried, towards Nineveh. At the gates of the city, a man approached me . . .

DAMIS: It was I, my dear master. I! and I loved you, on the instant! You were gentler than a girl, and as beautiful as a god!

APOLLONIUS (*who has not heard him*): He asked if he might come with me, as my interpreter?

DAMIS: But you answered that you understood all languages, and could divine all thoughts. And I kissed the hem of your mantle, and set my face to follow after you.

APOLLONIUS: Leaving Ctesiphon, we came to the country round about Babylon.

DAMIS: And the Governor cried out to see a man so pale.

ANTHONY (*aside*): And it meant . . . ?

THE TEMPTATION OF ST. ANTHONY

APOLLONIUS: The king received me, standing by a silver throne, in a circular hall, clustered with stars, and from the dome were hanging, by invisible cords, four great birds of gold, with outstretched wings.

ANTHONY (*dreamily*): Can there be such things in all the world?

DAMIS: There's a city for you! That Babylon! Everyone is wealthy! The houses, painted blue, have gates of bronze, and the steps go down to the river.

(Tracing lines on the ground with his stick :)

Like that! See? And there are temples and squares and baths and aqueducts! The palace-roofs are of red copper! And if you could but see inside!

APOLLONIUS: Upon the north wall rises a tower which supports a second, a third, a fourth, a fifth—and there are still three others! The eighth is a chapel where there is a bed. None may enter there save the woman chosen by the priests for the god Belus. The King of Babylon himself installed me there.

DAMIS: But nobody took any notice of me! And so I walked about the streets by myself. I became familiar with the customs of the place; entered the workshops; saw the mighty contrivances that carry water to the gardens. But it irked me to be separated from my master.

APOLLONIUS: In due time we left Babylon, and in the moonlight we suddenly saw a spectre.

DAMIS: Oh, yes! She sprang up and down on

her iron hoofs; brayed like a donkey; galloped about among the rocks. He shouted at her, and she disappeared.

ANTHONY (*to himself*): What are they driving at?

APOLLONIUS: At Taxilla, the capital of five thousand fortified places, Phraortes, King of the Ganges, showed us his guard of black men, each of them five cubits high, and in his palace-gardens, under a pavilion of green brocade, an enormous elephant, about whose toilet the Queens were busy. It was the elephant of Porus, which escaped after the death of Alexander.

DAMIS: And was found again in a forest.

ANTHONY: They babble like drunken men!

APOLLONIUS: Phraortes made us sit at his table.

DAMIS: And what a queer country it was! The lords, while they drank, amused themselves by shooting arrows round about the feet of a dancing child. . . . But I disapprove. . . .

APOLLONIUS: When I was ready to depart, the King gave me a parasol, saying: " On the Indus I have a stud of white camels. When you have done with them, blow in their ears, and they will come home."

We descended the river, walking at night by the light of the fire-flies which glittered among the tall grasses. The slave whistled a tune to keep snakes away; and our camels bent their backs beneath the trees, as though passing through little gateways.

One day a black child, with a herald's wand of gold in his hand, led us to the College of the Sages. Iarchas, their chief, spoke of my ancestors, of my most secret thoughts and deeds, of my several existences. Once, he said, he was the River Indus, and he assured me that I had been a boatman on the Nile, in the days of King Sesostris.

DAMIS: They said nothing about me, though, so that I know not what I may have been!

ANTHONY: There is something unsubstantial-looking about them, as though they were mere shadows.

APOLLONIUS: On the sea-beach we met the wild men who have dogs' heads. They were gorged with milk, and were returning from an expedition to the Island of Ceylon. The lukewarm waters rolled tawny pearls about our feet. Amber cracked beneath our steps. Skeletons of whales whitened in the crevices of the cliffs. The land, at length, became no broader than a sandal's width; and when we had sprinkled drops of ocean-water towards the sun, we turned to the right, on our homeward way.

And thus we came back through the Land of Spices, and through Bengal, past the promontory of Comaria, through the territories of the Sachalites, the Adramites and the Homerites—then, across the Cassanian mountains, the Red Sea and the Island of Topazon, we entered Ethiopia by way of the kingdom of the Pygmies.

ANTHONY (*to himself*): What a big world it is!

DAMIS: And when we got home, everyone that we used to know was dead.

(Anthony bows his head. Silence.)

APOLLONIUS (*goes on again*): And then I began

to be spoken of in the world. The plague was ravaging Ephesus; I persuaded them to stone an old beggar.

DAMIS: And the plague ceased!

ANTHONY: What! He drives disease away?

APOLLONIUS: At Cnidos I cured a fellow who was smitten by Venus.

DAMIS: Yes, a fool, who actually vowed that he would wed her! . . . To love a woman may be well enough; but a statue! . . . What foolery! . . . The Master put his hand on the man's heart, and his longing instantly died out.

ANTHONY: Why! He casteth out devils!

APOLLONIUS: At Tarentum, the body of a maiden was being carried out for burning.

DAMIS: The Master touched her lips, and she arose, calling for her mother.

ANTHONY: What! He raises the dead?

APOLLONIUS: I predicted to Vespasian his acquisition of power.

ANTHONY: Why! He foretells the future!

DAMIS: At Corinth there was . . .

APOLLONIUS: Being at table with him in the Baths at Baiæ . . .

ANTHONY: Forgive me, strangers, but it grows late!

DAMIS: A young man called Menippus . . .

ANTHONY: No! No! Begone!

APOLLONIUS: A dog came in, carrying in his mouth a severed hand.

DAMIS: One evening, in a suburb, he met a woman.

ANTHONY: Do you not hear? Go away!

APOLLONIUS: He prowled uncertainly round the couches.

ANTHONY: That will do!

APOLLONIUS: They tried to drive him away.

DAMIS: So Menippus went home with her, and they . . .

APOLLONIUS: And tapping the mosaic with his tail, he laid that hand upon the knees of Flavius.

DAMIS: But next morning, in school, Menippus was very pale.

ANTHONY (*jumping up*): Still more? Oh! Let them go on since there is not . . .

DAMIS: The Master said to him: "O beautiful youth, you fondle a serpent, and a serpent is fondling you! When is the wedding to be?" We all went to the wedding.

ANTHONY: I do wrong, I know, to listen to this!

DAMIS: In the vestibule, servants were fidgeting about, doors were being opened; and yet there was no sound of footsteps or of closing doors. The Master kept near Menippus. And then the bride became furious with the philosophers. But the golden plates and dishes, the cup-bearers, the cooks, the pantrymen, all disappeared; the roof flew away, the walls fell in; and Apollonius stood there alone, with that woman all in tears at his feet. She was a vampire who gave pleasure to beautiful young men, so that she might eat their flesh—for nothing better suits that sort of phantom than the blood of enamoured youths.

APOLLONIUS: If you want to know how to . . .

ANTHONY: I don't want to know anything!

APOLLONIUS: The night we arrived at the gates of Rome . . .

ANTHONY: Oh, yes! Tell me about the city of the popes!

APOLLONIUS: A drunken man greeted us, singing a melodious song. It was a marriage-song of Nero, with power to slay anyone who should listen to it carelessly. He carried, in a box upon his back, a string plucked from the Emperor's cithara. I shrugged my shoulders. He threw mud in our faces. Then I pulled off my girdle, and placed it in his hand.

DAMIS: Upon my word, that was very wrong of you!

APOLLONIUS: During the night the Emperor sent for me to his house. He was playing knuckle-bones with Sporus, leaning with his left arm on a table of agate. He turned towards me, and frowning with his blond eyebrows, asked me: "Why are you not afraid?" And I answered: "Because the god who made you terrible also made me intrepid!"

ANTHONY (*to himself*): Something terrifies me—something inexplicable!

(Silence.)

DAMIS (*begins again in a shrill voice*): All Asia, moreover, can tell you . . .

ANTHONY (*starting up*): I am ill! Leave me!

DAMIS: Just listen a moment! He saw them, while he was at Ephesus, killing Domitian, who was at Rome.

ANTHONY (*forcing a laugh*): Is it possible?

DAMIS: Yes, in the theatre, in broad daylight, on

THE TEMPTATION OF ST. ANTHONY

the fourteenth of the kalends of October, he suddenly cried out: "They are killing Cæsar!" and from time to time he would add: "He is rolling on the ground. Oh! how he struggles! He gets up and tries to flee; the doors are shut! Ah! it is all over! He is dead!" And as a matter of fact, Titus Flavius Domitianus was assassinated that very day, as you know.

ANTHONY: If it were not for the help of the Devil, certainly . . .

APOLLONIUS: He had meant to kill me, that same Domitian! Damis had fled, by my orders, and I was alone in my prison.

DAMIS: A most daring business, it must be confessed!

APOLLONIUS: About the fifth hour, the soldiers led me to the tribunal. I had my speech all ready, and was holding it under my mantle.

DAMIS: We others were then on the shore at Puteoli! We thought you were dead; we were weeping. When, at the sixth hour, you suddenly appeared, you said to us: "It is I!"

ANTHONY (*to himself*): Just as He said!

DAMIS (*very loudly*): Exactly!

ANTHONY: Oh, no! You lie, do you not? You lie!

APOLLONIUS: He came down from heaven. I ascend thither—by virtue of the power which has raised me to the level of the First Principle!

DAMIS: Thyana, where he was born, has instituted a temple in his honour, and a priesthood!

APOLLONIUS (*comes near to Anthony, and shouts in his ear*): It is because I know all the gods; all rites, all prayers, all oracles! I have descended into the cave of Trophonius, son of Apollo! I have kneaded the cakes which the Syracusan women carry to the mountains! I have undergone the eighty tests of Mithra! I have clasped in my bosom the serpent of Sabazius! I have received the scarf of the Cabiri! I have purified Cybele in the waves of the Campanian gulfs, and spent three moons in the caverns of Samothrace!

DAMIS (*laughing foolishly*): Ha-ha-ha! The mysteries of the Great Goddess!

APOLLONIUS: And now we begin our pilgrimage again!

We go to the north, among the swans and the snows, where on the white plains the blind men with horses' feet trample the blue herbage with their hoofs.

DAMIS: Come! The day dawns. The cock has crowed, the horse has neighed, and the sail is hoisted.

ANTHONY: The cock has not crowed! I hear the cricket in the sand, and I can still see the moon in the sky.

APOLLONIUS: We go to the south, beyond the mountains and the mighty waves, to search among the perfumes for the meaning of love. You shall breathe the odour of balsam which brings death to feeble folk. You shall lave your body in the lake of oil-of-roses in the Isle of Junonia. You shall behold, asleep upon the primroses, the lizard which awakens once in a hundred years when the carbuncle in its forehead ripens and drops to the ground. The stars sparkle like eyes, the fountains sing with the music of lyres, intoxication is in the breath of

THE TEMPTATION OF ST. ANTHONY

blowing flowers; and in your heart and upon your countenance will be shown how the mind of a man expands in that wide atmosphere!

DAMIS: Master, it is time! The wind rises, the swallows awaken, the myrtle-leaves have blown away.

APOLLONIUS: Yes, let us go!

ANTHONY: But I shall stay where I am!

APOLLONIUS: I will teach you where Balis grows, the herb which revives the dead.

DAMIS: Ask him rather for the blood-stone which attracts silver and iron and brass!

ANTHONY: Oh! How I suffer! How I suffer!

DAMIS: You shall understand the voices of all creatures, their roarings and their cooings!

APOLLONIUS: I will mount you upon unicorns and dragons, upon centaurs and dolphins!

ANTHONY (*weeping*): Oh! Oh! Oh!

APOLLONIUS: You shall know the demons that dwell in the caverns, that whisper in the woods, and those that move the waves and drive the clouds along.

DAMIS: Gird up your loins! Fasten your sandals!

APOLLONIUS: I will teach you the meanings of the divine appearances, why Apollo always stands upright, but Jupiter sits; why Venus is black at Corinth, square in Athens, cone-shaped at Paphos.

ANTHONY (*clasping his hands*): If they would but go! If only they would go away!

APOLLONIUS: Before your very eyes I will remove their wrappings from the gods; we will break open their sanctuaries; you shall violate the Pythia!

ANTHONY: O my God! Help! Help!

(He rushes towards the cross.)

APOLLONIUS: What do you desire most of all? Of what do you dream? Just think of it now, and . . .

ANTHONY: Jesus! Jesus! help me!

APOLLONIUS: And this Jesus! Shall I make him appear to you?

ANTHONY: What! How?

APOLLONIUS: It will be Jesus himself! Not another! He will lay aside his crown, and talk with us face to face.

DAMIS (*in a low tone*): Say you wish it! Tell him that you wish it indeed!

(Anthony is murmuring prayers at the foot of the cross. Damis walks round him, making enticing gestures.)

Come, come, good hermit, dear Saint Anthony! Illustrious man! Man so pure! Whom it were impossible to praise too highly! Be not shocked! I do but use a flowery fashion of speech which I learned in the Orient. But there is really no reason why . . .

APOLLONIUS: Leave him, Damis!

He believes, as do the beasts, in the reality of things. His fear of the gods hinders his understanding of them, and even his own god he debases to the level of a jealous king!

But do not you desert me, my son!

(He edges backwards to the brow of the precipice, and then beyond it, and hovers, suspended in the air.)

Underneath the outward appearances, farther off than the ends of the earth, higher than the heavens, lies the world of Ideas, filled by the Word! In a

THE TEMPTATION OF ST. ANTHONY 251

single bound we shall cross all intervening space; and you shall grasp in his infinity the Eternal, the Absolute, the Self-existent! Come! Give me your hand! Let us set out!

(Slowly, side by side, Apollonius and Damis rise through the air. Anthony, clinging to the cross, watches them go.
They disappear.)

V

ANTHONY (*walking slowly up and down*): Nothing in hell itself could equal that!

Nebuchadnezzar did not dazzle me so much. . . .

The Queen of Sheba could not charm me so completely. . . .

When he spoke of the gods, I longed to know them. . . .

I remember seeing hundreds of them at one time, in the Isle of Elephantis, in the days of Diocletian. The Emperor had granted a piece of territory to the wandering tribes, on condition that they should guard the frontiers; and the treaty was to be concluded in the name of " the Invisible Powers." For the gods of each were unknown to the others.

The barbarians had brought theirs with them, and they were camped on the sandhills along the river. We saw them nursing their idols in their arms, as though they were big crippled babies; or steering themselves through the cataracts on palm-trunks, with amulets, even at that distance, visible on their necks, and tattooing on their chests—and that was no worse than the religion of the Greeks and the Asiatics and the Romans!

When I was at the temple of Heliopolis I often examined the pictures on the walls: vultures bearing sceptres, crocodiles playing upon lyres, bodies of serpents with faces of men, cow-headed women prostrate beneath obscene gods; and those supernatural shapes allured my thoughts to other worlds. I longed to know what it was at which those calm eyes were gazing.

If a mere material representation can have such influence, it must assuredly contain a spirit; and so it seems that the souls of the gods are linked-up with their images.

Those who have outward beauty might ensnare a man! But what of the others, base or terrible—what about them?

(And close to the ground he sees moving leaves, stones, shells, branches of trees, indistinct outlines of animals, and then a company of dropsically swollen dwarfs: these are gods! And he bursts out laughing at them.

Another laugh breaks out behind him; and Hilarion appears—dressed as a hermit, and much taller than before—gigantic!)

ANTHONY (*who is not surprised to see him again*): How stupid a man must be, to worship such as those!

HILARION: Oh, yes! Very stupid indeed!

(Then there pass before them, in single file, the idols of all nations and of all time—of wood, of metal, of granite, of feathers, and of sewn skins.

The oldest, of days before the Deluge, are half hidden under sea-weed that hangs, like horses' manes, upon their necks. Some, too big and heavy for their feet, crack at the joints and break at the back when they try to walk. Others have sand running out from holes in their bellies.

THE TEMPTATION OF ST. ANTHONY

This gives abundant amusement to Anthony and Hilarion, who hold their sides for laughing.

Then come some sheep-faced idols, staggering along upon their crook-kneed limbs, with eyelids only half open; and these make noises like dumb men : " Ba ! Ba-a-a ! Ba ! "

The more nearly these idols approach the human form, the more do they anger Anthony, who strikes them with his fists, kicks them with his feet, sets furiously at them.

Some frightful figures appear—with high tufts on their heads, eyes that bulge, arms that end in claws, sharks' jaws.

And to these gods men are sacrificing men on stone altars; others are being pounded in great tubs, or crushed beneath the wheels of chariots. There is one, of red-hot iron, who swallows children.)

ANTHONY : Horrible !

HILARION : But gods must always have their victims ! Why ! Even your own god was pleased . . .

ANTHONY (*weeping*) : Stop ! Do not finish that . . . !

(The amphitheatre of the rocks changes to a valley. A herd of oxen feeds on the scanty grass.

The countryman in charge of them notices a cloud—and in a shrill voice utters some peremptory words to the sky above him.)

HILARION : Wanting food for the cattle, he tries by his incantations to compel the King of Heaven to release the fruitful rain.

ANTHONY (*laughing*) : What witless presumption !

HILARION : And why do you yourself use exorcisms ?

(The valley becomes a sea of milk, still and limitless.

In the middle of it floats a long cradle, formed by the coils of a serpent, whose many curving heads enshadow a god asleep upon its body.

He is young, beardless, more beautiful than a maiden,

and covered with transparent veils. The pearls in his head-dress shine softly like moons, a garland of stars is wound many times about his breast—and with one hand beneath his head and the other arm stretched out, he slumbers as one who has drunk deeply and who now dreams.

A woman crouches at his feet, and waits for his awaking.)

HILARION: It is the primordial duality of the Brahmans—the Absolute which may not be expressed by any form.

(Upon the navel of the god a lotus-stem has flowered; and within its cup appears another god with three faces.)

ANTHONY: What a strange conception!

HILARION:[1] Father, Son and Holy Spirit likewise are but one!

(The three faces vanish, and three great gods appear:—
The first, rosy-coloured, is biting the end of his big toe.
The second, blue, waves his four arms.
The third, green, has a necklace of human skulls.

In front of them at the same moment arise three goddesses, one wrapped in a net, another offering a cup, the third brandishing a bow.

And these gods and goddesses increase and multiply tenfold. Arms grow upon their shoulders, and from these arms spring hands, holding standards, axes, shields, swords, parasols and drums. Fountains issue from their heads, growing plants drop down from their nostrils.

Riding upon birds, rocked in palanquins, seated in state upon golden thrones, standing in ivory niches, they dream, they travel, they give commands, drink wine, inhale the scent of flowers. Dancing-girls go whirling; giants pursue monsters; hermits are meditating in the doorways of their grottos. Eyes confuse themselves with stars, and clouds with streamers; peacocks drink from rivers of gold-dust, the

---

[1] "Père, Fils et Saint-Esprit ne font de même qu'une *seule personne!*" Even Homer nods at times; but Flaubert should have allowed Hilarion to know better than that!—Trans.

broider-work of tents mingles with the spots of leopards; and in the air there are flying arrows and swinging censers and the criss-cross of multi-coloured glowing rays of light.

And all of this unrolls like a lofty frieze, resting upon the rocks, and reaching even to the skies.)

ANTHONY (*dazzled*): What a multitude! And what is it that they seek?

HILARION: The one who scratches his stomach with his elephant-trunk is the Sun God, who infuses wisdom.

That other, whose six heads carry six towers, and his fourteen arms a javelin apiece, is the Prince of Armies, Devouring Fire.

The old man on a crocodile cleanses the souls of dead men on the river bank. They will be tormented by that black woman with decaying teeth, who is Mistress of the Infernal Regions.

The chariot, drawn by red mares, and driven by a legless coachman, bears the Governor of the Sun through the heaven's azure height. With him goes the Moon God, in a litter to which three gazelles are yoked.

Kneeling on a parrot's back, the Goddess of Beauty offers to Love, her son, her rounded breast. There she is again, farther off, leaping joyfully in the meadows. See! See! With dazzling mitre on her head, she passes over the cornfield, over the waves, rises into the air, scatters herself in all directions!

Along with these gods are seated the presiding deities of the winds, the planets, the months, the days, and a hundred thousand more! And their appearances vary from time to time, and their transformations are speedy! One there is that from fish becomes tortoise; and then again he assumes the jowl of a wild boar, with the figure of a dwarf.

ANTHONY: And why?

HILARION: To preserve the balance of things—to combat evil. Life exhausts itself; outward forms wear away; and if they move onward they must move by way of metamorphosis.

(Suddenly appears A NAKED MAN seated in the midst of the sand, his legs crossed.

A halo, large and vibrating, swings behind him. The little ringlets of his black hair, through which flash bluish lights, go symmetrically round a prominence on the top of his skull. His arms, unusually long, hang straight down by his sides. His two hands, with open palms, rest flat against his thighs. The under parts of his feet resemble two suns; and he keeps perfectly still—in front of Anthony and Hilarion—with the gods round him, one beside the other on the rocks, as on the seats in a circus.

His lips open a little; and in a deep voice :)

I am the Great Almoner, the provider of all that has been created, and both to believers and to the profane I expound the law.

For the deliverance of the world I willed to be born among men. The gods lamented when I left them.

First of all I sought out a woman suitable: of warrior blood, spouse of a king, most good, most beautiful, well-formed of body, and with flesh compact as the diamond; and at the time of the full moon, without intervention of any other, I entered into her womb.

I issued forth from her right side. Some of the stars stood still.

HILARION (*under his breath*): " And when they saw the star, they rejoiced with exceeding great joy."

THE TEMPTATION OF ST. ANTHONY

(Anthony looks more closely at THE BUDDHA, who goes on :)

From a monastery away in the Himalayas, one who was a hundred years old came hurrying to see me.

HILARION: " A man whose name was Simeon . . . he should not see death, before he had seen the Lord's Christ."

THE BUDDHA: I was sent to school, but I already knew more than my teachers.

HILARION: " In the midst of the doctors . . . and all that heard him were astonished at his understanding and answers."

(Anthony beckons to Hilarion to be silent.)

THE BUDDHA: Unendingly did I meditate in the gardens. The shadows of the trees moved with the moving of the sun; but the shadow of the tree that sheltered me moved not.

None could equal me in knowledge of the scriptures, the enumeration of the atoms, the management of elephants, the working of wax, in astronomy, poesy, boxing, in every exercise, or in any of the arts!

According to the custom of my country, I took a wife—and I passed the days in my royal palace, covered with pearls, beneath showers of perfume, and cooled by the fans of three and thirty thousand women, watching my subjects from the height of my terraces, surrounded by the echoing of bells.

But the sight of the miseries of the world turned me aside from pleasure; and I fled.

I begged upon the roads, covered in rags which

I had gathered among the tombs; and when I heard of a most learned hermit I chose to become his slave; I kept his door, I washed his feet.

All sensation was annihilated, all joy, all weariness.

Then, turning my thoughts to wider meditation, I achieved an understanding of the essences of things, of the illusion of outward shapes.

I very quickly exhausted the science of the Brahmans. They are eaten up with covetousness under their apparent austerity—plastering themselves with filth, lying upon thorns, hoping to attain to happiness along the pathway of death!

HILARION: " Pharisees, hypocrites — whited sepulchres—generation of vipers!"

THE BUDDHA: I too! Some wondrous things I did—eating but a single grain of rice each day—and grains of rice were no bigger in those days than they are now—my hair fell out, my skin blackened; my eyes, sunk within their sockets, looked like the stars that men see at the bottoms of wells.

For six years I remained motionless, exposed to flies, to lions and serpents; and the great suns, the mighty floods, snows and thunderbolts, hail and tempest—all these things I underwent without the shelter even of my lifted hand.

Passing travellers thought that I was dead, and they stood and hurled clods of earth at me from a distance.

There remained the temptation of the Devil.

I summoned him.

His sons came—hideous, covered with scales, noisome as charnel-houses, howling, wheezing,

THE TEMPTATION OF ST. ANTHONY

bellowing, clashing their armour and rattling dead men's bones. Some spat fire through their nostrils, some threw shadows with their wings, some wore strings of chopped-off fingers, some quaffed serpents' venom from the hollows of their hands; they had the heads of swine, of rhinoceroses or of toads, all manner of forms that could inspire disgust or terror.

ANTHONY (*aside*): I also, in my time, endured all that!

THE BUDDHA: Then he sent his daughters—lovely, their faces beautifully painted, with girdles of gold, their teeth as white as jasmine, and their thighs as round as an elephant's trunk. Some stretched out their arms and yawned, to show the dimples on their elbows; some winked with their eyes, some began to smile, and some to unfasten their robes. There were blushing virgins, haughty matrons, and queens with great trains of baggages and slaves.

ANTHONY (*aside*): Ah! He too . . . ?

THE BUDDHA: Having overcome the demon, I subsisted for twelve years on perfumes only—and forasmuch as I had acquired the five virtues, the five faculties, the ten energies, the eighteen essential parts, and penetrated the four spheres of the world invisible, Intelligence became mine! I became the Buddha!

(The gods all bow themselves down; those with several heads bending all of them at once.

He raises an authoritative hand and resumes:)

For the deliverance of creatures I have made sacrifices by the hundred thousand. I bestowed silken robes upon the poor, and beds, and chariots, and houses, and heaps of gold and diamonds. My own hands I gave to the one-armed, my legs to the lame, my eyes to the blind; I cut off my head for the headless. When I was a king I dealt out provinces; when I was a Brahman, I despised no one. When I was a monk I spoke gentle words to the robber who slew me. When I was a tiger, I let myself die of hunger.

But now, in this last existence, having preached the law, there is nothing left for me to do. The great period is accomplished. Men, animals, gods, bamboos, oceans, mountains, grains of sand in the Ganges, with the myriads upon myriads of the stars, all shall die; and until the new births begin, a flame shall dance upon the ruins of worlds destroyed!

(Then a dizziness overtakes the gods. They stagger, go into convulsions, and vomit up their very beings. Their crowns split, their banners are blown away. They tear off their attributes, their sex, throw over their shoulders the cups from which they drank their immortality, strangle themselves with their serpents, vanish in smoke—and when all have disappeared . . .)

HILARION (*slowly*): You have now beheld the outward symbols of the faith of many hundreds of millions of men!

(Anthony is prostrate on the ground, his face in his hands. Standing by him, and with his back turned to the cross, Hilarion watches him.

A considerable time elapses.

Then a singular being appears, having a man's head on the body of a fish. It approaches through the air, upright, and thrashing the sand with its tail—and the venerable face with its tiny arm sets Anthony laughing.)

OANNES (*in a plaintive voice*): Honour me! I was contemporary with the beginning of things.

I dwelt in that unformed world in which slumbered hermaphroditic beasts, weighed down by an opaque atmosphere, in the depths of the dark waters—when fingers and fins and wings were all tangled together; and when eyes, belonging to no head, floated like molluscs, amongst bulls with human faces and serpents with the feet of dogs.

Over this assemblage of beings Omoroga, bent like a hoop, spread her womanly body. But Belus cut her in twain, making of one half the earth, and of the other heaven; and these two equal worlds face one towards the other.

I, the earliest consciousness that emerged from Chaos, rose from the abysm to give hardness to matter, and arrangement to form; and to man I taught fishing and sowing, and the art of writing, and the history of the gods.

Since then, I have dwelt in the pools left by the Deluge. But about those pools the desert enlarges; into them the winds blow sand, and the thirsty sun swallows them up—and I lie upon my slimy couch, and watch the stars through the water. And thither I return.

(He leaps in the air, and then disappears in the Nile.)

HILARION: That was an ancient god of the Chaldæans!

ANTHONY (*ironically*): Then of what sort were the gods of Babylon?

HILARION: You shall see them!

(And they find themselves upon the topmost platform of a four-sided tower which overlooks six other towers which, becoming narrower as they rise, form one prodigious pyramid. Beneath, a great black mass is visible—the city, no doubt—spread out upon the plains. The air is cold, the sky a melancholy blue; multitudinous stars are throbbing.

In the middle of the platform rises a column of white stone. Priests in linen robes pass and repass about it, so as to describe by their movements a turning circle; and with uplifted heads they gaze at the stars.)

HILARION (*points out some of these to Anthony*): There are thirty principal stars. Half of these look upon the upper parts of the earth, and half upon the lower. At regular intervals one of them shoots from the upper regions towards those below, whilst another leaves the lower and mounts towards the height.

Of the seven planets, two are beneficent, two evil, three of uncertain quality; and upon these eternal fires all mundane matters depend. From their positions and their movements in the sky, the future may be foretold—the soil on which your feet are fixed is the most venerable on earth—here met Pythagoras and Zoroaster; and from this place for twelve thousand years men have watched the skies that so they might better know the gods.

ANTHONY: But the stars are not gods.

HILARION: But yes! For so men say! All things round about us vanish; but the heavens remain, eternal and unchanging!

ANTHONY: But even they have their master.

HILARION (*pointing to the column*): He, Belus, the first ray, the Sun, the Male! That Other, whom he impregnates, is beneath him!

(Anthony beholds a garden, lit with lamps.

He is in the midst of a crowd, in an avenue of cypress-trees. To right and left, little pathways lead to huts built

THE TEMPTATION OF ST. ANTHONY

in a forest of pomegranate-trees, and sheltered by reedy trellises.

Most of the men wear pointed caps, and robes as gorgeous as the plumage of peacocks. But people there also are from the north, clad in bears' skins, nomads in dark woollen cloaks, pale men from the Ganges, with long ear-rings; and their categories would seem to be as various as their nationalities, for sailors rub shoulders with princes who wear tiaras of carbuncles and carry long rods with carved heads. But they all press forward with dilated nostrils, united in the one desire.

From time to time they step aside, to give way to long covered wagons drawn by oxen, or it may be to a donkey jolting on his back a heavily-veiled woman, who disappears, with the others, in the direction of the huts.

Anthony is afraid, and has half a mind to turn back : but an indescribable curiosity carries him on.

Beneath the cypress-trees are rows of women wrapped in deer-skins, each with a braided fillet of cords which she wears like a crown. Some, magnificently dressed, call loudly to the passers-by. Others, more timid, hide their faces in their arms, whilst older women behind them—their mothers, perhaps—speak words of encouragement. And there are yet others, with their heads hidden in black shawls and their bodies quite naked, who from a distance look like statues of flesh. As soon as a man has thrown some money into their laps, these women get up.

And among the foliage is heard the sound of kissing— sometimes a loud, sharp cry.)

HILARION : These are the virgins of Babylon who prostitute themselves to the goddess.

ANTHONY : What goddess is that ?

HILARION : Behold her !

(And he shows him, at the very end of the avenue, at the entrance to an illuminated grotto, a block of stone representing Venus Genetrix.)

ANTHONY : For shame ! How abominable is this attribution of sex to God !

HILARION: But yet you think of him yourself as a living person!

(Anthony finds himself again in darkness.
And then he sees, in the air, a luminous circle, hovering upon horizontal wings.
This circle surrounds, as though with a loose girdle, the loins of a small man, wearing a mitre and carrying a crown in his hand, the lower part of his body being hidden by large feathers spread round him like a petticoat.
This is ORMUZ, the god of the Persians. He flutters in the air, and cries:)

I am afraid! I caught a glimpse of his jaws!

I had triumphed, Ahriman! But now you attack me again!

When first you revolted against me, you destroyed the earliest of creatures, Kaiomortz, the Man-Bull. Next you seduced the first pair of human beings, Meschia and Meschiana; and you put darkness into the hearts of men, and sent forth your battalions against heaven.

But I, too, had my followers, the people of the stars; and seated on my throne I looked out upon all the marshalled hosts of heaven.

Inaccessibly remote, Mithra, my son, dwelt in a place where he received souls, and from whence he sent them forth, and each morning he arose to spread abroad his abundance.

The splendour of the firmament was reflected by the earth. Fire blazed upon the mountains—symbol of that other fire from which I had created all being. That it might remain pure and undefiled, no dead were to be burned; but birds carried them in their beaks towards heaven.

I had made all needful rules for the pastures, and

THE TEMPTATION OF ST. ANTHONY

for work, and as to wood proper for sacrifices, as to the shape of cups, and the words to be used by those who could not sleep—and my priests prayed continually, so that their worship might have part in the unending duration of God. Men purified themselves with water, offered meal upon the altars, and confessed aloud their sins.

Homa gave himself to mankind, to be their drink, and to impart to them his strength.

While the genii of heaven were fighting against the demons, the children of Iran pursued the serpents. The king, upon whom uncounted kneeling courtiers waited, took my personality and assumed my appearance. His gardens had the glories of a terrestrial paradise; and upon his tomb he was himself depicted in the act of slaying a monster —to represent the extermination of Evil by Good.

For, in the course of endless time, I was destined once and for all to vanquish Ahriman.

But the space that separates the two of us is shrinking! The darkness gathers! Help! Amschaspands, Izeds, Ferouers! Help! Mithra! Take up the sword! Caosyac, who shall return for the universal deliverance, defend me! What! . . . None to help? . . .

Ah! I perish! Ahriman, thou at last hast overcome me!

(Hilarion, who is behind Anthony, checks a cry of joy— and Ormuz plunges into the darkness.

Then appears THE GREAT DIANA OF EPHESUS, black, with glassy eyes, her elbows by her sides, her forearms turned outwards, her hands open.

Lions creep upon her shoulders; fruits and flowers and stars wreathe about her bosom; and beneath are three rows of breasts; from her belly to her feet she is encased in a tight-fitting sheath, from which bulls, stags, griffins and bees thrust forth a half of their bodies. She is revealed by the white light of a silver disc, round as the full moon, set behind her head.)

Where is my temple?

Where are my amazons?

What has happened to me—to me, the incorruptible, that faintness thus overwhelms me!

(Her flowers wither. Her fruit becomes overripe and falls. The lions and bulls bend their necks; the stags, exhausted, dribble at the mouth; the bees, buzzing, fall dead on the ground.

One after another, she squeezes her breasts, but they are all empty. In her desperate effort, her sheath bursts; she grasps it at the bottom, as though gathering up the front of a robe, throws into it her animals, her blossoms—then vanishes in the gloom.

And far away there are voices murmuring, scolding, roaring, braying, bellowing. The thickness of the night becomes yet thicker with the breath of living things; drops of warm rain fall.)

ANTHONY: How sweet are the odours of the palm-trees, the tremblings of the green leaves, the clarity of the springs! I would lie flat upon the earth, and feel her against my heart; and my life should be plunged anew in her eternal youth.

(He hears the sound of castanets and of cymbals—and amid a rustic crowd some men appear, clothed in white tunics banded with scarlet, leading a donkey richly caparisoned, its tail decked out with ribbons, its hoofs brightly coloured.

A box, draped in yellow linen, shakes about upon its back, between two baskets, one of which is open to receive the offerings placed in it: eggs, grapes, pears, cheeses, fowls, small pieces of money: the other being filled with roses,

THE TEMPTATION OF ST. ANTHONY

the leaves of which the drivers of the donkey pluck off and scatter before him as he walks.

They have ear-rings, large cloaks, matted hair, painted cheeks; wreaths of olive are fastened on their foreheads by medallions bearing small figures; there are poniards in their belts, and the whips which they flourish in their hands are ebony-handled, each having three thongs strung with knuckle-bones.

The hindermost of these men place upright upon the ground, like a candlestick, a tall pine-tree, alight at the top, under whose lowest branches a lamb shelters.

The donkey has stopped. The cloth is taken off, and underneath appears a second covering of black felt. Then one of the men in white tunics begins to dance, rattling his castanets; another, on his knees before the box, beats a tambourine, and—THE OLDEST OF THE COMPANY begins :)

Here is the Good Goddess, the archetype of the mountains, the mother of Syria! Draw near, honest people!

It is she who brings joy, heals sickness, bestows inheritances, and satisfies the longing of lovers.

We are the men who lead her through the lands, in fair weather and in foul.

Often we must sleep in the open air; and not for us, day by day, is there always a table spread. In the woods there are robbers. Wild beasts rush out upon us as we pass their dens. Paths on the edge of precipices are sometimes slippery. Behold her! Behold her!

(They raise the covering; and a box is seen, inlaid with small pebbles.)

Higher than the cedars, she soars in the blue ether. Vaster than the wind, she encompasses the world. Her breath exhales from the nostrils of tigers; her voice rumbles in the volcanoes; the pallor of her face it is which has whitened the moon. And it is she who ripens the harvests, swelling the skins and making the prickles grow. Make her an offering, for she hates miserly men!

(The box opens; and beneath a covering of blue silk is seen a tiny image of Cybele—glittering with spangles, with a lofty head-dress, and seated in a chariot of red stone, drawn by two lions with uplifted paws.
The crowd presses forward to look at THE ARCHGALLUS, who continues:)

She delights in the tinkle of tambourines, the stamping of feet, the howling of wolves, in echoing mountains and deep gorges, in the flower of almond-trees, in pomegranates and green figs, in the whirling dance, the plaintive sound of flutes, in the sugared sap and the salt tear—she delights in blood! Hail! Hail! Mother of the mountains!

(They scourge themselves with their whips, and the blows ring again upon their chests; the skins of the tambourines quiver as though about to burst. They seize their knives and slash their arms.)

She sorrows—let us also be sorrowful! For her pleasing let us suffer! So shall your sins be remitted unto you. Blood cleanses all things—scatter its drops about, like blossoms! She demands the blood of another—of some pure thing!

(The Archgallus raises his knife over the lamb.)

ANTHONY (*filled with horror*): Do not slay the lamb!

(A crimson jet spurts up.
The priest sprinkles the people with blood; and everyone —Anthony and Hilarion included—gathers about the burn-

ing tree to watch in silence the last convulsive movements of the victim.

From in among the priests comes forth A WOMAN—her appearance precisely that of the image in the little box.

She pauses at the sight of A YOUNG MAN wearing a Phrygian cap. His thighs are covered by close-fitting trousers, with regularly-placed lozenged openings here and there, tied with coloured knots. He stands languidly beside the tree, leaning his elbow against one of its branches, and holding in his hand a flute.

CYBELE throwing her two arms round his waist :)

The wide world over have I sought you—and famine ate up the countries where I passed. You deceived me, but yet I love you! Warm my chilled body! Embrace me!

ATYS: Spring comes not back, eternal Mother! For all my love I may not enter thine inmost self. I would cover myself in a painted robe like thine. I am envious of thy milk-swollen breasts, of thy flowing tresses, of thy mighty flanks from which living things come forth. Why am I not thyself? Why am I not a woman?

Nay! Never! My manhood terrifies me . . . !

(With a sharp stone he mutilates himself, then rushes furiously away, waving in the air the piece of his dismembered flesh.

The priests do as did the god, the faithful as the priests. Men and women exchange garments and embrace—and the whirlpool of bleeding bodies drifts away, though their voices, still persisting, become more clamorous, more strident, as the sound of voices heard at funerals.

A great catafalque, hung with purple, bears upon its summit an ebony bed, flanked by torches and filigreed silver baskets, full of green lettuces, mallows, and fennel.

On the steps round about it, from the top to the bottom, women are seated, all clad in black, their girdles loosened, their feet bare, holding with melancholy air great bunches of flowers.

At the bottom, at each corner of the low platform, urns of alabaster, filled with myrrh, are slowly smoking.

On the bed is seen the corpse of a man. Blood flows from his thigh. One of his arms hangs limply down—and a dog is licking the finger-nails, and whining.

Torches are so closely placed together in a row that he cannot clearly be seen; and Anthony is seized with anguish, fearing to recognize the face of someone that he knows.

The sobs of the women cease; and after an interval of silence, ALL chant in unison :)

Fair! Fair! Fair is he! But long enough has he slept! Lift now thy head! Arise!

Draw in the breath of our flowers—there are narcissi and anemones, gathered from thine own gardens for thy delight. Awake! You are making us afraid!

Speak! What would you have? Will you drink wine? Will you lie in our beds? Will you eat of honeycakes shaped like little birds?

Let us clasp him in our arms and kiss his breast! There! There! Can you feel us—our ring-laden fingers fluttering over thy body, our lips searching for thy mouth, and our hair brushing about thy thighs, thou swooning god, so deaf to our prayers!

(They utter cries, tearing their faces with their nails, and then fall silent—and only the howling of the dog is heard.)

Alas! Alas! The black blood trickles over the snowy flesh! His knees are twisted; his sides are sinking in! The bloom of his countenance is all soaked with purple! He is dead! Weep for him! Grieve for him!

(They come, one behind another, and drape their flowing

hair about the torches, until it seems, from a distance, as though many serpents, black or blond, were gathered together—and the catafalque slowly sinks to the level of a cavern, a shadowy sepulchre that yawns with open throat.

Then A WOMAN bends over the corpse.

Her hair, that was never cut, covers her from head to foot. She sheds so many tears that her grief is plainly not as that of others; it is something more than human, something infinite!

Anthony thinks of the Mother of Jesus.

She speaks :)

Out of the Orient you came, O Sun! and into your arms, all quivering with dew, you gathered me. About your azure mantle fluttered doves; our kisses made a wind among the trees; and I gave myself wholly to your love, rejoicing that I found myself so weak.

Alas! Alas! Why went you upon the mountains?

It was a wild boar that wounded you, at the time of the autumnal equinox! And now you are dead! The fountains weep; the trees bow themselves down, and through the naked briers whistles the winter wind.

Mine eyes shall close, now that, hidden in the shadows, you dwell on the under side of the world, where abides my most hated rival.

O Persephone, all lovely things are going down to thee, never to return!

(While she has been speaking, her fellows have raised the corpse to lay it in the sepulchre : but it seems to melt away as they hold it, for it was no more than an effigy of wax.

And Anthony thereupon feels greatly relieved.

Everything disappears—and the hut, the rocks and the cross are there again.

But on the other side of the Nile he can see A WOMAN—standing in the midst of the desert.

With her right hand she grasps the lower part of a long black veil that hides her face; while in the other arm she carries a babe to which she gives suck.

Beside her, a great ape crouches on the sand.

She lifts her head towards heaven—and in spite of the distance her voice is clearly heard.)

ISIS: O Neïth, beginning of all things! Hammon, Lord of eternity; Phthah, maker of the world, and Thoth, his intelligence; gods of Amenti—several triads of the Nomes—sparrow-hawks in the azure, sphinx beside the temples; ibis perched between the horns of oxen, planets, constellations, river-banks, murmurs of the wind, reflections of light, tell me where is Osiris!

I have sought him in the watercourses and by the lakes—and further still, even at Byblos of the Phœnicians. Anubis, the prick-eared, leaped about me, yelping and sniffing with his muzzle among the clumps of tamarinds. Thanks, good Dog-headed One! My thanks!

(She gives the ape two or three friendly pats on the head.)

Hideous Typhon of the red hair slew him, rent him in pieces, and we gathered up all his scattered members. But him who made me fruitful I have not!

(She utters bitter lamentations.)

ANTHONY (*becoming angry throws stones at her, reviling her*): Shameless one! Go away! Go away!

HILARION: Show her more regard than that! Hers was the religion of your own forefathers! In your cradle it was her amulets that you wore.

THE TEMPTATION OF ST. ANTHONY

Isis: In former days, when summer came, the flooding of the river drove the unclean creatures towards the desert. The dykes were opened, the boats bumped one against another, the panting earth drank thirstily. Thou god with the bulls' horns didst throw thyself on my breast—and the lowing of the eternal cow was heard.

Seed-time and harvest, threshing of the corn and the vintage, followed each other in succession, according to the change of the seasons. Great stars were ever beaming in the clear skies of night, and the days shone with never-ending splendour. As a king with his queen, the Sun and the Moon appeared above the ends of the horizon.

And we two then sat on our throne in a world sublime, twin-monarchs, wedded from out the womb of eternity—he, holding a sceptre with a conchophylla at the head, I one with a lotus-flower, both of us erect, our hands joined—and not even the crumbling of an empire could disturb us.

Egypt spread itself out at our feet, amazing and awful, and more long than broad, like the corridor of a temple, with obelisks on the right, pyramids on the left and its labyrinth in the midst—and everywhere rows of mighty monsters, forests of columns, massive gateways flanking doors that were topped by winged terrestrial globes.

In the pastures of Egypt were found the creatures of the zodiac, and her mysterious writings were full of their shapes and their colours. Divided into twelve districts, as the year is made up of twelve months—each month, every single day, having its own god—she initiated the unchanging orderliness of heaven; and her children, when they died, retained each his own likeness, for they were so steeped in spices that they became indestructible, and lay down to sleep for three thousand years in another Egypt, larger than the first, spread out under the earth.

Men went down thereto by stairways that led into halls where on the walls the joys of the righteous were depicted, and the torments of the wicked and all that happens in the third invisible world. Ranged along the walls, the dead in their painted coffins awaited each his turn; and souls, set free from further wandering, enjoyed a drowsy slumber till they woke to life again.

Osiris came sometimes to visit me, and it was by his shade that I was made the mother of Harpocrates.

(She looks closely at the babe on her arm.)

It is himself! Those are his eyes; and that his hair, twisted like rams' horns. You will go on with his work, my little one, and we shall flower again like the lotus. I am still the great Isis! None has yet lifted my veil! My fruit is the sun!

Sun of the spring-time, clouds darken your face! Typhon breathes upon the pyramids and they crumble. I saw, just now, the sphinx in flight, and he was running like a jackal.

I look in vain for my priests—in their linen vestments, with their great harps, carrying the little mystic boat adorned with silver pateræ. No more those festivals upon the lakes! Nor the illuminations of my delta! Nor cups of milk at Philæ! For a long while now, Apis has not been seen.

THE TEMPTATION OF ST. ANTHONY

Egypt! Egypt! The mighty shoulders of your silent gods are white with the droppings of birds, and the winds that blow over the desert sport with the ashes of your dead! . . . Anubis, guardian of ghosts, leave me not!

(The dog-headed creature has vanished.

She dandles the child up and down.)

But . . . what is the matter? . . . hands cold . . . head fallen back!

(Harpocrates has that moment died; and she sends out a cry so piercing, so mournful and heart-rending, that Anthony responds with another cry, and stretches out his arms as though to support her.
She is no longer there; and his head droops, weighed down by shame.

All that he has seen becomes confused, as in the mind of a man bewildered after a journey, or giddy with drink. He had wished to hate; and now a vague pity fills his heart and softens it. He begins to weep copiously.)

HILARION: Wherefore so sad?

ANTHONY (*after long search for an answer*): I think of the many souls lost through these false gods!

HILARION: But do they not seem to you . . . now and then . . . somehow to resemble the true?

ANTHONY: That is a trick of the Devil, by means of which he seeks to seduce the faithful. As he attacks the weak through their flesh, so does he assault the strong through the medium of the spirit.

HILARION: But lust, in its madness, is as unselfish as penitence. Frantic physical love does but hasten the dissolution of the body, which by its feebleness forbids attainment of the impossible.

ANTHONY: But what in the world has that to do with me! My gorge rises with disgust at these bestial gods, busy as they are with slaughter and incest.

HILARION: Don't forget, though, the many things in Scripture which offend you merely because you do not understand them. In much the same way, these other faiths may hide some spiritual truth beneath their guilty outward forms. There are others yet for you to see. Look round about!

ANTHONY: No! No! It is too perilous!

HILARION: Yet you wanted just now to know more about them! Do you fear lest their lies should make your faith to waver?

(The rocks in front of Anthony have become a mountain, of which all but the lower slopes are hidden behind layers of cloud.

Above this cloud rises another mountain, immense, brilliantly green, scooped out here and there by valleys, and having at its summit, in a grove of laurels, a palace of bronze, with a roof of golden tiles supported on ivory capitals.

Midway in the columned court, on his throne, JUPITER, tremendous, his torso bare, holds victory in one hand, thunderbolts in the other; while his eagle rears its head at his feet.

JUNO, beside him, rolls her large eyes beneath the diadem from which, like a vapour, her veil flutters in the wind.

Behind them, MINERVA, upright on a pedestal, leans against her spear. The Gorgon's skin covers her breast, and a linen peplum falls in regular folds to her very toe-nails. The far gaze of her grey-blue eyes, shining under the open visor, is steadily fixed.

On the right of the palace, OLD NEPTUNE rides upon a dolphin churning with its fins the clear expanse which may be either sea or sky—the blue of ocean being one with the blue of the ether—the two elements intermingle.

On the other side, fierce PLUTO, in mantle dark as night,

THE TEMPTATION OF ST. ANTHONY

with diamond tiara and sceptre of ebony, is seated on an island about which the shadowy River Styx goes winding, before it plunges into the gloom, into the vast black gulf below the mountain-side, into the void that has no form.

MARS, clad in brazen armour, and angry-looking, flourishes his great shield and his sword.

HERCULES, lower down, leaning on his club, looks up at him.

APOLLO, his face flashing forth rays of light, with outstretched right arm, urges on his four galloping white horses; and CERES, in her chariot drawn by oxen, comes to meet him with a sickle in her hand.

BACCHUS is behind her, in a low car, drawn softly by lynxes. Fleshy, beardless, and with vine-branches about his brow, he moves along, grasping a bowl from which wine overflows. SILENUS, close beside him, is balanced unsteadily upon an ass. PAN, with the pointed ears, blows upon his pipes; while the priestesses strew flowers and the Bacchantes, beating drums and with dishevelled hair, glance ever and again behind them.

DIANA, her tunic tucked up, comes out from a wood with her nymphs.

Deep in his cavern, VULCAN is hammering iron with his attendants round about him; here and there the ancient Rivers, reclining upon green rocks, discharge water from their urns; the Muses stand singing in the valleys.

The Hours, all equal in stature, go hand in hand; and MERCURY, seated sideways on a rainbow, has his wand and his winged sandals and travelling-cap.

But above the stairway of the gods, amidst downy clouds from whose whirling folds roses are falling, VENUS, freshemerged from the sea, gazes at her own face in a mirror, her eyes moving languidly beneath their lazy lids.

Her great blond coils of hair roll down upon her shoulders; her breasts are small, her build slender, her hips bell-shaped, with the graceful outlines of a lyre, her thighs perfectly rounded, dimples near her knees and about her delicate feet. Very near her lips a butterfly is hovering. The brightness of her body throws a halo of pearly light around her; while the whole of Olympus is drenched in a rosy dawn which now climbs imperceptibly upward into heaven's blue heights.)

ANTHONY: Ah! My heart expands! A joy that I have never known till now has come into the secret places of my soul! How beautiful it is! How beautiful!

HILARION: They used to lean down from behind their clouds to guide men's swords; one met with them by the roadside, and welcomed them in one's own home—and this commonness could make all life divine!

It had but the single purpose then, of being free and fine. Clothing was loose and did not hinder graceful movement. The voice of the orator, long exercised on the sea-beach, rolled in waves of sound against the marble porticoes. Young men, smeared with oil, wrestled naked in the full light of day. To show forth perfection of form was accounted always a most pious act.

And these were the men who showed respect for wives, for old men, and for those who begged for mercy. Behind the temple of Hercules stood an altar sacred to Pity.

Those who were about to offer victims in sacrifice had flowers twined about their fingers. Even memory itself was enabled to hold aloof from the dreadful details of death, for nothing remained but a handful of ashes, when the soul, mingling with the boundless ether, had risen towards the gods!

(Stooping to whisper in Anthony's ear:)

And they are still living! The Emperor Constantine adores Apollo. You will find the Trinity in the mysteries of Samothrace, baptism in the worship of Isis, redemption in the faith of Mithra, the martyrdom of a god in the festivals of Bacchus. . . . Proserpine is the Virgin! . . . Aristæus, Jesus!

(Anthony remains for a while with downcast eyes; then suddenly repeats the Jerusalem creed—as he remembers it—heaving a deep sigh at the beginning of each clause :)

I believe in one only God, the Father—and in one only Lord, Jesus Christ—first-begotten Son of God—who was incarnate and was made man—who was crucified—and buried—who ascended into Heaven—who shall come to judge the living and the dead—whose kingdom shall have no end—and in one only Holy Spirit—one baptism of repentance—one only Holy Catholic Church—the resurrection of the flesh—the life eternal! . . .

(And then the cross grows larger, and bursting through the clouds it casts a shadow upon the heaven of the gods.

All of them grow pale, for they feel that Olympus is rocking.

At its foot, Anthony can see vast chained creatures, either half hidden within caves or supporting the rocks on their shoulders. These are the Titans, the Giants, the Hundred-handed people, the Cyclopes.

A VOICE rises, indistinct and terrifying—like the sound of waves, like the noise of a tempest over the forests, like the roaring of the wind against the face of a precipice :)

We knew it, we knew it! The gods must have an end. Uranus was maimed by Saturn, Saturn by Jupiter, and Jupiter himself shall be annihilated. Each in his turn—it is destiny!

(And little by little they sink into the mountain, and are gone.

In the meantime the golden tiles of the palace wing their flight, and they too are gone.

JUPITER has come down from his throne. The thunderbolts at his feet smoke like firebrands on the point of extinction—and the eagle stretches out its neck to gather its own feathers that are falling.)

No longer am I master, then, of all—holiest, mightiest, god of the clans and of Greek peoples, ancestor of all the kings, Agamemnon of the skies!

Eagle of deifications, what breath from Erebus has blown you back to me? Or, flying from the Field of Mars, have you perchance brought me the soul of the last of the Emperors?

I will have no more dealing with the souls of men! Let the earth retain them, and still let them have their being on the level of its basenesses! Already they have the hearts of slaves—who forget injuries, neglect ancestors, break oaths! Everywhere the fickleness of mobs, the meanness of mankind, the hideousness of human breeds, have triumphed!

(His ribs are being torn asunder by his heaving breath, and he wrings his hands. Hebe, who is in tears, offers him a cup, which he seizes.)

No! No! As long as there is a mind, wherever it be, which can entertain a thought, which hates disorder and understands the Law, the spirit of Jupiter shall live!

(But the cup is empty, and he lets it rest in his hand:)

Not one drop more! When the nectar[1] fails, the Immortals depart.

(The cup slips slowly from his hand; he feels the approach of death; he leans against a column.)

JUNO: It was not good to have had so many

[1] *L'ambrosie*: It is JUPITER himself, this time, who is allowed to nod.—Trans.

THE TEMPTATION OF ST. ANTHONY

love affairs! Eagle, bull, swan, golden rain, cloud and flame—you have assumed all shapes, scattered your splendour over all the elements, grown old with uncounted bed-fellows! Our divorce this time is irrevocable,[1] and our dominion, our very being, is dissolved.

(She goes away in the air.

MINERVA no longer holds her spear; and some ravens that had rested in the carvings of the frieze wheel and peck at her helmet.)

Let me see whether my ships, cleaving the bright sea, have returned to my three harbours; and why the fields are deserted; and what the daughters of Athens are doing now.

In the month of the great public sacrifice, my entire people came to me, led by their magistrates and their priests. After them, in white robes and golden tunics, followed the long lines of virgins bearing cups, baskets, parasols; then the three hundred oxen for the sacrifice, old men waving green branches, soldiers clashing their armour, youths singing hymns, flautists, lyrists, rhapsodists, dancing-girls—and last of all, on the mast of a trireme that moved upon wheels, my great veil embroidered by virgins who for a year had been maintained with particular care; and when this had been shown in all the streets and squares, and in front of all the temples, in the midst of an ever-chanting procession it went step by step up the hill of the Acropolis, skirting the Propylæum, and entering at last the Parthenon.

[1] *Notre divorce est irrévocable cette fois!* The decree has been made absolute!—Trans.

But confusion of mind has seized me—me, the intelligent one! What! What! No single idea of any sort occurs to me! And I am trembling like an ordinary woman!

(She becomes conscious of the fall of some building behind her; cries out as she turns; is struck upon the forehead; and falls backward to the ground.

HERCULES has cast aside his lion-skin; and setting his feet firmly, arching his back, biting his lips, he makes terrific efforts to sustain Olympus as it crumbles to pieces.)

I vanquished the Cercopes, the Amazons and the Centaurs. I have slain many kings. I subdued Achelous, a great river. I have cut through mountains and joined oceans. I have set free nations that had become enslaved, and peopled lands that were empty. I scoured Gaul, and traversed thirsty deserts. I have defended the gods, and freed myself from Omphale. But Olympus is too mighty for me! My arms are cracking! I die!

(And he is crushed beneath the fragments.)

PLUTO: It was your fault, O son of Amphitryo! Why came you into my dominions?

The vulture feeding upon the liver of Tityos lifted its head; Tantalus moistened his lips; the wheel of Ixion stood still.

At the same moment the Keres stretched out their claws to intercept the departing ghosts; the Furies in despair twisted the serpents coiled about their heads; and Cerberus, whom you yourself fastened with a chain, was near to death, slavering from each of his three mouths.

It was you who left the door ajar, so that others

THE TEMPTATION OF ST. ANTHONY

could enter. Tartarus is thrown open to the light of day!

(He founders among the shadows.)

NEPTUNE: No more shall my trident stir up the tempests. The monsters that were once so terrible lie rotting at the bottom of the sea.

Amphitrite, whose white feet went swiftly over the foam, the green Nereids on the horizon, the scaly sirens who stopped ships and beguiled sailors; and the old Tritons winding their wreathed horns—they all are dead! The gaieties of the sea are for ever gone!

Nor will I now survive! Let the great Oceans receive me!

(He vanishes beneath the blue waters.)

DIANA (*habited in black, and with her dogs—now turned into wolves!—about her*): The freedom of the great forests has sickened me, with their reek of wild beasts and the exhalations from their marshes. The women, over whom I watched when they were pregnant, now bring dead babies to the birth. The moon wavers on her way beneath the incantations of witches. My longing is for violence and desolate places. I would quaff poisons, lose myself in vapours, in nightmares . . . !

(And a passing cloud hurries her off.)

MARS (*bareheaded and bloodstained*): In the olden days, caring not for countries or nations, I fought for sheer joy of battle, single-handed, and arousing whole armies by my insults.

I had comrades afterwards who marched to the

music of flutes, in good order, keeping step, breathing over their bucklers, holding their plumes aloft and their lances at the slope. Like great eagles crying aloud, we would throw ourselves into the fight. War was then a gladsome thing, a festival!—as when against the whole of Asia three hundred of us stood and were unafraid!

But now the Barbarians return, in myriads and millions! And their numbers are the stronger, with wicked engines of war and mean cunning; and so let me bravely make an end!

(He kills himself.)

VULCAN (*wiping the sweat from his brow with a sponge*): The world grows cold. We must stoke up the sources—the volcanoes and the streams of molten metal underground!—Hit your hardest! Put your strength into it! With all your might!

(The Cabiri injure themselves with their hammers; are blinded by sparks; go groping about, and lose themselves in the darkness.)

CERES (*standing in her chariot, which is drawn by wheels which have wings at their hubs*): Stop! Stop! Good reason to shut out strangers and atheists and Epicureans and Christians! The mystery of the basket is uncovered, the sanctuary profaned, all is lost!

(She goes slipping down a steep slope—despairing, shrieking, tearing her hair.)

Lies! All lies! Daïra was not given back to me! And now the trumpets summon me to join the dead. This is another Tartarus! And from it there will be no return. Horror!

THE TEMPTATION OF ST. ANTHONY

(The abyss engulfs her.)

BACCHUS (*laughing frantically*): Never mind! The Archon's wife is my spouse! The Law itself is drunk! A new song for me, and multifarious shapes!

The fire that devoured my mother flows in my veins. Let it burn ever more brightly, though it consume me!

Boon companion with you all, male and female, my priests and priestesses, you shall take care of me! And the vine shall go twining round the tree-trunks! Howl! Dance! Split yourselves! Let loose the tiger and untie the slave! With furious teeth, bite into flesh!

(And Pan, Silenus, the Satyrs, the Bacchantes, the Mimallones and the Mænads, with their serpents and their torches and black masks, throw flowers at one another, expose their ceremonial symbols and embrace them—they beat timbrels, wave their ivy-wreathed wands, pelt each other with shells, munch grapes, strangle a he-goat, and then tear Bacchus in pieces.)

APOLLO (*lashing his coursers, with pale locks streaming*): I have left stony Delos behind me, so chaste that it seems all but dead; and I hasten to Delphi ere the divine influence of its vapours shall be wholly lost. Mules browse on its laurels. My priestess has wandered away and she cannot be found.

But more powerfully will I turn my mind thereto, and thence shall come sublime poems and everlasting memorials—all that exists shall thrill to the vibrations of my cithara!

(He strikes the strings thereof; but they snap, and the

ends lash across his face. He casts it aside; and furiously whipping his team :)

No! Enough of outward symbols! Further yet! To the very summit! To the realms of pure thought!

(But the horses back and rear, and smash the chariot; and, entangled in fragments of the broken pole and the twisting together of the harness, he falls head downward towards the abyss.

The heavens are darkened.)

VENUS (*shivers, blue with cold*): My girdle it was which once encircled the horizon of Hellas.

Her fields shimmered with the roses of my cheeks, her shores were carved to the pattern of my lips; and her mountains, whiter than my doves, sang beneath the sculptor's chisel. My spirit was manifest in the cycle of their feasts, the way in which they dressed their hair, the dialogues of their philosophers, the constitutions of their republics. But too carefully have I cherished mankind! It is by Love itself that I have now been put to shame!

(She throws herself backwards, weeping.)

It is a hateful world! I cannot breathe!
O Mercury, inventor of the lyre, and guide of souls, bear me away!

(She puts her finger to her lips, and drops through a tremendous curve into the abyss.

There is no more to be seen, since the darkness is now complete; save that from the eyes of Hilarion two red beams of light shine forth.)

ANTHONY (*at last noticing his great stature*):

THE TEMPTATION OF ST. ANTHONY

Several times, now, while you have been speaking, it has seemed to me that you grew taller—and it was no illusion! Tell me why it was . . . for your presence terrifies me!

(Footsteps approach.)

What is that?

HILARION (*stretches out his arm*): Look!

(Then, in the dim moonlight, Anthony sees an endless company filing over the rocky crest—and each wayfarer, one behind the other, falls down the steep into the gulf.

First of all are the three great gods of Samothrace grouped together, Axieros, Axiokeros, Axiokersa, masked in purple and with uplifted hands.

Æsculapius moves with a dejected air, nor does he notice Samos and Telesphorus, who ply him with agonized questionings. The Eleatic Sosipolis, in the form of a python, rolls its coils towards the edge. Doespœne grows dizzy, and hurls herself down. Britomartis, shrieking with terror, clings to the meshes of her net. The Centaurs come up at a gallop and topple pell-mell into the black pit.

Behind them, limping, comes the mournful assemblage of the nymphs. The meadow-nymphs are all dusty, and the wood-nymphs, moaning, bleed from wounds they have received beneath the hatchets of the woodcutters.

The Gelludes, the Strygii, the Goblins, all the infernal goddesses, their fangs and torches and vipers tangled in a pyramid together, with Eurynome at its top, on a vulture's skin, blue of face as flies that crawl upon meat, gnawing the flesh of her own arms.

Then, in one whirling mass disappear the bloody Orthia, Hymnia of Orchomenus, the Laphria of the Patræans, Aphia of Ægina, Bendis of Thrace, the Stymphalians with birds' legs, Triopas, with his three orbits from which the eyes have disappeared, Erichthonius, with his legs hanging loose, drags himself, like a cripple, upon his wrists.)

HILARION: What luck for us, eh? To see them all in their low estate and in agony! Come with me up on this rock; and let us be like Xerxes reviewing his army!

Down there, in the distance, among the fogs, do you see a fair-bearded giant lowering his sword, red with blood? That is the Thracian Zalmoxis, between two planets, Artimpasa—Venus, and Orsiloche—the Moon.

And farther off, coming forth from the wan clouds, are the gods whom the Cimmerians worship, beyond ultimate Thule.

Their lofty halls were warm; and by the gleam of naked swords that covered the walls they drank honeyed water from horns of ivory. They ate whales' liver in copper dishes beaten out by demons, and listened to captive sorcerers strumming upon stone harps.

They are weary! They are old! Their bear-skins are weighted down with snow, and their toes are pushing through the holes in their sandals.

They weep for the meadows where on grassy hillocks they were wont to recover breath in intervals of battle; the long ships whose prows broke through the icebergs; and the skates they used when they followed the circle of the poles, bearing at arms' length the entire firmament as it turned with them.

(A wintry squall surrounds and hides them.
Anthony looks in another direction, and sees, outlined in black against a scarlet background, some strange creatures, chin-strapped and gauntleted, who are tossing balls to each other, playing leap-frog, making grimaces, dancing idiotically.)

HILARION: Those are the gods of Etruria, the innumerable Æsars.

There is Tages, the contriver of augury. He seeks with one hand to multiply the divisions of the heavens, and with the other he leans upon the earth. Let him re-enter therein!

Nortia looks closely at the wall in which she hammered nails to mark the passage of the years. Its whole surface is now covered—the last period is ended.

Like two storm-tossed and trembling travellers, Castor and Pollux shelter themselves beneath one mantle.

ANTHONY (*closing his eyes*): Enough! Enough!

(But with a great noise of wings, all the Victories of the Capitol pass through the air—hiding their faces with their hands, and letting fall the trophies that hang from their arms.

JANUS—lord of the twilight—flees away upon a black ram; and, of his two faces, one is already become corrupt, the other has fallen asleep with fatigue.

SUMMANUS—god of nocturnal lightnings—whose head has disappeared, presses to his heart a stale cake shaped like a wheel.

VESTA—beneath a cupola in ruins, strives to rekindle her extinguished lamp.

BELLONA—slashes her cheeks, but no blood spurts out to purify her devotees.)

ANTHONY: Mercy! They weary me!

HILARION: And yet, not so very long ago, you were interested!

(And he shows him, in a thicket of whitebeam, a naked woman on all fours, like a beast, covered by a black man who holds a torch in each hand.)

That is the Nymph Aricia, with the demon Virbius. Her priest, the king of the wood, himself must be assassin—and fugitive slaves, robbers of corpses, brigands on the Salarian Way, beggars on the Sublician bridge, and the human vermin in the stews of the Subura, had no god whom they loved more dearly!

In Mark Antony's days, patrician women preferred Death.

(And then he shows him, beneath cypress and rose-bush, another woman—clad in gauze. She smiles, and round about her are mattocks, stretchers, black hangings, and all the implements of burial. Her diamonds sparkle from far off through spiders' webs. Hobgoblins, like skeletons, show their bones between the branches; and the Lemures, who are spectres, spread their bat-like wings.

At the side of a field the god Terminus, uprooted, totters, all covered in filth.

Midway in a furrow, red dogs are devouring the huge corpse of Vertumnus.

The gods of the countryside go off, weeping: Sartor, Saritor, Vervactor, Collina, Vallonia, Hostilina—all wrapped in little hooded mantles, and each carrying either a grubbing-axe, a pitchfork, a hurdle, or a boar-spear.)

HILARION: It was these spirits who prospered country-houses, with their dovecots, their enclosures of dormice and snails, their poultry-yards protected by nets, their warm stables smelling sweetly of cedar.

They watched over all the wretched folk who dragged their fettered limbs across the flints of the Sabine territories, the swineherds with their horns, the grape-gatherers who must climb to the very tops of the elms, those who drove along the little lanes their asses laden with dung. The labourer, panting over the handle of his plough, prayed to them that they would strengthen his arm; the cowherds under the shade of the lime trees, with

THE TEMPTATION OF ST. ANTHONY

milk-filled calabashes at their sides, one after another sounded their praises upon pipes of reed.

(Anthony sighs.
And in the midst of a chamber, on a low platform, is seen an ivory bed, surrounded by figures holding pinewood torches.)

Those are the deities attendant upon marriage, and they wait the coming of the bride!

Domiduca must lead her to her husband's home; Virgo will loosen her girdle; Subigus will place her on the marriage-bed; while Præma, whispering sweet words in her ears, gently draws her arms apart.

But she comes not! And they dismiss the others: the nurses Nona and Decima; the three Nixi, guardian deities of women in labour; Educa and Potina, who watch over the food and drink of children; and Carna, the protectress of family life, whose bunch of hawthorn wards off evil dreams from the child.

Later, Ossipaga should have strengthened his knees, Barbatus given him his beard, Stimula his first desires, Volupia his earliest pleasures, Fabulinus would have taught him to talk, Numera to count, Camena to sing, and Consus the making of plans.

(The chamber is empty; and beside the bed remains only Nenia—a hundred years old—mumbling on her own account the dirges she was wont to murmur by the beds of aged dying men.
But soon her voice is overborne by the shrill cries of THE GODS OF THE HEARTH, crouching at the back of the entrance-hall, clad in dog-skins, their bodies wreathed with flowers, their clenched hands held against their cheeks, and crying with might and main :)

Where is the allowance of food that once was ours at every meal? And where the careful kindness of the waiting-maids, the matron's smile, and the merriment of little boys playing knuckle-bones on the courtyard mosaics? As they grew older, they would hang about our necks their baubles of leather or of gold.

What happiness when, on the evening of some triumph, the master as he came again beneath his roof would turn his shining eyes towards us! He would tell about his combats; and the humble home became important as a palace, holy as a temple.

How pleasant were those family repasts, especially on the eve of the Festival of the Dead! In their tenderness towards the departed, all discords died away; and men embraced as they drank to the glories of the past and to their hopes for the future.

But gradually, the painted waxen effigies of ancestors, shut up behind us, have become covered over with mildew. Newcomers, avenging upon us their own incredulities, have smashed our cheeks; beneath the teeth of rats our wooden bodies are crumbling away.

(And the thronging deities on guard at the doorways, in the kitchen and the cellar, and round the stoves, scatter in every direction—in the semblance of enormous ants running rapidly, or like moths that escape.)

CREPITUS (*is heard speaking*): I, too, was held in honour once. Offerings were made to me. I was a god!

The Athenian hailed me as a presage of good fortune; while the pious Roman, with uplifted hands, cursed me; and the Egyptian priest, who never ate

THE TEMPTATION OF ST. ANTHONY

beans, trembled at my voice and grew pale at the smell of me.

When the soldiers' vinegar trickled over their unshorn chins, when men regaled themselves on acorns and peas and raw onions, and chopped goats' flesh stewed in the shepherds' rancid butter, no one was embarrassed, nobody bothered about his neighbours. Solid foods produced sonorous digestions. In warm country sunshine, men relieved themselves at leisure.

And so without offence I was accepted, as are other common needs of human life: as Mena who torments virgins, and gentle Rumina who guards the breasts of nursing mothers, swollen with blue veins. I was jovial. I evoked laughter! And stretching himself in comfort by my assistance, the guest expressed his merriment in most natural ways.

I had my great days, too! Good Aristophanes brought me upon his stage, and the Emperor Claudius Drusus gave me place at his table. Under the broad-striped tunics of the patricians I moved majestical! Golden vases resounded like tambours beneath my touch—and when, full of lampreys and truffles and pies, the master's body cleared everything noisily out of its way, a world in waiting understood that Cæsar had dined!

But now—I find welcome only with the common folk—and men cry out upon me, even at the mention of my name!

(And Crepitus departs, with audible expression of his grief.
Then comes a clap of thunder.)

A Voice: I was the God of Armies, the Lord, the Lord God!

I pitched the tents of Jacob upon the mountains, and nourished amongst the sand-hills my people when they were in flight.

It was I who burned Sodom! I who swallowed up the world beneath the Deluge! I it was who drowned Pharaoh, with all the princely sons of kings, the war-chariots and their drivers.

A jealous God, I utterly detested other gods. I pounded the unpure as in a mortar; beat down the proud; and my desolating anger ran about to right and left, like a camel set loose in a field of corn.

For the deliverance of my people Israel, I chose simple men, and my angels with wings of flame spoke to them from out of the bushes.

Smelling of spikenard and cinnamon and myrrh, in diaphanous robes and with high-heeled foot-gear, brave-hearted women went forth to kill captains.

The winds, as they passed, breathed messages to my prophets.

My law was graven on tables of stone, and by it were my people enclosed as in a citadel. They were my people and I was their God! The earth was mine, and all the men that lived thereon—with their thoughts, their works, the very tools with which those works were done, and their posterity.

My ark rested within a threefold sanctuary, behind hangings of purple, and surrounded by lighted candelabra. For my service there was a whole tribe of censer-swingers; and the High Priest, in a robe of hyacinth, used to wear a breastplate of precious stones set symmetrically in order.

THE TEMPTATION OF ST. ANTHONY

But alas! and alas! The Holy of Holies has been entered, the veil rent, and the smell of the holocausts is wasted upon every wind. The jackal whines among the sepulchres: my temple is destroyed, and my people scattered!

The priests were strangled with their own girdles: the women carried captive: the holy vessels have been melted down!

(Dying away in the distance, the Voice repeats:)

I was the God of Armies, the Lord, the Lord God!

(Then there is a tremendous silence, a night that is profound.)

ANTHONY: They have all gone.
SOMEONE: But I remain!

(And he sees before him Hilarion—transfigured, beautiful as an archangel, luminous as a sun—and so tall that to look in his face ANTHONY must throw back his head and gaze upward.)

Who are you, then?
HILARION: My kingdom is as wide as the universe: and there is no limit set to my desires. Ever onward I go, setting free the minds of men, weighing worlds in the balance, without hatred, without fear, without pity, without love, and without God—and men call me Science.

ANTHONY (*recoiling from him*): Rather should they call you—the Devil!

HILARION (*fixing him with his eyes*): Would you look upon him?

(Anthony, who is seized by diabolical curiosity, cannot tear his eyes away. His terror increases, and yet his desire increases also, and at last is almost beyond measure.)

If I were but to see him—but once to see him . . . ?

(*Then, with a spasm of anger*): My horror of him will deliver me from him for ever and ever! . . . Yes, in very deed . . . !

(A cloven foot appears.

Anthony now regrets his boldness; but the Devil flings him across his horns and carries him away.)

VI

(Flying beneath him, spread out like a swimmer, the Devil with two vast wings wide unfurled and hiding him entirely, seems to Anthony like a cloud.)

ANTHONY: Whither go I? . . .

Was it of the Accursed One that I caught a glimpse a moment ago?

No! It is a cloud that carries me away. It may be that I have died, and am on my upward way to God . . . ?

Ah! How easily I breathe! The unstained air expands my very soul! No more heaviness of mind, no more suffering in my body!

Far below, underneath me, the thunder bursts, the horizon broadens, the rivers interlace. That brown smear is the desert, that paltry puddle the Ocean.

Other oceans are rising into sight, great regions of which I know nothing. I can see the black countries, smoking like braziers, and the zone of snows eternally hidden by the fogs. I must try to find the mountains where each evening the sun goes to his rest.

THE DEVIL: The sun never goes to rest!

THE TEMPTATION OF ST. ANTHONY 297

(Anthony is not surprised at this voice. It seems to him but the echo of his own thought—a response uttered by his own memory.

The earth, meanwhile, assumes the shape of a ball; and he beholds it in the midst of the azure, turning upon the poles, revolving about the sun.)

THE DEVIL: And now you see that it is not the centre of the universe! Pride of man, bow thyself down!

ANTHONY: I can scarcely see it at all now, for it has mingled with other moving fires!

The firmament is but a tissue of stars!

(They are still rising.)

No sound! Not even the cry of an eagle! . . . Nothing! . . . and I lean out to listen for the harmony of the planets.

THE DEVIL: You will not hear it! Nor will you see the antipodes of Plato, the focus of Philolaus, the spheres of Aristotle, or the seven heavens of the Jews, with the great waters above the crystal vault!

ANTHONY: From below it seemed as solid as a wall. But now I am passing through it, sinking into it!

(And he comes abreast of the moon—which resembles a rounded mass of ice, glowing with steady light.)

THE DEVIL: It was once the dwelling-place of souls. The admirable Pythagoras himself would have filled it with the singing of birds and the magnificence of flowers.

ANTHONY: And I can see nothing but empty plains, and jet black craters under a jet black sky.

Take me towards those stars that shine so gently,

that I may see the angels holding them, like torches, in their outstretched arms.

THE DEVIL (*carries him into the midst of the stars*): They mutually attract and repel each other; and the activity of each results from and contributes to that of all the others—with no need of any outside help, but by sheer force of law, by virtue of order alone.

ANTHONY: Yes—yes! I grasp that! And it gives me joy greater than any mere pleasure of the emotions! My breath fails me with wonder at the immensity of God!

THE DEVIL: As the firmament which ever rises while you yourself ascend, so will he become greater to you with the extension of your thought—and this discovery of the universe, this enlarging for you of the infinite, will cause your joy to grow greater and ever greater!

ANTHONY: Ah! Higher! Higher! Ever higher!

(The sparkling stars multiply. Overhead the Milky Way stretches like a great belt, with mighty holes here and there; and within these interruptions of its brightness vast shadowy spaces of darkness spread themselves. There are showers of moving stars, trails of gold dust, luminous drifting vapours that float and then fade away.

Now and then a comet passes, suddenly—and then the tranquillity of the uncountable glittering points begins again.

Anthony lies stretched upon the Devil's two shoulders, and his open arms exactly match their span.

He scornfully recalls the ignorance of earlier days, the insufficience of his own imaginings. Here, quite close to him, are those lit spheres he had so often watched from below! He makes out the intercrossing of their paths, the intricacy of their courses. He sees them coming from afar

THE TEMPTATION OF ST. ANTHONY 299

—and, caught up like stones in a sling, describing their orbits, fulfilling their course.

With one sweep of his eyes he sees the Southern Cross and the Great Bear, the Lynx and the Centaur, the nebula of the Gold Fish, the six suns in the constellation of Orion, Jupiter with his four satellites, and the triple ring of great Saturn! All the planets and all the stars that will some day be discovered by men! He fills his eyes with their light, and bewilders his brain with calculations of their distances; then bows his head :)

What purpose is behind all this?

THE DEVIL: There is no purpose!

How should God have purposes? What experience could have taught him, or what reflection have decided him?

Before the beginning he could not act, and action now would be useless.

ANTHONY: Yet he it was who created the world, once for all, by his word!

THE DEVIL: But the beings that people the earth come thereupon one after another. In heaven, after like manner, new stars arise—different effects from various causes.

ANTHONY: And this variety of causes is none other but the will of God!

THE DEVIL: And yet to concede several acts of will in God is to admit various causes, and so to destroy his unity!

His will is not separable from his essence. He cannot have as it were a second will, since he can have no second essence—and since he exists eternally he also acts eternally.

Look upon the sun! From its surface flames shoot forth to tremendous heights, casting off sparks, which scatter and become new worlds—and farther than the farthest of these, beyond those depths in which you now see only night, there is the whirling of other suns—and yet others behind them—unendingly . . . !

ANTHONY: Enough! Enough! I am afraid! I shall fall into nothingness!

THE DEVIL (*stops; and gently rocking him*): There is no nothingness! Empty space does not exist! Everywhere are bodies moving upon the unchangeable depths of Space—since, if Space were bounded by anything, it would be no longer Space, but a body—therefore is it without limits!

ANTHONY (*wide-mouthed*): Without limits!

THE DEVIL: Rise upward in the heavens for ever and for ever: never will you reach the summit! Go down beneath the earth for billions of billions of centuries: never will you arrive at the bottom—since there is no bottom, no summit, neither height nor depth, no " end "; and Space is comprised in God, who does not fill a portion of Space, larger or smaller, but who is Immensity.

ANTHONY (*slowly*): Matter—then—would be a part of God?

THE DEVIL: Why not? Can you conceive any limits to God?

ANTHONY: I prostrate myself in humility before his power!

THE DEVIL: And yet you pretend that you can persuade him! You speak to him, you even deck him out with virtues, goodness, justice, mercy, instead of acknowledging that he possesses all perfection!

To conceive something beyond him, is to conceive

THE TEMPTATION OF ST. ANTHONY

God beyond God, being above being. He therefore is the only Being, the sole substance.

If the Substance could be divided, it would thereby be changed, it would no longer be itself, God would no longer exist. He is therefore indivisible as well as infinite—and if he had a body he would be built up of parts, he would be no longer one, he would not be infinite. And so he is not a person!

ANTHONY: What! My prayers and sobs, my bodily suffering, my transports of affection, have all these gone forth to a lie—into space—uselessly—like the cry of a bird, or as the whirling of withered leaves?

(He weeps.)

Oh, no! There is a someone above all things, a great soul, a Lord, a father, whom my heart adores, and by whom I must be loved!

THE DEVIL: You are wishing that God were less than God—for if he could have experience of love, or anger, or pity, he would thereby pass from one perfection to another that was either greater or smaller. God cannot descend to a feeling, nor be contained in a form.

ANTHONY: Some day, nevertheless, I shall see him!

THE DEVIL: Together with the blessed, you mean? When the finite shall perceive the infinite, on some limited spot, which will then contain the Absolute!

ANTHONY: There must at least be a paradise for goodness, and a hell for wickedness!

THE DEVIL: Are the unreasonable demands of

your reason to constitute the final court of appeal? Surely it must be plain that God cares but little about wickedness, since he endures that the earth should be filled with it!

Do you imagine that he puts up with it because he has no choice; or is it just because he is cruel, and so approves of it?

Do you think of him as continually tinkering with the world, as one might try to readjust a machine that was working badly? Or that he keeps his eye on everything, from the flight of a butterfly to the inmost thoughts of men?

If he did create the universe, then his providence is superfluous. If there is a Providence, then that means that creation is defective.

But evil and good are merely your own private concerns—just as day and night, pleasure and pain, dying and being born, are all relative merely to some particular point in space, to some definite surroundings, to some personal interest. Since only the infinite can be permanent, the Infinite exists—and that's all there is to it!

(The Devil has gradually stretched out his long wings, until they now cover the whole of space.)

ANTHONY (*no longer sees anything. He becomes faint*): A deathly chill freezes the very depth of my soul, exceeding the extremity of pain! It is like a death beneath death. I roll in tremendous darkness. It enters into me. My consciousness is bursting asunder in the presence of this nothingness which seems to spread in all directions!

THE DEVIL: But only by the intervention of your mind can you become aware of anything at all; and

THE TEMPTATION OF ST. ANTHONY

your mind, like a concave mirror, distorts things—and you have no way of checking the accuracy of your results.

Never can you know the universe in its full extent; and therefore you can possess no adequate idea of its cause, no clear notions about God; nor can you even venture to say that the universe is infinite—for first of all you would need to know what the Infinite is!

It may even be that Form is an error of your senses, and Substance a mere fancy of your thought.

Unless indeed, the world being a perpetual flux of things, appearance on the other hand may not be the whole of truth—illusion the only reality.

But are you quite sure that you see? Can you even be certain that you live? It may be that nothing really exists!

(The Devil has seized Anthony; and holding him at arms' length looks fixedly at him, with jaws open as though ready to devour him.)

Adore me, then! And curse that phantom which you call God!

(Anthony lifts his eyes in a last agony of hope. The Devil leaves him.)

VII

(Anthony finds himself stretched upon his back, at the edge of the cliff. The sky begins to glow.)

Is it the brightness of dawn, or no more than the shining of the moon?

(He tries to rise, but falls back; and with chattering teeth :)

I am so tired—as though my every bone were broken!

Why?

Ah! It was the Devil! I remember—and how he repeated to me all that I learnt from old Didymus about the opinions of Xenophanes, and Heraclitus, and Melissus, and Anaxagoras—about infinity, and creation, and about the sheer impossibility of ever really knowing anything!

And yet I used to think that I could unite myself with God!

(*Laughing bitterly*): Ah! Madness, madness! Is the fault my own? Prayer is intolerable to me! My heart is more hard than a rock! And yet there was a time when it overflowed with love! . . .

The sand, at morning time, would smoke on the horizon like the cloud from a censer; at setting of sun, flowers of fire blossomed upon the cross—and through the night hours it seemed to me that all beings and all things gathered themselves into one great silence and joined with me in adoration of the Lord. O joy in prayer, delight in ecstasy, O goodness of heaven, what has become of you?

I remember a journey I made with Ammon, in search of solitude where we might build a monastery. It was the last evening, and we quickened our steps, in silence, except that as we went along side by side we now and then would softly sing a hymn. As the sun went slowly down, our two shadows stretched out like obelisks, growing taller and taller, moving in front of us. Here and there we fixed small wooden crosses, made of fragments broken from our staffs, to show where the cells were to be. Night

THE TEMPTATION OF ST. ANTHONY

was slow in coming, and black waves spread over the land, even though wonderful rosy lights were still filling the sky.

As a child, I had played at building hermitages with stones; and close at hand my mother would watch me.

She must often have torn out her white hair by handfuls, and cursed me for leaving her.

And her corpse lay neglected in the middle of the hut, under the thatch of reeds, between decaying walls. Through a hole, a hyena, sniffing, pokes his muzzle . . . horror! horror!

(He sobs.)

No! For Ammonaria will not have left her!

Where is she now—Ammonaria?

She may be in the warm chamber of the baths—putting off her clothes—one by one—first the mantle, then the girdle, the outer tunic, the lighter undergarment, all her necklaces; and the evaporation of cinnamon wreathes her naked limbs. She lies down at last upon the warm mosaic. Her hair reaches to the curves of her hips—like a black fleece—and she stifles in the overheated atmosphere—and she begins to pant—her figure arched, her two little breasts pointing up. . . . What!—does my flesh rebel again? In the midst of grief am I tortured also by lust? Two torments at one single time? It is too much for me! I cannot any longer bear myself!

(He leans over, and looks down the precipice.)

If one should fall down there he would be killed! . . . Nothing easier, if I were but to roll over to the left—one single movement—just one!

(Then appears AN OLD WOMAN.

Anthony struggles to his feet with a start of terror—he fancies that he is looking upon his mother, risen from the dead.

But he sees that this woman is much older, and incredibly wasted.

A shroud, knotted about her head, hangs down, together with her white hair, and reaches her legs, which are as thin as crutches. Her shining teeth, the colour of ivory, make her discoloured skin, by contrast, look yet darker still. The orbits of her eyes are full of shadows, and in their depths two tiny flames are wavering, like lamps within a sepulchre.)

Well! (*she says*), what hinders you?

ANTHONY (*stammering*): I am afraid—for it would be a sin!

SHE (*makes answer*): But King Saul killed himself! Razias, a righteous man, killed himself! Saint Pelagia of Antioch killed herself! Dommina of Aleppo and her two daughters, all three of them saints, killed themselves; and remember, too, all the confessors who delivered themselves up to the executioners, so greedy were they of death. That they might be embraced by death the more speedily, the virgins of Miletus strangled themselves with their shoe-strings. The philosopher Hegesias, at Syracuse, preached death so persuasively that men forsook the brothels to go hang themselves in the fields. The patricians of Rome arranged death for themselves as though it were a debauch.

ANTHONY: Yes, the attraction of death is sometimes strong indeed! Many and many a hermit has given way to it.

THE OLD WOMAN: A thing which makes you equal to God himself—think of that! It was he who

made you; but you yourself will destroy his work—
you by your courage, of your own free will. The
enjoyment of Erostratus was inferior to this. And
then your body has so often mocked your soul that
you may rightly now take vengeance on it at the last.
You will feel nothing. It will so soon be over!
What do you fear? A large black hole! It is
empty, perhaps!

(Anthony has heard; but he answers nothing; and on
the other side of him appears ANOTHER WOMAN. Young
and beautiful—amazingly beautiful. For the moment he
takes her for Ammonaria.

But this woman is taller, her colour fair as honey, very
plump, with paint on her cheeks and roses in her hair.
Her long robe, trimmed with spangles, gives back metallic
flashings; her thick lips are a burning red, and her heavy
eyelids seem so drowned in languor that one might almost
think her blind. She murmurs:)

Live rather, and be joyous! Solomon commends
joy! Follow whither your heart would lead you,
and walk according to the desire of your eyes!

ANTHONY: What joy could I hope to find? My
heart is heavy, and my eyes are dim!

SHE (*replies*): Make for the suburb of Racotis,
push open a door that is painted blue; and when
you have entered the hall where a fountain plashes
a woman will appear—in a splendid upper garment
of white silk striped with gold, her hair loose, her
laughter like the clatter of castanets. She is expert!
When she has caressed you, you will know the pride
of the initiate, and the appeasing of all desire.

No need thereafter that you should be intent upon
adulteries, climbings in and out, abductions; but you
shall enjoy possession, in its simple state, of that

from which you would have shrunk, were it all decked out and disguised.

Have you ever strained to your bosom a virgin who loved you? Do you recall her modest surrender, and the vanishment of her scruples under sweet floods of tears?

Can you imagine yourself walking with her now in the woods by moonlight? With each pressure of your joined hands a shudder goes through you both; your eyes, as they meet, pour out, each unto other, incorporeal waves, and your heart fills to overflowing, until it seems near to bursting; it is a delicious whirl, an overwhelming frenzy . . . !

THE OLD WOMAN: No need to possess joy in order to know its bitterness! But to look upon it from afar begets disgust thereof. You must be weary of the monotony of the same things to be done, of the long days, of the ugliness of life, of all the stupid business under the sun!

ANTHONY: Ah, yes! I hate everything that he shines upon!

THE YOUNG WOMAN: Hermit! Hermit! You can find diamonds among the pebbles, fountains beneath the sand, and pleasures amid these dangers that you despise; and there are even parts of this earth so lovely that you long to press her to your heart!

THE OLD WOMAN: And every evening, when you lie down upon her to sleep, you hope that before long it will be she who will cover you!

THE YOUNG WOMAN: And yet you believe in the resurrection of the flesh, which is the carrying over of life into eternity!

THE TEMPTATION OF ST. ANTHONY

(The Old Woman, while speaking, has become even more emaciated; and above her skull, which no longer has any hair upon it, a bat goes circling in the air.

The Young Woman has become fatter. Her robe flashes iridescent hues, her nostrils quiver, her eyes gently flicker.)

THE FIRST (*says, as she opens her arms*): Come, I am consolation, rest, forgetfulness, everlasting calm!

THE SECOND (*and offering her bosom*): I am the giver of sleep; I am joy, life, happiness unfailing!

(Anthony turns his heels on them to flee.

Each lays a hand on his shoulder.

The shroud drops away, discovering the skeleton form of DEATH.

The robe is rent asunder, revealing the uncovered limbs of LUST, with slender figure, and huge flanks, and long waving hair that flies about her.

Anthony stands motionless between the two, deliberating.)

DEATH (*says to him*): In a little while, or after a long while, what odds! You are mine, as are the suns, the nations, the kings, the snow on the mountains, and the grass in the fields. I fly higher than the sparrow-hawk; I run faster than the gazelle; I even outdistance hope; it was I who overcame the Son of God!

LUST: Resist me not; I am the omnipotent! The forests resound to my sighs, the waves move beneath my sway. Virtue, courage, piety—all these dissolve in the sweetness of my lips. I go along with man every step of his journey—and on the very threshold of his tomb he turns again to me!

DEATH: I will find out for you what you have tried so long to grasp, in the light of torches, on the face of the dead—or when you spent your time, wandering beyond the Pyramids, over the great sand composed of human debris. Now and then a broken bit of skull would crack beneath your feet. You gathered up the dust, and let it trickle through your fingers; and your thoughts, mingling with it, were lost in nothingness.

Lust: My gulf is deeper still! Marble statues have inspired obscene loves. Men go gladly to encounters that terrify. They rivet fetters which soon they learn to curse. Whence comes the fascination of courtesans, the extravagance of dreams, the greatness of my sorrow?

Death: My satire leaves all others far behind! There are convulsions of joy at the burials of kings, at the utter destruction of a people—and war is made with music and plumes and flags and golden harness, a show of ceremony that they may thereby pay me greater homage.

Lust: My anger is as great as yours. I howl, I bite. I sweat in agony; and sometimes I even look like a corpse.

Death: It is I who give you your importance; let us embrace!

(Death chuckles, and Lust shouts aloud. They catch each other by the waist, and chant together :)

It is I who hasten the dissolution of matter!
And I make easy the scattering of germs!
You destroy—so that I may begin again!
You conceive—that I may have something to destroy!
Active is my power!
And fruitful my rottenness!

THE TEMPTATION OF ST. ANTHONY 311

(And their voices, with echoes that spread forth and fill the horizon, become so loud that Anthony is stunned by them.

A shock, several times repeated, makes him open his eyes; and he sees before him, amid the shadows, a sort of monster.

It is a death's-head, crowned with roses, above the trunk of a woman, pearly-white. And beneath, a shroud starred with particles of gold, like a tail—and the creature undulates, like a gigantic worm that might hold itself erect.

The vision grows fainter, and then vanishes.

ANTHONY rises.)

Yet once again 'twas the Devil, in his twofold shape: the spirit of fornication, and the spirit of destruction.

Neither of these twain can frighten me, for I have renounced the lust of the flesh, and I know myself to be immortal.

And so death itself is but an illusion, a veil that here and there conceals the continuity of life.

But if Substance be one, why all these varied Forms?

There must be, somewhere, rudimentary figures, whose bodies are only images. If one could but see them one might understand the linking of matter with thought, in which Being consists!

Such were the figures in Babylon, painted on the walls of the temple of Belus; and there were others in a mosaic upon the harbour at Carthage. I myself have sometimes seen in the sky the shapes, as it were, of spirits. Travellers in the desert meet incredible animals . . . that are . . .

(And opposite, on the other side of the Nile, suddenly

appears the Sphinx. He stretches out his paws, shakes the fillets on his forehead, and crouches low upon his belly.

Leaping, flying, spitting fire from her nostrils, and with dragon-tail lashing against her wings, the green-eyed Chimera circles, barks.

Her long ringlets, tossed back on one side, mingle with the hair on her loins, and on the other side hang right down to the sand, and wag to and fro with the movements of her body.)

THE SPHINX (*motionless, gazes at the Chimera*): Here, Chimera; stop!

THE CHIMERA: No, never!

THE SPHINX: Do not run so swiftly, nor fly so high, nor bark so loudly!

THE CHIMERA: Call me no more, call me no more, since you remain for ever mute.

THE SPHINX: Cease this casting of flames into my face, these howlings in my ear; you cannot melt my granite!

THE CHIMERA: You cannot seize me, terrible Sphinx!

THE SPHINX: You are too crazy, you cannot stay with me!

THE CHIMERA: And you are so heavy that you could not follow me!

THE SPHINX: And where would you go, running so fast?

THE CHIMERA: I gallop in the corridors of the labyrinth, soar above the mountains, skim upon the waves, yelp at the bottom of precipices, hook my jaws to the skirts of the thick clouds; with tail trailing I scratch the shores; and the hills catch their curves from the shape of my shoulders.

But you! I find you ever unmoved, or it may

be making alphabets with the tips of your talons on the surface of the sand!

THE SPHINX: True! I keep counsel! I dream and I reckon up.

The sea swings back into his bed, the corn sways to the wind, the caravans go by, the dust is awhirl, cities come to nothing—and my gaze, unswerving, stretches beyond surrounding things to a horizon that none shall ever reach.

THE CHIMERA: And I—I am joyful and light of heart! I offer to the eyes of men dazzling visions of paradise in the clouds, and happiness far off. I pour into their souls eternal madness, plans of blessedness, schemes for the future, dreams of glory, and vows of love and good resolves.

It is I who urge them to perilous adventure and to mighty enterprise. I have chiselled with my claws the wonders of architecture. It was I who hung the bells on Porsenna's tomb, and flung a wall of yellow copper round the Atlantean quays.

I search out fresh odours, finer flowers, unimagined pleasures. If anywhere I find a man whose mind dwells quietly with wisdom, I straightway fall upon him and I strangle him.

THE SPHINX: And I have devoured all those who were distracted by the love of God. The bravest of them, who would climb even to the level of my royal brow, clamber on my ribbed mouldings as upon the steps of a staircase. But weariness takes them by surprise; and of their own weakness they fall, and are undone.

(Anthony begins to tremble.
He is no longer in front of his hut, but in the desert—

and by his side are these two monstrous creatures, their jowls grazing his shoulders.)

THE SPHINX: O Fantasy, bear me away on wings, that I may be freed from sadness!

THE CHIMERA: O Unknown, I am enamoured of those eyes! As a lustful hyena I go round about you, craving those fruitful gifts for lack of which I waste away! Open your jaws, lift up your feet, get up on my back!

THE SPHINX: My feet have been so long upon the ground that they can rise no more; the lichen, like a ringworm, grows upon my jaw; and I have thought about so many things that I have nothing more to say.

THE CHIMERA: You lie, O hypocrite Sphinx! How comes it always that you summon me but to deny me?

THE SPHINX: It is yourself, you wild and wilful one, who pass and repass like a whirlwind!

THE CHIMERA: You blame me? How? Let me be!

(She barks.)

THE SPHINX: You move away, you avoid me!

(He growls.)

THE CHIMERA: Let us try! . . . You are hurting me!

THE SPHINX: No! Impossible!

(And sinking slowly down, he disappears in the sand—whilst the Chimera, creeping along with her tongue hanging out, at last gets right away, describing circles as she goes.

The breath from her mouth has caused a fog: and in

THE TEMPTATION OF ST. ANTHONY

this fog Anthony perceives a curling as of clouds, and certain indistinguishable shapes.

At last, he makes out something that looks almost like the bodies of men; and then, first of all, approach :)

THE MOUTHLESS GROUP (*like bubbles of air through which the sunlight shines*): Do not breathe too hard! Raindrops bruise us, false notes jar upon us, in a dim light we are blind. We are compact of breezes and of perfumes, and we roll and float along—something more than dreams, yet something short of actualities.

THE HALF FOLK (*have but one eye, one cheek, one hand, one leg, the half of a body, half of a heart, apiece. Their voices are very loud, and they say*): We dwell at our ease in our own halves of houses, with our half-wives and our halves of children.

THE BLEMMYES (*who have no heads at all*): Our shoulders are all the larger—and there is no ox or rhinoceros or elephant could carry what we can!

We have something that resembles features, and the dim likeness of a face imprinted on our breasts—but that is all!

For brains, we have our digestions; and for imagination there are our glands. God, in our way of thinking, floats peacefully amid our inward bodily secretions.

Straight upon our way do we march, passing over the muddy places, skirting all the gulfs—and of all the people in the world it is we who work the hardest, and are the happiest and most respectable!

THE PYGMIES: We little fellows swarm about the world like lice upon a camel's hump.

They burn us, drown us, squash us: but always

there we are again, livelier and more numerous than ever—terrible by our mere multitudes!

THE SHADOW-FOOTED FOLK: Bound to the earth by our flowing locks, which are longer than the bindweed; our whole existence is spent beneath the shadow of our own feet, which are as big as parasols; and such light as reaches us comes from between our toes. There is no bustle or confusion amongst us, nor can there be any work! . . . Keep your head as low down as you possibly can—that's the way to be happy!

(Their heaving limbs are like the trunks of trees, and they go on increasing in number.
And so a forest appears. Great ape-like creatures are crawling about on all fours among the branches—they are men, though they have the heads of dogs.)

THE DOG-HEADED FOLK: We leap from bough to bough, sucking eggs and plucking the little dicky-birds; and then we stick their nests on our heads, as if they were bonnets.

We never miss chances to tweak cows' udders, or put out the eyes of lynxes; our dung drops from the tops of trees, and we delight to display our depravity in full sight of the sun!

Tearing flowers asunder, smashing the fruit, befouling springs, raping women—we are masters of all by reason of strong arms and pitiless hearts!

With a will, good fellows! With a will! Let your jaws go chattering!

(Blood and milk run over the edges of their lips; and the rain pours down their hairy backs.
Anthony inhales the freshness of the young leaves.

There is movement among the trees, and branches are

THE TEMPTATION OF ST. ANTHONY

pushed about. Suddenly there appears a great black stag, with the head of a bull, and a tangle of white horns between his ears.)

THE SADHUZAG: My four-and-seventy antlers are hollow—like flutes.

When I turn towards the south, there come forth from them sounds which bring the enraptured beasts around me. Serpents come and twine about my legs, wasps cling to my nostrils, and parrots and doves and ibises alight upon my branches. . . . Listen!

(He throws back his horns, and music comes forth from them, deliciously sweet.

Anthony presses both hands to his heart, and feels as though the melody would bear his soul away.)

THE SADHUZAG: But when I turn me to the north, my horns, that are more bushy than a battalion of spears, give forth a sound of howling; and then the forests tremble, rivers run backwards, the pods of fruits crack open, and blades of grass stand up on end like hairs on the head of a coward. . . . Listen!

(He bows his branching antlers, and dreadful grating noises issue from them. Anthony feels as though he were being torn asunder.

And his horror heightens as he sees:)

THE MARTICHORAS (*a gigantic red lion, with human face, and three rows of teeth*): The sparkles of my scarlet coat are mingled with the flashings of the mighty sands. I snuff up through my nostrils the fearsomeness of solitary places. When armies adventure themselves in the deserts, I eat them all up!

My claws are twisted like gimlets, and my teeth notched like saws. My tail, which is all crooked, bristles with darts, and these I hurl to the right and to the left, before me and behind. . . . See! See!

(The Martichoras discharges quills from his tail, which shoot about in every direction. Drops of blood fall, splashing on the leaves.)

THE LOOKER DOWN (*a black buffalo, with a drooping pig's-head that is joined to his shoulders by a long, lean neck, flabby as an empty gut. He wallows flat on the ground; and his feet disappear under the enormous mane of hard hairs that covers his entire face*): Gross, melancholy and very fierce, I enjoy always beneath my belly the warmth of the mud. My head is so heavy that I cannot carry it erect, and so I roll it round about me, slowly—while with open jaws I snatch with my tongue at the poisonous plants which my breath waters. Once, unawares, I devoured my own feet.

No living man, O Anthony, has seen my eyes; for the few who ever saw them are dead. If I did but raise my eyelids, red and swollen, on that instant you would die!

ANTHONY: Oh! That . . . a . . . a! As if I should want . . . ! And yet his utter stolidness attracts me. . . . No! No! I will not!

(He looks steadily towards the ground.

But the grass catches fire, and amid the twisting flames arises :)

THE BASILISK (*a great violet serpent with three-lobed crest, and two fangs, one above and one below*): Take care, or you will fall into my jaws! I drink fire. I am fire—and I draw it in from everywhere,

THE TEMPTATION OF ST. ANTHONY

from the clouds and the stones and the dead trees, from the fur of animals and from the surface of the marsh. It is my warmth that keeps volcanoes in being: I who am the cause of the glint in precious stones and the gleaming of metals.

THE GRIFFIN (*a lion with vulture's beak and white wings, red paws and blue neck*): I am master of hidden splendours, and I know the secret of the tombs where the old kings sleep.

Their heads are held upright by chains fixed in the wall. Near them, in basins of porphyry, upon black waters, float the bodies of the women that they loved. Their treasures are set in order in vast halls, arranged diamond-shape, in little piles, or in pyramids; and down below, far beneath the tombs, and to be reached only after treading long passages in stifling darkness, are rivers of gold, and forests of diamonds, fields of carbuncles and lakes of mercury.

With my back against the door of the vault, and my claws outspread, I mark, with flaming eyes, those who would approach. The wide open plain is whitened to the farthest edge of the horizon by the bones of travellers who came too near!

But for you the folding-doors of bronze shall open of themselves; you will breathe the fumes of these mighty excavations and go down into the caverns. . . . Quick! Quick!

(He scoops out the earth with his paws, crowing the while like a cock.

A thousand voices answer him. The forest trembles.

And all manner of frightful beasts arise: the Tragelaphus, half stag and half horse; the Myrmecoleo, lion in front and ant behind, whose genitals are reversed; the python Aksar, sixty cubits long, that frightened Moses; the great weasel Pastinaca, whose stink kills trees; the Presteros, whose touch imparts madness; the Mirag, a horned hare, inhabiting the islands of the sea. The spotted Phalmant bursts his belly with the force of his howling; the Senad, a three-headed bear, tears her young to pieces with her tongue; the dog Cepus spills blue whey from its breasts upon the rocks. Mosquitoes begin their humming, toads their hopping, and serpents their hissing. Lightning flashes. Hail descends.

There come whirlwinds, bringing with them wondrous forms: heads of alligators upon roebucks' feet, owls with snakes' tails, hogs with tigers' muzzles, goats with the crupper of an ass, frogs as shaggy as bears, chameleons huge as hippopotami, calves with two heads—one of which weeps while the other bellows, a quadruple progeny that hold together by their navels and spin round like tops, winged paunches that flutter like gnats.

They rain down from the sky, they come up out of the earth, they drop from the rocks. All round about, eyes gleam, jaws growl; breasts swell, claws stretch out, teeth gnash, flesh flaps. Some are bringing forth, some are mating, and there are those who devour one another at a mouthful.

Stifled by their own numbers, multiplying by contact, they crawl one over another—and all of them swim rhythmically about Anthony, as though the ground were the deck of a ship. He feels against his calves the sliminess of snails, on his hands the chilliness of vipers; and spiders spinning their webs entangle him in their net.

But the portentous circle opens, the sky in a moment becomes blue, and :)

THE UNICORN (*presents himself*): Gallop! Gallop!

I have hoofs of ivory, and teeth of steel; my head is a bright purple, and my body white as snow; and the horn on my forehead is straked like a rainbow.

I travel from Chaldæa to the desert of Tartary, on the banks of the Ganges and in Mesopotamia. I

THE TEMPTATION OF ST. ANTHONY

outrun the ostriches. I run so fast that I drag the winds behind me. I rub my back against the palm-trees. I roll among the bamboos. With a single bound I leap over rivers. Doves fly about me. None but maidens can bridle me. Gallop! Gallop!

(Anthony watches him race away.
And with eyes still raised, he sees all the birds that live upon the wind: the Gouith, the Ahuti, the Alphalim, the Iukneth from the mountains of Caff, the Homaï of the Arabs, which are the souls of murdered men. He hears parrots speaking with human tongues, and the great Pelasgic swimming-birds that sob like children or snicker like old women.
Salt air assails his nostrils. The seashore is now before him.

In the distance whales are spouting; and from the far horizon come:)

THE BEASTS OF THE SEA (*round, like wine-skins, flat as shoulder-blades, toothed like saws, lumbering over the sand and drawing near*): Come with us, into the vastnesses where never yet has man gone down!

Many peoples dwell in the countries of the Ocean. Some inhabit the abode of tempests: others swim in the open sea amid the transparency of the cold waves, browse like oxen on the coral plains, suck in through their trunks the ebb of the tides, or bear upon their shoulders the burden of the sources of the sea.

(Phosphorescence glows in the whiskers of the seals and on the scales of fish. Sea-urchins spin round and round like wheels, Ammonite horns uncurl like cables, oysters creak their hinges, polypi unfold their tentacles, medusæ float like quivering crystal balls, sponges bob up and down, anemones spout water; seaweed and moss have shot up.

And all kinds of plants stretch themselves into branches, twist themselves into tendrils, lengthen into points, round themselves off into fans. Pumpkins take on the appearance of breasts, creepers interlace like serpents.

The Dedaïms of Babylon, which are trees, bear human heads instead of fruit; mandragoras sing, the root baaras runs about in the grass.

Vegetation can no longer clearly be distinguished from living animals. Polypous growths, with the appearance of sycamores, have human arms among their branches. Anthony thinks he sees a caterpillar between two leaves; but it is a butterfly in flight. He is about to step on a pebble; and a grey locust springs into the air. On one shrub are insects that look like rose-petals; the fragmentary remains of mayflies form a snowy layer on the soil.

And there are plants, too, which mingle themselves with the rocks.

Lumps of stone look like brains; stalactites like beasts; and a mass of some sort of ironstone suggests a patterned carpet.

In pieces of ice, he sees crystal flowerings, and the impress of leaves and shells—but cannot tell whether they be impress only, or the very things themselves. Diamonds twinkle like eyes, and minerals sparkle.

And he is no longer afraid!

He throws himself at full length on the ground, leans upon his elbows; and, hardly daring to breathe, looks about him.

Insects, without stomachs, nevertheless go on feeding; withered ferns begin to flourish again; missing limbs sprout forth once more.

And last of all he perceives some tiny globular bodies, no bigger than the head of a pin, and all fringed round about with hairs which are thrilling and vibrating.)

ANTHONY (*in great excitement*): Oh, joy! Joy! I have seen life at its birth, and movement in its

THE TEMPTATION OF ST. ANTHONY

beginnings. My veins are at the point of bursting, so loudly throbs my pulse! I fain would fly, swim, bark, bellow, howl! Oh, that I had wings! Or that a shell were mine, or a rind! That I might breathe out smoke, wave a trunk, have a body that writhed along the ground, portion out my being everywhere, exist in everything, spread myself abroad in perfumes, develop as do the plants, flow like water, vibrate like sound, shine as the light, assume all shapes, enter each atom, make my way to the inmost kernel of matter—be, I myself! *be* matter!

(The day at last appears: and as curtains are swept aside from the door of a tabernacle, so do the golden clouds remove, in great spiral whorls, and heaven stands unveiled.

In the midst, against the disc of the sun itself, shines the face of Jesus Christ.

Anthony makes the sign of the cross, and betakes himself to prayer.)

THE END